PRAISE FOR THE FAMILY UNIT AND OTHER FANTASIES

"A playwright, graphic novelist, and mystery writer, Laurence Klavan has long enthralled audiences with his extraordinarily fertile imagination, insight, and style. He is also an admired short-story writer. *The Family Unit and Other Fantasies* brings together his best work, reminding us of the pleasure of unplugging, putting your feet up, and living someone else's life for a while."
—T. J. Stiles, author of the Pulitzer-winning *The First Tycoon: The Epic Life of Cornelius Vanderbilt*

"I have this secret addiction to the short stories of Laurence Klavan, which sneak up on me at odd moments in little magazines and small presses. Attention, all! Give these stories big magazines and big presses. They are full of unexpected joys and always leave me feeling terribly uneasy and blissfully satisfied."
—John Guare, Tony Award-winning author of *Six Degrees of Separation* and *The House of Blue Leaves*

"These are wonderfully strange tales—cunningly written—eerie and satiric by turn—often evoking tremendous pathos."
—David Greenspan, five-time Obie Award-winning author of *The Myopia*

"Laurence Klavan knows all too well that the world is changing too fast to offer us much in the way of shelter. To remind us of this, he's written an impressive collection of stories—some playful, others tender or sobering, all of them shrewd and surprising and wise."
—John Dalton, author of *The Inverted Forest* and *Heaven Lake*

"A masterful, unnervingly funny collection set in a society with no place to hide: in other words, our own."
—Irina Reyn, author of *What Happened to Anna K.*

"Laurence Klavan uncovers the places you didn't know exist, the gaps between everyday life and existential horror, where the disconnect between reality and the weird operates its quiet and subtle magic."
—Maxim Jakubowski, author, and editor of *The Mammoth Book of Erotica*

"Disturbing, surprising, and unflinchingly intimate, Laurence Klavan's stories make the mundane bizarre and are absolutely engrossing."
—Danica Novgorodoff, author of *The Undertaking of Lily Chen*

PRAISE FOR THE CUTTING ROOM

"A witty spoof. . . . Klavan gleefully slices and dices every known specimen of the Hollywood film trade. . . . Worth its weight in popcorn."
—*The New York Times Book Review*

"Highly entertaining . . . Klavan knows his turf. . . . Sure to put a smile on any movie buff's lips."
—Leonard Maltin

"Brimming with engaging tidbits of movie trivia. . . . This tongue-in-cheek whodunit marks the long overdue second coming of a gifted novelist."
—*Publishers Weekly* (starred review)

PRAISE FOR THE SHOOTING SCRIPT

"Hilarious. . . . [A] wholly entertaining sequel: a frenzied encore for suspense fans and an edifying indulgence for seasoned film buffs."
—*Publishers Weekly*

"Hard-boiled nerd Roy Milano is back in another screwball adventure... Enough delightful insanity to please fans of silly suspense (from Jonathan Lethem to Kinky Friedman.)"
—*Booklist*

PRAISE FOR WASTELAND (co-authored with Susan Kim)

"A *Lord of the Flies* for future generations, *Wasteland* is an irresistible and complex novel that I just couldn't put down."
—Karin Slaughter, *New York Times* bestselling author

"Kim and Klavan's world-building enticingly trickles through the brutal, fast-paced, multilayered plot, which is fueled by a sweet romance between brooding Caleb and spunky Esther and plenty of mysteries. . . . The first in a planned trilogy, *Wasteland* raises plenty of captivating questions and doesn't shortchange readers on satisfying answers."
—*Booklist*

PRAISE FOR BRAIN CAMP
(co-authored with Susan Kim; Illustrated by Faith Erin Hicks)

"Smart, disgusting fun . . . sly social commentary with a fizzy dash of stomach-lurching horror."
—*Kirkus Reviews*

"A throwback to the kind of paranoia that *Rosemary's Baby* and *The Stepford Wives* capitalized on. . . . Kim and Klavan, who balanced adventure and kids' social issues so well in *City of Spies* (2010), do the same in another well-rounded adventure here, as the far-out (and kind of gross) climax mixes with genuine insight into dealing with parents, fitting into a new crowd, and handling the pressures of performance."
—*Booklist*

PRAISE FOR CITY OF SPIES
(co-authored with Susan Kim; Illustrated by Pascal Dizin)

"[An] excellent graphic novel—it has a great plot, interesting characters and fantastic artwork."
—*Wired.com*

"It is hard to know which to praise more in *City of Spies*, the grand, old-fashioned story crafted by Susan Kim and Laurence Klavan, or the enchanting artwork by Pascal Dizin. . . . The tale of Nazi spies in New York is full of a Golden-Age Hollywood ambiance, like some lost Hitchcock or Hawks film. Mixing romance, humor, suspense, and pathos, this graphic novel should be handed out to every young reader you know—after you've enjoyed it yourself."
—*Asimov's Science Fiction*

"A terrific adventure story. . . . Rip-roaring fun."
—*Publishers Weekly* (starred)

"Told with seat-of-the-pants, graphic-novel immediacy, [this] is an artful melding of jewel-box illustration with noir atmosphere—Tintin directed by Hitchcock. Still, the story's slant is all its own. . . . The snappy, uncluttered tale has a rousing visual flow and plot depth on a variety of fronts. Plus, the Nazis wind up swimming with the fishes. Pow! Pow! Pow!"
—*Kirkus Reviews*

FIRST EDITION

Distributed in Canada by
HarperCollins Canada Ltd.
1995 Markham Road
Scarborough, ON M1B 5M8
Toll Free: 1-800-387-0117
e-mail: hcorder@harpercollins.com

Distributed in the U.S. by
Diamond Comic Distributors, Inc.
10150 York Road, Suite 300
Hunt Valley, MD 21030
Phone: (443) 318-8500
e-mail: books@diamondbookdistributors.com

Library and Archives Canada Cataloguing in Publication

Klavan, Laurence, author
The family unit and other fantasies / Laurence Klavan. -- First edition.

Short stories.
Issued in print and electronic formats.
ISBN 978-1-77148-203-5 (pbk.).--ISBN 978-1-77148-204-2 (pdf)

I. Title.

PS3561.L3343F36 2014 813'.54 C2014-902687-0
C2014-902688-9

CHIZINE PUBLICATIONS
Toronto, Canada
www.chizinepub.com
info@chizinepub.com

Edited by Andrew Wilmot
Proofread by Sam Zucchi

Canada Council for the Arts Conseil des arts du Canada

We acknowledge the support of the Canada Council for the Arts which last year invested $20.1 million in writing and publishing throughout Canada.

Published with the generous assistance of the Ontario Arts Council.

Printed in Canada

THE FAMILY UNIT AND OTHER FANTASIES

ChiZine Publications

LAURENCE KLAVAN

THE FAMILY UNIT

AND OTHER FANTASIES

for Susan

CONTENTS

The Family Unit 13
Hole in the Ground 25
What the Wind Blew In 31
Stray 43
The Unexpected Guest 56
Long Story Short 75
Versatility 81
Modern Sign 96
The Happy Hour 102
Alert 111
Bomb Shelter 132
Old Tricks 146
The Dead End Job 157
The Son He Never Had 173
Home Invasion 184

Acknowledgements 192
Publication History 193
About the Author 194

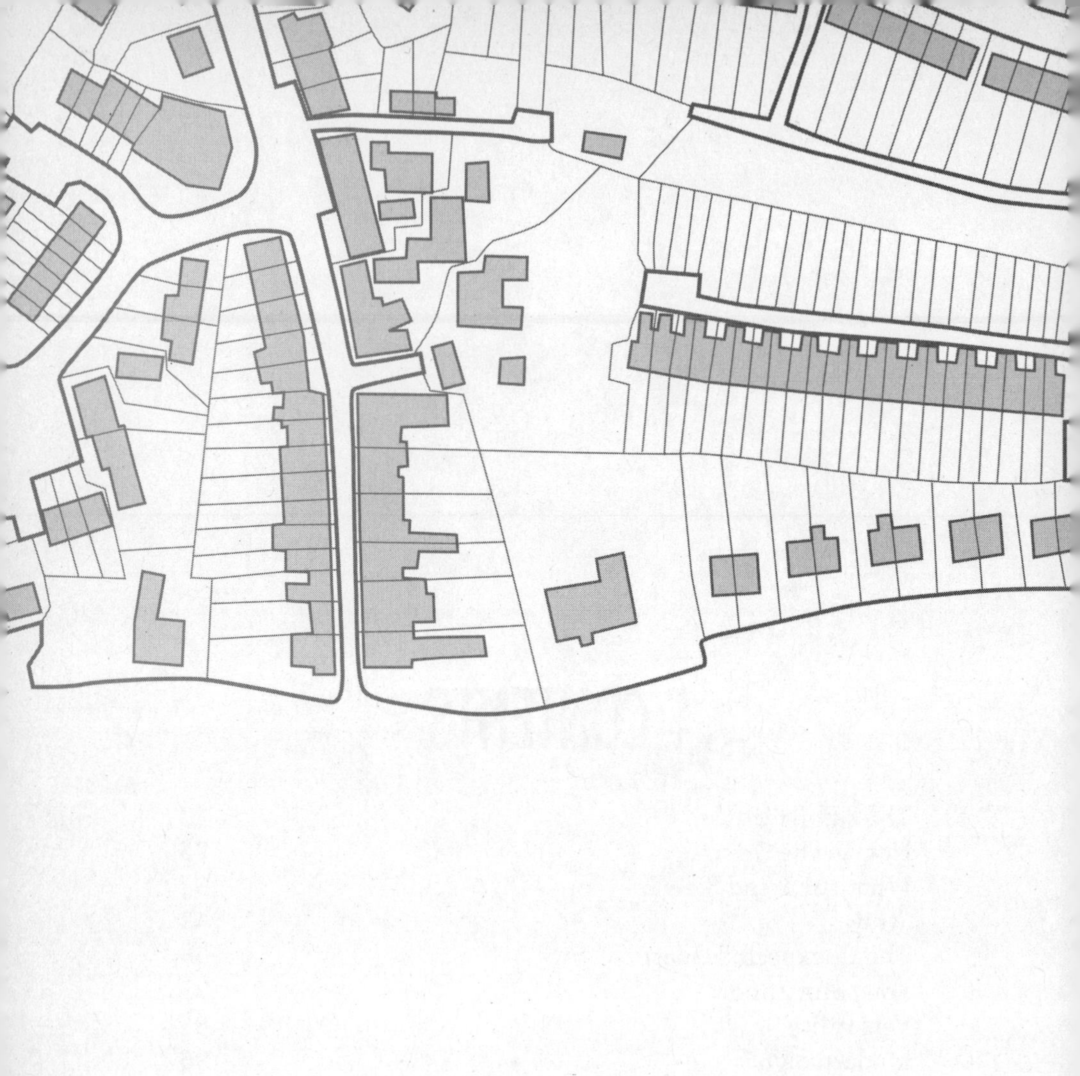

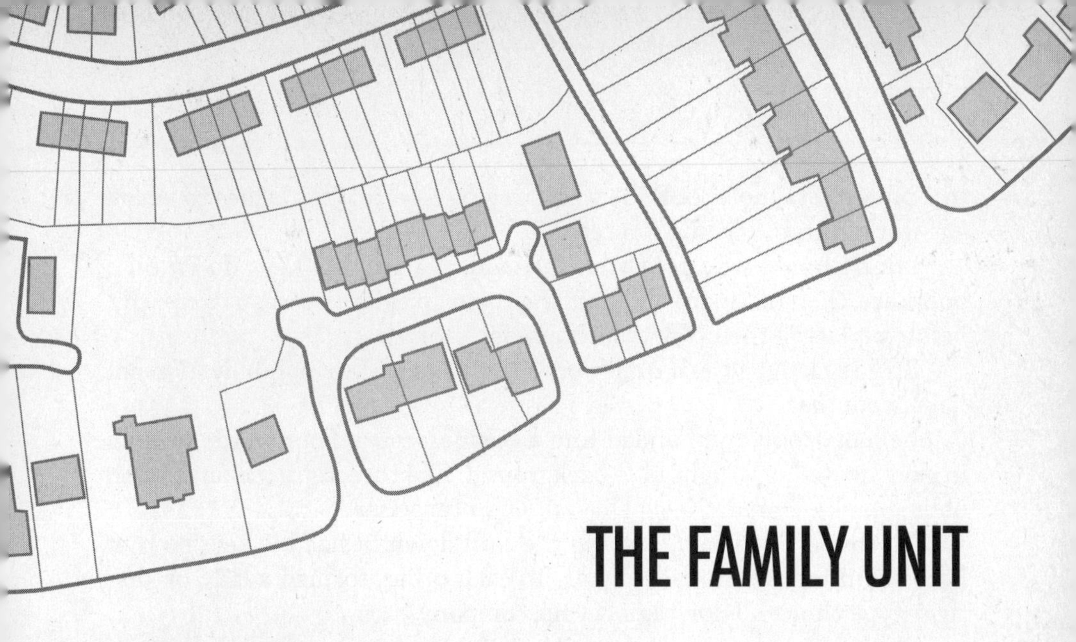

THE FAMILY UNIT

It was unclear what the woman wanted, sitting in the Wiltons' house. She said that Bode had let her in, though he'd been taught not to do so, to politely close the door and get his parents if he did not know someone. (If Sarabeth was home alone, she was only to call through the closed door and not open it at all.) It was a safe neighbourhood, nothing ever happened there (except for that one home invasion and armed robbery, and that was at that contractor's house on the day his payroll was delivered; it was obviously organized crime, no one was ever arrested, cops turned a blind eye, and the man and his family—Arch couldn't remember their names—had moved away soon after); it was safe, but still. The woman said Bode had been on his way to baseball practice and sort of run into her on his way out; Arch and Celinda would have to talk to him about that.

Still, as Arch entered and saw her on the sofa, he really couldn't blame the boy: the woman was perfectly presentable, fit right into the suburban setting, even almost blended into the country-style plaids and stripes Celinda had selected. The woman was so at ease in fact that she did not seem surprised to see him and only smiled, sweetly and incidentally, before speaking.

"Hi, Arch. How are you?"

Arch quickly took in whatever information was available, which was the woman's age (middle) and the way she was attired: her checked blazer, soft grey slacks, and black pointy-toed shoes—plus the portfolio covered in a pink plastic notebook she was carrying—were visual clues to where she worked and what she wanted.

"I don't know who told you," he said, placing his keys down on a bookcase, then instinctively snapping them up again, he wasn't sure why, before replacing them. "But the house isn't for sale."

"Oh." She laughed as if Arch were a child and endearingly silly. "I'm not here about *that*."

She half-stood and handed him a business card. Four words printed in grey floated on a light blue background, like threatening clouds in an oblivious sky: Brenda Keen, Diversified Enterprises.

"I'm sorry," Arch said, putting the card down beside his keys so that they sat in unintentional contrast to each other, formed a lady-or-the-tiger-type choice. "I don't know your company."

"Oh, yes, you do," she said, easily, sitting down again. "Every day."

Arch glanced around the room, an action she seemed to be encouraging. What had her company made? The windows? The leather in the chairs? The paintings of stubby, gnarled yet valiant New England fishermen Celinda had selected? All of it? More? When he looked back, Brenda had already opened her portfolio and was spreading pages with surprising indelicacy across their coffee table.

"Now, we've done the assessments," she said, "and I think you'll be impressed by the advantages of this arrangement. The fuchsia chart represents the potential first quarter growth in . . ."

She continued like this, in the foreign language of finance—foreign to Arch, anyway, who edited a tennis magazine and left the management of their money to others—until she ended by looking up, the pages as if by magic reshuffled and placed again in the portfolio, which she was handing him. "So I think you should seriously consider letting us acquire your family, and the Wiltons becoming a wholly-owned D.E. subsidiary."

Arch took the portfolio silently, his grasp so limp that he almost let it fall before he snapped it up again. He was thrown but not shocked; he had heard of this happening to other families, he had just never thought his own would be the target of a takeover—or was that too antagonistic? Wouldn't they be beneficiaries?

Indeed Brenda counted off the positive reasons for the offer: Arch's job at *Ace* magazine, lucrative but not suffocatingly corporate; his quirky habit of collecting and restoring old radios; his five-day-a-week use of an exercise bike that controlled his cholesterol; his twice-a-week lovemaking with Celinda, impressive after twenty years of marriage. Celinda, too, rated kudos (according to Brenda and, by extension, D.E.) for her therapy practice that still left her time for Arch and the kids; her diligent care of her elderly mother, now in a nearby facility; her Eastern cuisine cooking class and classic novel book club. Even Celinda's use of an anti-depressant after her father's death (Arch read along in the portfolio) had been sensible and short-lived; she now relied on yoga for mental and physical health. As for Bode and Sarabeth, the boy at twelve was a playful and good-humoured Little Leaguer (coached without bellicosity by Arch), and the sixteen-year-old a dedicated high school thespian whose most recent role, Emily in *Our Town*, had been well received—plus she was still a virgin, and (this was stressed in italics) *by choice*.

This kind of consistency made the Wiltons a safe investment, a valuable property, and one that would be a good fit beneath D.E.'s umbrella of international assets. As Brenda became quiet and put her hands into her lap, Arch couldn't help it, he felt pride.

"We'll give you all some time to talk it over," she said, standing. "But you should know we don't make this kind of offer often—and certainly not with such unanimity on our board. You got fifteen out of fifteen—first time!"

After shaking his hand—and refusing coffee or a cookie or even a glass of water, and they lived in a dry climate—Brenda left, giving one last, particularly knowing and appreciative look at the painting of the fisherman hanging above their hearth.

—~—

"Okay, okay, great," Bode said enthusiastically, tapping his foot during the family meeting. "Whatever, whatever, let's do it."

"You know, that is really annoying," Sarabeth said, pointing at the foot. "Mom and Dad, will you please make Bode stop doing that?"

"We'll be done in a second," Arch said. "But not before we take a family vote on this."

Bode's hand immediately shot up, which only further annoyed his sister.

Arch saw Celinda discreetly check the caller ID on a cell phone pulsing on the coffee table; she seemed as eager to get to work as Bode did to the ball field. Arch thought for a second that his family was being a little rowdy this morning, at a time when their high quality had deemed them worthy of purchase. Then he thought, this is what they want, it's us, the Wiltons, so what am I so worried about?

"Now all in favour—"

"Will I get my own credit card?" Sarabeth asked suddenly and, as usual, dramatically. "Will I? I'll die if I don't."

"We've told you no, sweetheart," Celinda said. Then she added, analytically, "We already give you credit. Do you feel as if we don't?"

She didn't speak fast enough to keep the girl from picking up the portfolio pages lying on the table that she had heretofore ignored. After a cursory rifling, Sarabeth stopped and pointed to one line. "It says yes. So I vote aye," and she raised her hand.

"I vote ear," Bode said goofily, and grabbed his bat.

Arch looked at his wife, who was clearly disconcerted by this particular benefit of the deal—though, to be fair, she hadn't asked more than a few questions and had seemed just as excited and immediately okay with it as the kids.

"Oh, all right," she said, shrugging. "Sure. Aye."

"Now here's how it'll—" Arch started to say but soon found he was alone, his cheeks having been quickly kissed by his wife and daughter, his hand shaken with comical gravity by his son.

Though the specific financial terms were vague to Arch, he knew that there would be a cash payment, that the family's stocks and savings would be transferred to D.E.'s control and each member would be in fact issued a new credit card that featured a hologram of his or her face—and came with strict spending restrictions for the kids, to Celinda's relief. The shifts in their routines would be otherwise imperceptible, except that all four were provided square, red-bordered stickers for their clothing, bags, notebooks, and cars that contained their names and underneath, "A Diversified Enterprises Subsidiary."

In the week ahead, to get everything off on the right foot, representatives of the company appeared at the family's daily events. A man in a three-piece suit sat in on *Ace*'s editorial meeting and vocally approved of Arch's suggestion of a feature on overweight ball boys. Another politely stepped forward to dispute a strike called during Bode's Little League at-bat. A woman gave line readings to cast members at a rehearsal of *Harvey* to bolster Sarabeth's performance. And Brenda Keen herself observed Celinda's session with a particularly voluble patient and piped up that he should "stop talking and listen to Dr. Wilton for a second." All of this was what had been meant, Arch and the others understood, by the line in the portfolio that said, "D.E. will stick by you."

Friends who read of the Wiltons' acquisition in the local paper's "People on the Move" column were either resentful or openly admiring but, in any case, envious.

At the end of the month, Brenda Keen again appeared, this time in the Wiltons' den. She said the cleaning woman had let her in, though Arch thought it was Magdalena's day off. What she said next made him forget any such concerns.

"This is your first quarter review." She opened a new blue plastic notebook. "And I have to say your performance has been exemplary." She lauded the stability and success maintained in their work and recreational lives. "Congratulations."

Arch was too pleased by her approval to speak, though he felt slightly sheepish about feeling such pride. Knowing he sounded obsequious but unable to stop himself, he blurted out, "How can we improve? Tell me. We want to do even better."

"Just keep doing what you're doing." Brenda uncrossed her legs, once more clothed in grey slacks, and stood. "Now—there's something I'd like to show you."

In a gas-efficient sedan, Brenda chauffeured Arch to another suburb twenty miles away. She drove with smooth and ruthless efficiency, tailgating or swiftly passing stragglers without ever using her horn. They reached a house that was similar to the Wiltons' but conspicuously more run-down.

Inside, she introduced him to a couple of Arch and Celinda's ages named Red and Karina Blum.

"The Blums are the first proud owners of a Wilton franchise," Brenda said. Arch could indeed see satisfaction—and what he now recognized as intimidated shyness—on the couple's pale, smiling, sweaty faces. By Red's side there sat a newly delivered box of old radios for his restoring; Karina nervously held and twiddled her fingers on a curled yoga mat.

"We'd appreciate any tips," the husband was bold enough to say to an original Wilton. "Anything at all."

"We're off to a good start," Karina threw in, encouraged by her husband's temerity and by the easy atmosphere Brenda had made sure existed. "But, well, Red, you had something—"

"Right." Red grew even more relaxed. "Arch, right now, I work for a glass jar company. I know that's not well paying yet fun. Can you recommend something else for me to do for a living? I mean, unfortunately tennis is out, because I've never watched an entire match in my life—"

"Bowling?" Karina offered.

"Right. We were thinking, a bowling magazine. Is there even one? And if any of this is too much, please let us know."

Arch was initially reluctant to give them notes (as Brenda would later call "constructive criticism") but soon accepted his new responsibility and warmed to the task. He offered many helpful ways they could approximate his family's habits, and even comforted them about one child's resistance to try out for school plays as both the Blums' children were boys. He was on the verge of recommending Red replace his comb over with the kind of close-to-the-head haircut he himself sported, which was better he felt for the balding, but held back out of courtesy.

"And they'll be the first of many," Brenda said, beaming as she backed out of the driveway. "If we could, we'd have Wiltons on every corner."

As it disappeared, Arch saw the family's mailbox, which now had the name "Wilton" caboosed behind "Blum," and both names above the initials "D.E."

That night, Arch was exhausted from the trip; Celinda was similarly spent from work and her book club. As they lay in bed, nodding off, Arch suddenly realized: they'd only had sex once that week. Twice was the Wilton way.

He woke Celinda, who had been smiling slightly in her sleep.

"I was having a dream," she said, quietly, "that I was reaching for a piece of pound cake across a canyon, but you woke me up before I could get it."

Arch explained and then said, seriously, "I think we better do it," and started to arrange himself.

The next week, Celinda's mother died. The end came peacefully and in her sleep. Celinda took the news without any overt emotionalism, kept to her work schedule, and went to yoga class. "What good will it do to stay home?" she asked, evenly. She accompanied Arch to pick out a coffin and plan the funeral, and even called to tell relatives and friends, though Arch had volunteered.

The morning after the interment, Arch found his wife sitting in her nightgown before the bedroom mirror, staring at her reflection as if into the eyes of the utterly irrational.

"Don't you think," he said, gently, "we should maybe get going? You have a nine o'clock."

Celinda did not move for more than an hour, and when she did, it was only to stand in silence at the window and watch with great interest as clouds covered and uncovered the sun.

"Don't you think—" Arch began but never finished his sentence.

Celinda was admitted to a local psychiatric facility after a colleague pulled some strings. She was released a few days later, more animated and on medication, though still somewhat distant. She passed her patients onto other therapists, and Arch found the classic novel from her book club—*The Magnificent Ambersons*—sitting in a basket near the bedroom toilet, its bookmark lying on the floor. While he tried to be compassionate, he was secretly a bit impatient for her to snap out of it and become her old self again.

"This has hit your mother hard," he told the kids, "but she'll be fine." They at least said that they believed him.

Not long after, Arch and other employees were called into *Ace*'s main conference room and told that the magazine was making changes. A print journal, it would soon be online only. There would be layoffs and buyouts, and those who remained would have to add twenty-four-hour blogging to their duties at no extra pay. Arch survived the cut but knew his hours in the office would increase and he would also have to work from a computer at home, cutting into his time with his family and old radios.

He kept the news from Celinda, fearing she wasn't yet up to hearing it. It had been more than two weeks since they'd made love and that, in addition to the change at work, had started to make him irritable and sleepless.

The next time he went to Bode's baseball game, he saw his son slide into home and get called out. Though he had never done so before, he found himself bounding from the stands and onto the field.

"Hey, Helen Keller," he said to the umpire, a local fry cook, "he was safe by a goddamn mile!" and then he was ejected.

As he was driving Bode home, stopped at a light, Arch looked over and saw his funny son was in tears.

"Please," he said, feeling an unfamiliar fear, "don't do that."

—~—

Brenda contacted Arch again, this time by telephone, appearing on Call Waiting while he interviewed a retired doubles team. Arch immediately took the call, and by the time he got back to the players they were gone.

"There's nothing to worry about," Brenda said, referring to recent unsettling events. "But you might want to—well, I'm sure I don't have to tell you anything—"

"Absolutely not," Arch said quickly, having nervously anticipated this "meeting."

"With Celinda, especially, it's not that we're not sympathetic—"

"I know. Of course you are."

"But we really think her continuing a practice that leaves her time for her family, doing yoga for health, the book club and cooking class for eccentricity—"

"Right." Arch didn't say that Celinda had decided to drop out of the cooking class.

"—would really be the best way for her."

"I agree."

"And as for the magazine's restructuring, well, it'll be just as engaging yet lucrative online."

"I know. I'm sure it will."

"We still like the Wiltons. More soon. Be well."

"Thank you. You too. Bye, Brenda." Arch felt chastened by the call and also relieved that it had not been worse. Yet as he walked into the living room—for he had been working at night from home—Brenda's use of the words "still" and "like" rattled him. "Like" seemed mild—why hadn't she said "love"? And "still" implied a weakening of the company's loyalty, while at the same time it had been used to reassure him of its strength. When the phone rang again, he feared it would be Brenda with new disquieting words, but it was his doctor.

Arch had had a check-up that week and some results concerned Dr. Clay. The PSA levels in Arch's blood work were high, implying a possibility—and only that, Dr. Clay stressed—of prostate cancer. Would he come in for more tests? Arch agreed and made an appointment.

Afterwards, he walked into the bathroom he and Celinda shared. He opened their medicine cabinet and removed the sleeping pills she had recently been prescribed—two of which she had taken an hour before, at six P.M. Arch glimpsed her prone body in the bed beyond the bathroom door. He took two pills himself, neglecting to read the side effects warnings on the bottle's side.

Four hours later, sleepwalking, Arch crashed into a half-opened closet door near their bed, cut his upper lip and broke his nose.

The next night, when Arch attended the opening of Sarabeth's play, his nose was swollen and slightly blue, and his mouth distended and purple. Still, he thought it important that someone show up, and Celinda had been sleeping too deeply to be awakened. Also, he thought the play might distract him from Dr. Clay's looming diagnosis. His follow-up appointment had been made for six days away, as if he had all the time in the world. This should have comforted Arch but instead made him think that Dr. Clay didn't care about him.

Watching *Harvey*, Arch thought Sarabeth was big, bubbly, and agreeably over-the-top as the main character's hysterical sister. This reassured him as he was not sure but thought he had seen a D.E. employee—the one who had come to rehearsal—milling apart from other audience members outside.

Backstage, Arch watched his daughter share flowers, kisses, and squealed compliments with the rest of the cast. Her heavy stage makeup, running from sweat, suddenly made Sarabeth look adult, worldly, even badly used. It scared Arch. Caught in a crowd, he saw a short blemished boy who had played the head of the insane asylum ask—in a voice obscured by noise—to see Sarabeth socially sometime. Sarabeth didn't respond, just gave him a dismissive, incredulous look. The boy slunk away, his blush apparent even under makeup. Closer now, Arch heard Sarabeth to another actress, in a voice calmer and colder than she had ever used at home, refer to the boy as "a stinky little twat." Then she turned and made a display of surprise at seeing her father.

"Daddy!"

Sarabeth hugged him tightly and wept with joy, but her tears seemed like those she had shed onstage. Arch offered to drive her home to see her mother and celebrate, but she pouted, pointed to her friends and said, "But—I want to have *fun*. Okay, Dad?"

Her tone made it sound as if their home was the last place to find such a thing. Just now? Or always? Arch didn't know. He was tempted to mention his high PSAs (as he had told no one else) but held his tongue. Sarabeth clearly meant to soothe his bruised face by kissing it but she made his wounds sting instead.

Arch walked out alone onto the high school grounds. All at once, he had little desire to go home himself. When a group of five other parents, most of whom he knew, called from a car to "come get a drink!" he waved and agreed.

They went to a nearby bar next to a Christian exercise salon for women in a mini-mall. While Arch appreciated the company, he sensed the others stood at a jealous distance from him since his acquisition; it was a subtle thing but noticeable. He could only answer tersely such insinuating questions as "Where's Celinda?" and "What happened to your face?" He felt relieved when the party broke up.

Arch reluctantly agreed to drive home one of the mothers, Bethel-something, he could never remember her name. She was a heavy, somewhat melancholy woman whose husband had recently died. Even though he didn't ask why she had hitched a ride with the others, she apologized and told him, sadly, "I never learned to drive."

Beth reminded Arch of the recent disruptive episodes in his life. He drove quicker than usual to her house.

"Would you mind seeing me inside?" she said, to his dismay. "My son is out with the cast, and . . ."

Arch sighed, upset to perceive the solitude to which she was clearly only slowly adjusting; he did not care to identify with it. He agreed with a sigh and a grunt.

Arch meant to turn back once she was over the threshold. But as she snapped on the light in her living room, he saw a television and near it the controls of an intriguing new game he'd heard about. With it you could "play" sports on the TV screen—golf, tennis, lacrosse—by moving animated characters with controls held with a strap around your wrist.

"You don't have it?" Bethel asked, surprised. "I mean, being bought and all, I thought . . ."

Arch didn't reply; he was annoyed by her ignorant presumption about the deal. D.E. didn't give us *everything*, he felt like saying. Instead, with an inquisitive gesture toward the tube, he asked, "May I . . . ?"

"Oh, absolutely," Bethel said. "Just don't hurt your face—"

It was an unthinkingly silly thing to say, but protective; Arch appreciated it. Feeling less hostile, attaching the strap, he politely challenged Bethel to a game of tennis.

"Well, I'm not very good—it's only for my son, but . . ."

Soon they were deep into a match, making motions while cartoons actually functioned for them. When the set was over—Arch over Bethel, six-love—they felt almost as fatigued as if they had been on a court themselves.

"That was fun," Arch panted.

Breathing heavily and smiling, Bethel said, "Would you like a glass of water? And there's some coconut cake, too, homemade, my own recipe."

A few minutes later, she was gently smearing the icing on her surprisingly small, almost non-existent nipple, which looked like a beautiful mosquito bite on her bare right breast. Tenderly restraining her wrist with the strap still around it, holding her down upon the living room couch, "This isn't like me," Arch said.

"Yes," Bethel said, kissing his nasty nose and guiding him inside her, "it is."

All Arch thought afterwards was how he had never known he liked the taste of coconut.

Further tests turned up no more evidence of illness: Arch got the good news from Dr. Clay's nurse in a message on his machine. While relieved beyond words, he felt the lack of a personal touch in how he had been contacted, as if Dr. Clay had simply passed him onto others. He sat on the bed beside his sleeping wife and whispered his prognosis to her, but she didn't hear it, as she had never heard of his worries in the first place.

Later that day, Arch was called by the local police to come get his son, who had been arrested for shoplifting a video game from a store. At the precinct, he paid the surprisingly high bail and took Bode home. The boy's eyes were so red he looked as if he had been crying for hours.

Passing their car in the parking lot, in the custody of his own father, was another boy, Lon, who played on Bode's team. Sniffling, Arch's son looked at this boy with a mixture of anger and subservience that made Arch uncomfortable.

"Why?" he asked in an almost inaudible voice and got no reply.

Bode ran quickly upstairs and slammed the door of his room—in order to wake his mother? Arch didn't know. Then he heard his son start to cry again. Rounding the corner to the living room, he found Brenda Keen sitting where she had the first time they met.

"Celinda let me in," she said, and Arch knew it wasn't true. He didn't pursue it and simply stood shaking before her, his head bowed like a prisoner about to be executed.

"I might as well be blunt here, Arch—we're all adults. I'm afraid this isn't working out." As evidence, she pointed to a new portfolio, this one tangerine. "We were hoping you could maintain the levels we need to retain the Wilton brand, but our board sees a dismaying inability on your part to do so. And if *you* don't care, then how can we help you?"

"But I do care," he barely choked out.

"The financial terms of dissolving the agreement were spelled out in the original paperwork. The only thing we need to iron out between us is what to do about your name, as that will still be owned and is trademarked by D.E. Do you want to do that now or later? It's all the same to us."

"Later—no, now." Arch smarted under Brenda's harsh, indifferent tone, as if she had already dismissed and forgotten him. He wanted to please her even more than he wished to delay their final parting, though it was irrational; she would not be mollified, and he knew it.

"You can change one letter if you like, that's what we've done in the past. If it makes it less disorienting. It's really no problem for us."

There was a quick negotiation in which Arch barely participated—and of which he knew Brenda would have gotten the better, anyway, having what seemed like legal training. Finally, weeping, Arch agreed to take on the new family name of "Wiltog."

With a razor blade in his trembling hand, Arch scraped the D.E. sticker from the side of his car, as the contract required, leaving a splotch from the adhesive that looked like the white guts of a pigeon he had once seen squashed in the street, a permanent stain.

Days or hours later, he drove a route he remembered by instinct. At dusk, he pulled up a few feet short of a house, not wanting to park directly in the driveway. Then he walked stealthily over a precisely mown lawn to a stone path parallel to a side window. There he half knelt and looked inside.

In an eat-in kitchen, the Blum family was getting ready for dinner. Red was turning on a radio that dated from the Art Deco era; a novel in a Penguin edition was spread open on a counter near where Karina stirred a pot. One son laid aside a catcher's mitt as he took his place at the table; the other, already sitting, faintly hummed a show tune.

In exile, Arch Wiltog hid as the father stepped forward to draw a curtain, as if indeed upon a stage play. The drape was decorated with a swirling pattern of D.E. logos, which were almost undetectable in its elegant design. Soon the sun went completely down, causing the light from inside to glow even brighter on the family no longer visible. It illuminated the window, which was now a mirror. Arch crouched, unmoving, his mouth open, and stared at the image of himself, which was all he had left.

HOLE IN THE GROUND

“Closed for Renovations.” He had always thought it one of the great and unappreciated lies, up there with putting things in the mail and not in your mouth. Was he alone in thinking it? Barry Bumgardner felt alone, standing before the shuttered Steen’s, which had been his local green grocer for the past—how many? Twenty?—years. Sometimes it was “Under New Management,” but always recognizably Steen’s, the aisles never altered enough to look like any other store, the new owners always too lazy to change the name, the identity of the original owner of no interest to the new Asian, Latino, and now Albanian owners, as unimportant as the meanings of expressions one used every day—“Break a leg!” “Down the hatch!”—and didn’t question.

This time, however, was different—brown wrapping paper was taped over all of Steen’s windows, though not well enough to prevent Barry from peeking through. Today he saw a dark, abandoned interior, with paper boxes strewn about unassembled and a few steel racks fallen over like robbery victims, the Terra Chips and Pirate Booty and low-fat pretzels gone from their shelves. Unopened mail lay in a small pile near the front door—bills, Barry figured, and the real reason for the owner’s rush exit.

“Closed for Renovations.” The sign would probably stay there until a new store showed up; at some other places it had taken years, time definitively exposing the lie of the sign, which nobody believed in the first place, the way time caught people in lies nobody ever bought—"My wife is visiting relatives" (for ten years)—but were too polite to challenge.

Still, pondering the future didn't change his present quandary: where to buy milk now that Steen's was gone—the organic kind, without the cow hormones or whatever was bad. He turned, his feet feeling heavy, and walked at the pace of a man twice his age (forty-five—his age, not twice his age) to, well, he guessed Green Harbor was the nearest place now, though the milk was hormonal, the bananas were always brown, and he saw a mouse in there once.

Barry's head throbbed. The four blocks seemed to take forever—because, of course, he didn't want to go, Steen's had been just fine with him, and so his resistance increased time, and not in a good way. Other people might not mind as much, Barry thought, because they didn't work at home, they only passed Steen's on the way to and from their jobs, whereas he actually entered the place three or four times a day, since he never shopped in bulk—where did he live, the suburbs? What did he have, kids?—and went in for one item at a time: salt, a sponge, this morning, milk. Truth be told, he liked to leave his apartment, which sometimes seemed suffocating and was where he spent all day writing freelance brochures for U.S. stamps, and besides, going up and down the stairs was the only exercise he got, being somewhat plump and pasty, so why not spread it out?

Then something cheered him up on the way to Green Harbor, distracting him from the endless length of the trip.

He realized he would be passing Elegamento's, his usual newspaper store, and that today was the second week of the month and thus the time for new magazines to come in. He rarely if ever bought magazines, preferred to just stand and read them right there in the store, but he always bought *something*—usually a single small pack of tissues—to pay Elegamento's for its time. (With irony, he thought that tissue packets represented free-market capitalism at its best, since their price from one end of town to the other ranged from twenty-five cents to a dollar, and Elegamento's, at sixty cents, was right in the comfortable middle—another reason he liked the store.) If the owners seemed to witness his behaviour with something less than pleasure, they always at least recognized him, and that was all that mattered.

But when Barry reached Elegamento's, he read the sign, dumbfounded: "Coming Soon: A New Drugall's."

There was no prevarication, no pride; there was no brown wrapping paper, either; Elegamento's was simply closed, shut, kaput, he thought. Inside, the place was dark, but he could see that all was in suspended animation, the magazines—last month's, not new—candy and paperbacks just sitting there, like those recreations of parts of Pompeii he had seen on TV, only without any ash. A small pile of mail lay on the floor near the door, apparently the universal symbol for an absconded owner.

Barry was more than dismayed; he was mad. Where would he be known for reading magazines for free now? The nearest place was News Buddy, six blocks over, and it was so narrow you couldn't move your arms enough to open a magazine, let alone read one!

At least Elegamento's was honest about what had happened: its landlord had obviously jacked up the rent and a chain was taking over. No wonder they'd blown off that month's bills, they were mad as hell—as mad as Barry. How many Drugall's were there in the neighbourhood now anyway? Ten? (The stores had originated ninety miles north of New York and were spreading everywhere, like an illness or an awful catchphrase.) Each one was alike—how much eczema shampoo and imitation aspirin and scented toilet paper did one neighbourhood need? (And why were the interiors always heated to what seemed like a hundred degrees? And why was there always a long line, even when you were the only one there?!)

He bet Steen's would be one soon, too, or some other national outlet for clothes, coffee, or whatever else. In the twenty-odd years he had lived in the neighbourhood, he had seen individuality and small ownership dwindle—and who knew in what homogenized hell it would all end up? What had happened to his little microcosm of Manhattan, the two or three blocks around his apartment house? Who had stolen his little city?

Barry's vision briefly blurred and affected his balance. His fingers scrambled in his pocket for a pill but found none. These fits of anxiety, depression, and paranoia— other people's words, not his—were eased but not erased by the prescription. He resented having to take the pills in the first place: he was only being honest, after all—chain stores *were* taking over everything, it was true! Still, not even having the option of ingesting one unnerved him, especially since he'd been chastened by losing his job at the Philatelic Society a year before and going on disability. He would have to go home and find the small bottle he had left—intentionally? Arrogantly?—in his other jeans; the prospect of returning to the tiny room increased the unhappiness that now left him leaning limply against the wall of the new, upcoming Drugall's.

The search for the pills soon gave Barry hope, however. In the pocket, his fingers felt a small piece of paper, stuck deeper down. It was a ticket from his dry cleaners, where he had left his one good shirt. It would be ready today, that's what the man said (he was pretty sure), and retrieving the shirt would give him a positive new chore to perform and take his mind off the appalling industrial encroachment he seemed to encounter at every turn today in, as he thought of it, his little city.

The dry cleaners were, what, up two blocks or over one? Were they on Second and not Third? The pills, regardless of their effect in other areas, had always focused his attention, snapped him to, so now—in addition to the extremes of emotion he was pinballing back and forth between—he groped for simple surety as to the way he should walk, at last reaching the dry cleaners by instinct only, like a dog whose owner has uprooted him and finds his old home from many, many miles away.

The balloons outside the store were the first indication that something was awry, their merry aspect a kind of awful harbinger. The name was still the generic "Dry Cleaners," but that gave Barry small comfort when he took out his ticket inside.

"That was from the old owner," said the man behind the counter—Asian, like the last proprietor, but male, tall, and young, not female, squat, and old. "Sorry."

"What do you mean?" Barry said, surprised by the sudden sound of his own voice, since he had been silent for days at home. "What about my shirt?"

"I don't know what to tell you," he shrugged, regretful but only a little.

Barry had no answer; he just kept crumpling the ticket until it was a small ball in his hand. It had always been a guarantee, a laundry ticket, a way to get things back that had been so close to his skin they were almost a part of it, a way to get them back better. He was the one who had to worry about losing it; if he had the ticket, he was home free. What happened to his things when it didn't work that way, when no one cared if he kept his part of the bargain? Had *he* left the shirt there too long? Or had someone rewritten the rules here, too, as they were doing in the rest of the neighbourhood?

This was the worst yet, for it upended Barry's assumption that big business was all to blame; this was a small shop owner. And it wasn't enough that his places of convenience and ritual were being withdrawn, now his *stuff* was being abandoned, lost and forgotten, along with everything else! How had a piece of him disappeared with the old dry cleaners, like water down a dirty drain?

"Where is my shirt?" he kept asking. "Where is my good shirt?"

He was in danger, he had to escape—and that meant travel, the only way he knew how. He had to reach the garage in which he kept his mother's car, a 1991 Volvo, which had been his inheritance after her death two years ago, along with enough money in carefully stipulated installments to keep it housed, cleaned, and filled. Sometimes Barry felt that the car was his mother's real survivor, not he, so lovingly did she allot the money and spell out the method for its upkeep. "At least the car works," she once told him.

Though he rarely drove it, Barry made to do so now, nearly sprinting the ten blocks to the garage, which bordered the highway and so allowed easy access for getting out of town.

He had actually been standing in the garage for several minutes before he realized where he was—and how could he have known when it had been so utterly transformed, as totally shifted in shape as a balloon animal, one minute a dachshund, the next a giraffe?

It was a city park now, covered in fake grass and featuring cheery green benches, swings, and slides, a distinct improvement over the old grey garage, but a change so drastic that it almost made him lose consciousness and have to sit on one of those swings, the leather slingshot kind that sinks along with you.

He knew it was possible that he had not heeded the warnings, that he had discarded the letters that told him to remove his mother's car or else—he often tossed out envelopes unopened that seemed official and might mean he owed money. But now, along with his locations, routines, and clothes, his *past* was being dumped in the junkyard in the form of a car that, though a hated rival for her love, was all he had left that was tangible and touched by his mother.

And who could object to how it happened? Who didn't like a park? This was a pro-public civic gesture, not some crass commercial grab by a corporation or an individual. This was a good thing, even *he* knew that; the fact that he couldn't blame anybody caused him to cry tears of bitter and lonely helplessness.

Barry cried until he could cry no more. The discombobulating process seemed complete. There was only one place to go now: home, which while small enough to entomb him was also familiar enough to embrace him. He would bring back to it no milk or shirt but it might not matter; his dusty, cluttered, and overheated studio would at least allow him—or force on him, with the entrancing fumes from its radiator, the moderating knob of which had long since ceased to turn—the protective sleep he felt was his last, best, and at this point only possible action.

Drying his tears on a coffee-stained napkin—from the old Steen's?—he found in his back pocket, and averting his eyes from a child who now stood staring at him, horrified, at the base of the slide, Barry stood and started for the sidewalk. His Metro Card had fifty cents too little on it for the bus.

He stopped a few blocks from his home, panting from the effort, though he had walked at a reasonable rate. Unable not to, he pulled a little cell phone from his pocket, one which needed repair, one which for some reason was stuck on speakerphone and so blared his business to the world at large—which was most often the ringing of his home phone, as he checked for messages that were never there. Then he pressed in his personal PIN.

This time, there was a message. Barry turned to muffle the booming voice from any nosey passerby.

"This is Dr. Hagel's office. Please call at your earliest convenience. Thank you."

That was all the woman, clearly a receptionist, said in a tone neither comforting nor alarming, with a neutrality she had been trained—or with which she was naturally gifted and hired in the first place—to perform.

It was, he knew, the results of the tests he had taken since complaining of horrible headaches and dropping things during dinner—the kinds of symptoms ignored by others when you're the nervous type, and that even you yourself hope bizarrely are just more mental problems, more maladjustments, and not something worse, something in your brain that little pills can't cure.

It was the call, Barry admitted to himself, that he had left the apartment to avoid; his milk would have lasted until tomorrow.

Now he felt the cold touch of fear. Wouldn't the doctor have left a message *himself* if it were nothing? Wouldn't he feel that leaving bad news on a machine was too blunt, too callous, and, most of all, too cowardly? Of course, Barry thought—and his fingers trembled so much he had to struggle to put the phone away.

Then, suddenly, uncharacteristically, he caught himself. Why was he jumping to conclusions? Calm down, he thought, see it clearly. There were other opinions to get, other tests to take. Hadn't his cousin contracted something bad and survived? Mightn't he improve his diet, eat more greens, add more exercise? All was not lost; there were things he still could do.

Bolstered by this unique bucking up of himself, he started to take the few steps left toward home to return the call. He turned the final corner, his heart beating more from weird—to him impressive—hope than panic.

His building was gone.

All that was left was a giant hole in the ground, as wide and deep as the building itself had been. The residences to the right and left remained; it was as if the one between had simply been pulled out, as cleanly and completely as a tooth from a person's mouth.

Barry went to the edge and looked in, looked hundreds of feet down to a floor of solid earth, looked into the emptiness. Then he looked back up and stared without fear straight into the raging sun.

He had no doubt what was about to happen to him.

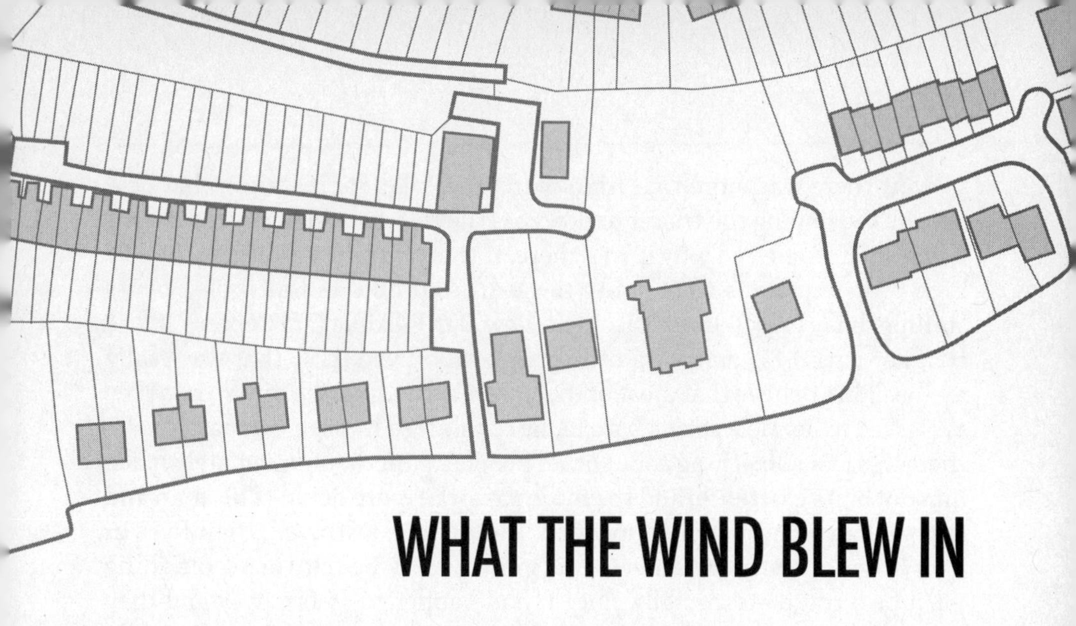

WHAT THE WIND BLEW IN

"But why would they be *here*?" Alan asked, trying to keep his voice calm.

"I don't know," Annabelle, his wife, replied. "The government put them here."

"But it happened a long way from here. It doesn't make any sense."

"I didn't say that it did."

There would be no settling the issue, Alan knew, partly because Annabelle didn't know the answer and partly because she didn't care. If two survivors of a hurricane half a country away—almost the whole country, really—had been resettled in their town ninety miles north of New York, then that's what had happened, and that's all there was to it.

"The government doesn't know what it's doing," she said. "That's obvious, isn't it? So why would this make any more sense than anything else they do?"

Alan shrugged; she had him there. That wasn't the point, anyway, not to Anna: it was the fact of the couple's suffering, and the fact that it could be eased and that they might help ease it. Alan didn't believe these were facts, but he didn't say. He just let Anna go on, establishing the basis for what she was suggesting they do.

"We have empty rooms. I can move my sewing stuff out of the den. Or you can move your toy theatres. It just seems criminal that two people who've been through so much should have to stay in a trailer park, and for God knows how long."

Now there was more that Alan didn't say. Like, for instance, that he'd never liked having the trailer park across the two-lane highway from their house, had wondered why it was there, if this was what their notoriously high property taxes were going toward. (And no one was fooled by its smiling daisy logo and its title: "The New Day Flexible Life Center." It was a trailer park!) He distrusted the people who lived in it, that was really it—he didn't believe that most of them were actually in the dire straits they professed to be. He wasn't a blamer, he considered himself compassionate; there was just something about other people's pain that immediately made him doubt its existence, and the more pain, the more doubt. This man and woman had been suddenly upended, their home destroyed, their lives in a place ended perhaps forever, and so inevitably he felt the whole thing must be a fraud—especially since it had happened so far away and they were now here. *And* because Annabelle wanted the people to temporarily move in with them. But he said none of this.

A year before, he would not have been so discreet. In those days—that is to say, in the twenty years of their marriage leading up to a year ago—he would have railed, scoffed, put his foot down, and Anna would have politely endured it and then backed down or compromised in a way that pleased him more than her, for he was always more negatively "invested" in his argument than she was positively in hers. But that was before Anna got cancer and things changed.

The suspicion and petulance that characterized much of Alan's conversations had been all along, it turned out, a kind of voodoo, a way to ward off the pain he saw in others and dreaded experiencing himself, even the pain involved in considering their pain. It was a form of subservience to pain, abject weakness before it. So when pain visited him, as it was always going to anyway, no matter what he did, visited Annabelle and so him, he had to switch tactics; now he did and did not question anything Annabelle wanted, as an equally ineffective way to keep the cancer, and thus the pain from returning. This was what closed his mouth or changed what he said—though it could not change what he thought, the pattern of suspicion being too well established within him not to manifest someplace.

"You're being awfully quiet," Anna said, surprised.

Anna, on the other hand, had responded to circumstances differently. Before her diagnosis and treatment (it was breast cancer, she was forty-eight, the radiation was over now, she'd been clean for six months, no hair loss), she had been more open to and less frightened of life than her husband. In the time since, she had shown signs of passivity and depression. The hurricane couple's appearance in town had brought back—even increased—her old intrepidness. She felt a new and invigorating alliance with them because they also suffered, felt they deserved all the help they could get. And since she was still here on Earth, she was here to help. Others in town had merely had them to dinner; Anna was willing to complete the permits to move the couple. This was its own mystical trade-off—help for health—but whatever its motive it tested Alan's own superstitions and his new vow of silence. So far, he had passed.

"I wasn't being quiet. I was just thinking," he said, and this at least was true.

"And?" she said, apparently eager to get going with her plan.

"I—" And here he swallowed a hundred objections, questions, and jokes, effectively ending his sentence as it began. He placed a hand on Anna's hand, which was still as elegant and pale as the day they met, though he hadn't noticed until a year ago. "Sure. Whatever you want."

~

When he met the couple, he was no more convinced of their veracity—less so, if that were possible. The Lynches were white, and hadn't most of the hurricane survivors been black? That was the first thing. Secondly, they both dressed as if they had stepped out of a photograph from the 1930s or something—the dust bowl, the Oakies, the WPA, or whatever: denim shirt and jeans with rolled-up cuffs for the man, a simple sleeveless gingham dress for the woman. And even though they were probably in Alan and Annabelle's mid to late forties age range, they looked twenty years older, with leathery skin tanned to a perilous crisp and rings beneath their eyes so deep they seemed to have been whittled out of wood.

The man in particular, Sam Lynch—and it was such an all-American name, wasn't it, appropriate to that earlier decade; too right, Alan thought, too clever—had a sculpted look, six feet tall and *sinewy*, that was the word, with the skin of his forearms stretched so tight that his veins had a protruding and snake-like look, phallic, if you must know, and his ropey neck was the same way. It bothered Alan to look at him: basic man, penile all over, and unembarrassed about it; show-offy, he would have said, if he had said anything to Annabelle.

The woman, on the other hand, Dorothy, was less resilient looking, with lank brown hair, crepey upper arms, her breasts already the "dugs" of the elderly, her facial features hangdog and hopeless, as if she had given up expecting to be remembered. It all seemed an imitation: iconic images of the Depression-era man and woman, wax figures in a diorama of America's most miserable. Alan couldn't stop these thoughts; they were piling up in his head like planes on a runway, for they couldn't fly out of his mouth.

All he allowed himself to say to them was, "Welcome to our home."

And Anna seemed so glad they were there, clasping both of their hands in her own and then hanging onto and swinging them a little, girlish in her happiness. She even seemed to choke back a tear or two, and the sight made Alan place a fond and gentling hand on her back, cynicism falling from the holes in his head like sifted flour.

"You can have the downstairs bedroom," she said. "Alan's moved his toy theatres."

Alan winced a little, hearing this. His hobby—and Annabelle couldn't have children and they didn't want to adopt, so yes, they both had hobbies, hers were sewing and dollhouses—suddenly seemed erudite and even effeminate before this couple of careworn, indomitable, apparently exiled Americans. Even the house itself seemed excessive and elitist (and it was only two storeys and they had earned it; owning a hardware store wasn't easy, especially these days, with chains taking over, even upstate, just look at the Drugall's and Super Buy 'n' Fly in town). But who were the Lynches to complain? Hadn't they been plucked out of a government-issued trailer, and before that, supposedly, from the drink?

And they weren't complaining. They were very grateful.

"Thank you so much," Dorothy said with a Midwestern or southern twang that sounded to Alan like American speech before it had been flattened by TV. Then, with dry, cracked lips, she placed a short, abashed, but clearly sincere kiss on Annabelle's cheek.

For his part, Sam performed a physical gesture so difficult Alan wasn't sure he'd ever seen it done before. He winked with *feeling*, as a taciturn way of giving thanks. Winks were usually—weren't they always—a form of snideness or flirtation. To wink with *feeling*—and slowly enough to reveal the veins in Sam's eyelids that were once again reminders of hardship and erections—that took talent. Alan, of course, didn't share this reaction, only reflexively—and it was a mistake, and he knew it the second before he did it, not after, before—winked back. *This* wink, of course, was a normal one and so completely inappropriate. It seemed to cast a pall over the kitchen in which they all stood before Annabelle saved the day by saying, "Well. You'll want to get moved in."

Minutes later, Alan couldn't help but peek in to see their belongings, whatever they had left of them: a few bundles wrapped up in old newspaper and tied with what seemed baling wire were sitting in an orderly line near the bed of the spare bedroom, placed so as to be as unobtrusive as possible—placed respectfully, that was it, *too* respectfully. In his and Annabelle's bedroom, Alan had piled his little theatres modelled on Broadway houses less carefully: a stage punctured here, a balcony bent there. (And don't ask him why he'd started building them; he'd barely seen a play in his life. Maybe they were dream-like expressions of his critical nature, temples in his religion of judgment; Alan wouldn't have been the one to say.)

When Alan walked in, he saw Annabelle standing by their window, looking out absently at the backyard. Soon after her surgery, he would sometimes catch her standing like this, hugging herself, her arms crossed with her fingers in her armpits, one palm covering the place where the lump in her breast had been removed. She looked weirdly Napoleonic, he thought, perhaps as a way to stop the heartbreak he felt in seeing it. He didn't know how to touch her himself in those days, didn't want to offend or cause harm but also didn't want to seem too squeamish, either: again, pain's dithering supplicant. Today he was pleased that her arms were crossed normally, her hands at her opposite elbows. So he crept up behind her and fully embraced her, as if he could magically keep the rest of her from slipping away as one piece already had.

She placed her head back against his chest, perhaps casting her own spell but in any case breaking his. "I'm so glad," she said, "that they're here."

To keep himself quiet, Alan concentrated on smelling her hair, taking in deep inhales that he imagined filled his mind with her scent, freshening and obscuring his bad thoughts. "Me too."

—~—

That night, Anna made a veritable feast, the kind of food the two rarely if ever had and certainly never had at home. It was a meal of "classics": pork chops, mashed potatoes, peas, what Alan thought Anna thought the Lynches would have eaten before all was lost. It was delicious, Alan had to admit, almost exotic after so much pasta and broiled chicken. He even delayed taking in a second hefty bite when Sam started saying grace, something no one had ever done beneath their roof before. Annabelle listened with a curious and appreciative smile, so Alan let it go then quickly dug back into the juicy meat, which he had painted with potato.

"That was wonderful," Dorothy said after a final bite of pecan pie.

"Absolutely," Sam said, leaning back and patting his stomach in overalls he had changed into. It was clear to Alan that if the Lynches ate in such a way they hadn't done so in years, since way before the hurricane. So he didn't hold it against them when Sam now lit up a pipe with only the most cursory head cock to ask permission. Anna touched Alan's hand, secretly, to say allow it, though she hated smoke in the house even more than he did.

Perhaps to further show his appreciation, Sam then brought out a banjo and strummed and sang some American standards, from "Polly Wolly Doodle" to "This Land is Your Land" and "Stardust." Sometimes Annabelle sang along in a voice Alan hadn't heard (or maybe just hadn't listened to) in years, one as pure and unaffected and touchingly flat as a child's. Then the Lynches said goodnight with a stalwart handshake (Sam) and a heartfelt hug (Dorothy) and went to bed.

As he did the dishes, Alan looked out the kitchen window at the clear night sky. A storm said to be crossing the country toward them was changing course, he had heard, maybe heading out to sea. Maybe the hurricane had been the worst of the "extreme" weather that summer. He heard Annabelle leave the table and, humming a little of Sam's last song, go upstairs.

When he reached their bedroom himself, Alan realized that he had left his watch downstairs. He tiptoed back to the living room, hoping that the creaks wouldn't awaken Annabelle, who had passed out—smiling—the second she lay down.

On the first floor, where the Lynches were, the bedroom door was shut, the light out. But a light still conspicuously shone from beneath the bathroom door beside it.

Alan looked for the watch in the places he usually set it: the side of the kitchen sink where pots still soaked, the arm of the living room chair on which the day's paper was piled. However, he couldn't get to his third usual place, the rim of the tub in the downstairs john.

The bathroom door suddenly opened and he hid in the shadows of the dark living room.

The light stayed on for a second and displayed with almost vulgar overtness a naked Sam Lynch. His body was a map of a male physique devoted for decades just to action and forbearance: flat where it was not muscular, scarred, with no place for the results of self-indulgence, no spare flesh, all of it in use. Even his penis—"weathered" was the only word for it—seemed more a weapon or utensil than an instrument for his pleasure or anyone else's.

The one jarring exception was his right hand, which Alan swore gripped the glittery and frivolous gold of his watch. With his other hand, Sam reached up and—his tortured bicep flexed—turned off the light; everything, including truth, disappeared.

The next morning, Alan was awakened by the clock radio, static-y and stuck between stations. He made out that the weather forecast had changed a bit: the storm might not pass the Northeast entirely. He turned it off, quickly.

He waited until Annabelle had cleared the breakfast dishes (bacon, toast, even an omelette, not just bran cereal). He studied Sam for any sign of guilt or any other kind of nefarious behaviour—and Dorothy, too, for she might be if not his active partner then his acquiescent accomplice. But the couple did nothing untoward or odd; they ate with the same deep and quiet appreciation of the food as they had their dinner. And did they have to say grace before every meal? Wouldn't food sort of *stay blessed* from before? Watching and coarsely wondering was easier for Alan than looking at Anna, because her pleasure at serving (saving?) the Lynches made him feel ashamed. Still, his watch hadn't turned up and he instinctively rubbed his bare wrist now in response. (It was a good one, waterproof, a fortieth birthday present from his sister.) He hadn't mentioned it to Annabelle.

Alan excused himself before the others, drifted to the bathroom, then pivoted in secret to the spare bedroom. Standing in the doorway, he checked the space out: most of the bundles still sat where they'd been, some shabby clothes hung in the closet; the Lynches had made the least and most humble use of the place. Checking behind himself, he cautiously entered.

A chest of drawers was the only piece of furniture except the bed; its top was clean. Alan opened the skinny first drawer; saw just a few pairs of men's underwear, neatly folded, and one old wedding night-type slip, placed at a discreet distance from them. He closed it then knelt slightly to open a bottom drawer more likely to be used for hiding.

"Wonderful breakfast," someone said.

Alan looked up, suddenly, and saw Sam in the threshold—looked *up* at him, for he was now unfortunately fully on his knees. The man stood casually cleaning his gums with a toothpick, one he must have brought with him for they kept none in the house (or had Annabelle bought a box just for them?).

"Yes," Alan said, blushing. He awkwardly started to stand and closed the drawer he had not had time to examine. It was his house, he could do in it as he pleased; perhaps the whole thing would go unmentioned?

It did not. "Did you leave something in here you wanted?" Sam asked with—unless Alan were crazy—a touch of insinuation.

Well, he had asked; why not answer? "Yes, actually," Alan said, now at his full height which was still less than Sam's. "My watch."

"Your watch."

"Uh-huh. Gold. Engraved. Have you seen it?"

Sam seemed to snort mirthlessly. He stopped using and merely rolled the toothpick around in his mouth. Then he answered but indirectly. "I had a watch once. An old watch. A gift from my dad. Even hung on its own chain. Fob, I guess they call it. It meant a lot to me. I have to admit that, when Dorothy and I were sitting on our roof after the hurricane, holding up our signs for help, the watch crossed my mind. Funny, isn't it, since we'd lost everything we owned, even living things, our dog? I remembered it was kind of ironical how careful I had been with that watch. Even kept it in its own little box. Why? Why had I bothered when everything is so easily washed away? I should have been careless with it. I should have left it, I don't know, just sitting on the side of a bathtub or someplace."

At this, he looked directly and unapologetically at Alan with eyes that said he had seen more bad times than his host—maybe more than anyone ever—and was angry and afraid of nothing.

"The government tried to give us things, to make it up to us," he said. "But they never can. There's no end to what we're owed. But, at any rate, this house is a lot better than where we were."

He smiled then, and the toothpick stuck more obviously out of his mouth like a small second tongue, one more way to say too bad and screw you. The veins in his neck grew hideously outlined, and Alan suddenly felt he could see inside him.

"Good luck in finding it," Sam said. This time, his wink was a mix of the snotty and sincere, which was much more disturbing than being one or the other.

—~—

Like one of those bible characters God tells to slay his son or something—Anna had been the occasional churchgoer, not him, and then mostly for the music—Alan felt he faced his greatest obstacle yet to mastering his new belief and its rituals. He was on the verge of blurting out what had happened, establishing why the Lynches must immediately leave—backsliding, as it were, results notwithstanding—when Annabelle prevented it. It was after she saw him more agitatedly rubbing the faint white circle on his wrist where the watch had been.

"You might as well know," she said. "I gave your watch to him."

"What?" Alan looked up, now holding the wrist hard.

"I'm sorry, but . . . maybe I'm not. He has so little—both of them do—and asks for so little. When I look at them and speak to them, I see that they've been made better, or—what's the word?—ennobled by all they've been through and the acceptance that there will be more: why wouldn't there, you know? Sam refused your watch at first, of course, but then I kind of folded it into his big palm and placed his fingers over it. Why not let them know that there can be good along with the bad? He almost wept—he wouldn't, you know, not him. But she did, though it was a dry kind of crying; maybe she has no real tears left. She hugged him from behind. Then we all stood embracing in a circle of what I can only call thanks."

She touched Alan's hand, to free the circulation-stopping chokehold he now had on his opposite wrist. "You can always get another watch."

Anna's face was—well, beaming, was the only way to describe it. Alan literally bit his lip as people are said to do in stories, to keep from speaking. Or maybe he wanted to cause himself pain—that self-flagellating thing that supplicants or novice nuns do—to remind himself of what he was trying to repel. When he finally stopped biting, it was at the same moment Anna separated his hands. Then he nodded, which meant it was okay, about the watch. In truth, he no longer knew which one of them was right, what was true and not, what Sam had really said and to whom: which one of their magics was going to work?

The next day, Alan crossed the highway to the trailer park. He looked up at the darkening sky; heavy rain was now being forecast from the oncoming storm, targeting New York directly. As he entered, he felt on guard, conscious as he almost never was of his class (which was what? Working-middle-upper?) and how it would distinguish him. But he found he was dressed virtually the same as everyone else, polo shirt, jeans, and sneakers being a new American uniform. He didn't feel as observed as he had anticipated, less the detective or undercover agent as he had feared. He tried not to judge—or its flip side, fear—the people he saw beside the American flags, the clothes on lines, the cars on blocks. He tried to keep an open mind.

In truth, he wanted his visit to end as soon as possible and provide him with answers, or at least more information. But he found, when he started asking about the Lynches, that they had made little impression on people except provoking a gossipy interest in some, and in others doubts similar to Alan's own (were they hustlers looking for a government handout? Why white? Why here?). For a few, there was also an extra element of resentment: they hadn't liked their own hardships diminished by the Lynches' example. These people in particular were glad the couple was gone.

Only one person had more than a few syllables to say. He was a man about thirty, an inhabitant of one of the shabbier trailers. His wife—a hugely fat woman of twenty-five or so—was eager to introduce him to Alan, if only it seemed to be saved from being with him herself. She whispered that after having difficulty finding work, he had attempted suicide and a few days earlier had been released from a mental hospital farther upstate. His memory of the event and many other things, including his identity, was now faulty. Her marriage had brought her more than she'd bargained for, but she distrusted authorities too much to completely relinquish the man to them, so she was stuck. As a reflection of his fragility—or was it her own embarrassment?—she kept him in the back of her trailer on a couch piled with pillows, as if he were a cat in a closet having kittens.

"I know all about them," he said authoritatively, his head moving spasmodically now and then. "They cause everything."

"What do you mean?" Alan asked.

"Everything bad."

Alan looked at him: trim, almost handsome, the hair on his head growing back in patches after being shaved during his stay upstate. "Like the—"

"The hurricane. And that thing down in the city. And this." He rolled up a sleeve, long for a summer day, to reveal slash marks that started on his wrists and ran up to his elbow. "They made me do this. They came here from hell."

Alan couldn't help but be repelled by the display of his injuries and was immediately dismissive of his "information." Yet it was so different from the beliefs he and Annabelle held that he found himself compelled and even a little frightened by it.

And he continued to be so when the man, shifting forward on the couch far enough to get close to Alan's face, ended with, "Good to see you, Phil."

"That's his own name," the woman said, outside again with Alan. "Sorry."

"I see."

"Don't take him too serious. He harps on your friends for what happened to him. He thinks the end times are near, and they're the cause. I think he'd have a pretty good case against his *parents* if he could remember something real."

She looked off, seeming to consider her options. Alan nodded, seriously, and thanked her. Then he hurried from the park. He felt as if he'd been to an old-style carny sideshow, complete with fortune teller (the country fair the town hosted didn't have them anymore and had become benign and cautious with healthy food booths and hand sanitizer soap stands near the petting zoo). Yet he didn't entirely scoff. Did this lunatic know something he and Anna didn't? Preoccupied, he had to dodge cars coming in both directions to get home, the rain already starting to fall.

~

Alan was pretty well soaked by the time he reached the driveway of his house, thunder sounding. On his way in, he saw the Lynches sitting dry beneath the roof of his—his and Anna's!—porch, Sam rocking and smoking that foul smelling piece-of-crap pipe, Dorothy staring off with a peacefulness he had not seen in her before and which he could not help but deeply resent. Yet mixed with his contempt was a little bit of fear of them now, as he again heard the claims and saw the rolled up sleeve of the crazy guy in the trailer.

Once inside, he slowed at the entrance to the spare room. After checking through the front hall window and seeing the relaxed backs of the Lynches, he walked into where they slept. Something immediately caught his eye through the now half-shut closet door. It was a burst of sharp colour, sharper than the faded denim and dusty browns of the Lynches' wardrobe.

He walked toward it, his fingers twitching with anticipation. Then he yanked the door completely open.

He saw his own purple button-down shirt. It was the one he'd bought down in the city one night, admittedly when he was a little drunk, after dinner. Still, he wore it, usually on special occasions and mostly to prove to himself that it had not been a terrible mistake. What did it matter? It was his—his alone!

Alan turned on his heel and coldly approached the chest of drawers. As if he were a policeman frisking a suspect, he pulled open the top drawer—and before he could even get to the more likely offenders near the floor, he saw Annabelle's amethyst necklace. It was the one that she—well, he couldn't remember where she got it, if he had even given it to her. He only knew that it was hers, just as the—what colour was it? A funny name for green—ring beside it and the pair of pearl earrings beside *it* were hers.

Alan slammed the drawers, forgetting that he meant not to attract any attention. He glanced at the doorway, nervously, and on the way, saw something else: a large leather bag sitting in a corner. It contained his golf clubs—the expensive set he had used only once and not well about a year ago, when he had decided to get more exercise. He cursed out loud but the sound was obscured by a shout of thunder that rattled the entire house.

Alan burst from the room and went into the main sitting area, past the dining room, convinced that everywhere he went he saw items missing—a glass ashtray owned by Annabelle's aunt from the coffee table, a pair of his nylon sneakers from under a chair, a broken umbrella from a stand—things that were now obviously rolled up in the Lynches' lousy bales of belongings. The rain fell so heavily on the roof it seemed like more anger and confusion trying to enter his mind, which was already stuffed to overflowing with them.

Out the window, through the obscuring sheets of water, he thought he saw Sam Lynch. He was standing and looking in with an expression of angry entitlement. Or was it something else, something worse? Like pride of ownership—of the rain itself? Alan felt faint.

"Alan?"

He stopped suddenly, responding to the familiar voice. He had not even noticed Annabelle standing at the window and watching the storm. Her arms were not folded this time: one elbow was in one palm and the other palm was at her cheek, Jack Benny-style. It was her most benign and least anguished stance so far.

"Yes?" he said, thrown by seeing her.

"I want you to know," she said, smiling in a certain way that was, well, adorable to him and always had been, and what it was like was not even worth trying to explain to anyone else, they would never understand. "I felt they needed some more of our things."

He was about to scream at Anna. Maybe it was worse than that the Lynches couldn't be trusted; maybe they were to be feared. Maybe she had invited into their home the very pain they had been trying in their own opposing ways to scare off, that their guests were who or what had been spreading it around the world for centuries, ever since the start of time, ever since the day they invented death. But before he could open his mouth, a javelin of lightning was thrown across the sky, and it exposed and electrified the living room like an old-fashioned flash bulb from the world's biggest camera.

Then they heard the sound. It was more than a boom or a crack or a funny sound effect from a cartoon. It was a tragic clash between giants equal in nature, the murder of something in the earth by something from the sky. Alan and Anna felt the house shake brutally—they were two tiny figures in a snow globe, that's how little power they had and had always had—as the top half of the old oak tree in their backyard, which had just then been killed by electricity, broke off and crashed into the roof, landing in their attic.

The lights flickered for a few seconds but stayed on. Soon, the house settled and was still, though Alan felt in his feet what he was sure were aftershocks. They heard the rain again, which was letting up, as if having made its big statement it had nothing else to say.

Both the faiths they had invented had been removed from within them; all that was left was the physical reality that existed outside. Both Alan and Anna said nothing, only wept, overwhelmed by fear of her disappearing from the world in pain, of his following after, of their showing up again nowhere, of their being lost forever and never even knowing. The setting sun was suddenly and again revealed. They looked outside and saw no one.

But they heard something, and it wasn't organic. A car was being started. They both ran to the window and saw their Subaru pulling out of the garage. At the wheel was Sam Lynch, Dorothy beside him. They didn't wear seat belts, as if they were new inventions they didn't understand. Their things and many of Alan's and Annabelle's were stuffed in the back seat and overflowing from the trunk. Given? Taken? And what about the new storm clouds that Alan could swear he saw forming before them?

Alan reached over as the Lynches drove away. His hand found and tightly held Annabelle's. Now these were mysteries for other people never to solve.

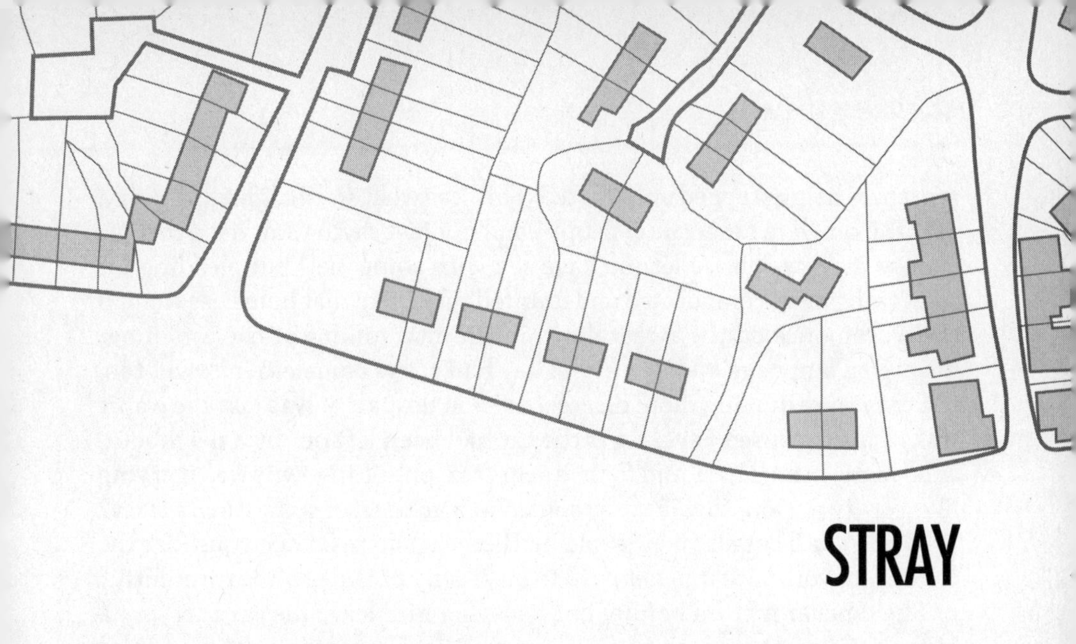

STRAY

She couldn't remember when she first heard the sound, but once she had that was all it took. Faye lived on the first floor of the Gleeful Terrace apartment complex, a—even she acknowledged—somewhat shabby development in a town ninety miles north of New York. It had been inserted into fields that also played host to several houses similarly stuck into the countryside a few years before (like those long houses—hotels!—you stuck on a Monopoly square; that's how ill-fitting and arbitrary they looked, though just as in the game whomever had stuck them there did so as a symbol of success). Wild life still roamed the area—mostly deer, raccoons, and skunks—perplexed by the change in their surroundings and adapting to it only in the sense of now feeding on what their new human neighbours threw or left out instead of on the living prey that had been scared away. Less exotic creatures also ran around, some in fact not wild at all, some belonging to the people who'd moved in and were merely let out to play and hunt frivolously, not to forage for food to survive—and by creatures she meant cats, because that's definitely what she'd heard crying. (Faye had had cats as a kid but not since then, so it had been a long time since she'd heard the sound and still hadn't forgotten it—probably close to thirty years, for she was thirty-four.)

It wasn't the usual cat crying, which had a repetitive, automatic pilot or broken car alarm quality. This one made a plaintive sound, broken up into what seemed like words, with spaces in between them to suggest sentences being stopped and started. This was what she imagined, anyway, as if the cat were beseeching people, and not just saying say "feed me!" or "house me!" or "please let me have sex with someone!" but pleading for something more complicated and unintelligible, like that homeless woman she'd seen once on the street down in the city, talking at the top of her lungs in a language all her own. (They had a few homeless in town, too, but they were quieter, more discreet even in despair, it was just the way it was.) This confused Faye, for if the cat had been left out by a neighbour, as so many others had, and for the same reason—fun—why was it crying like a crazy person, that is to say someone homeless, or some*thing*, a stray?

"Well, that's because it is," explained her neighbour, Ed Koch (just like the old city mayor). "But it never used to be, it only became this way recently."

She'd never met Ed before, but had seen him leave his car carrying a big bag of dry cat food, and so she assumed he'd know something and had stopped him in the parking lot.

"He was part of a litter that used to belong to someone here."

Ed seemed about fifty but could have been any age, for he had a timeless, dishevelled look: straggly greying beard, comb over, and wrinkled checked shirt untucked over chinos above sneakers. He wore glasses that made him look like a retired academic, though he seemed too young to be retired (but if he wasn't, why was he at home in the afternoon mid-week?). Anyway, this was how he spoke, too, in a precise, learned sort of way, not snooty but smart and with a slight lisp. Though Faye knew it all was silly: wearing glasses didn't mean people were smart; she wore them, was supposed to, anyway, and she wasn't smart, well, not book smart anyway.

"What do you mean, used to belong?" she asked, a little guilty that he stood there holding the cat food bag the whole time, but he could have put it down, she wasn't stopping him.

"Well, the recent young super—Ronnie, not the old super, Tim—"

"I moved in three months ago, right after Tim left, like he had one day to go, that's when."

"Well—and it wasn't a family reason by the way, they just made Tim take the fall for the string of robberies here, and then for the boiler explosion in the winter, though God knows they weren't Tim's fault."

Faye was quiet. She hadn't known about either thing—the real estate broker hadn't mentioned them—and she felt a little annoyed and even a little scared hearing about them. Still, if nothing else, the information proved that Ed knew a lot about the complex and so could be trusted to tell her about the cat. Frankly, she wished he'd get to it already.

"Then Ronnie, his replacement, only lasted six weeks, because they caught him selling ecstasy out of the back of his truck."

"*Really?*" The unpleasant facts about her home kept coming, made better or worse by Ed's matter-of-fact delivery, she wasn't sure.

"Yes, and when they fired Ronnie—and I'm not sure if he's going to be prosecuted or was just told to skedaddle, you know—he left his cats behind."

Faye was quiet again, this last imparted fact the most disturbing of all. Since it was obviously just the beginning of a longer, even more upsetting story, she braced herself for it, knowing she had to hear it even though she dreaded hearing—and besides, with his detached and intellectual air, Ed didn't seem the type to avoid upsetting details to spare anyone's emotions. He almost seemed to enjoy giving the awful specifics, rubbing his audience's nose in them—or was he rubbing his own? After all, he had hoisted the heavy cat food bag up on his shoulder instead of putting it down. Why, so he could feel pain as he expressed someone else's?

"Ronnie had adopted a cat in his office. The cat had kittens. They were royalty for a while. They had the run of the place. And when he got fired, he just abandoned them. Someone said they saw the mother cat dead by the highway; they said they could recognize her by her red-and-white stripe. Most of the offspring disappeared. A few were taken in—the friendly ones, savvy to the ways of humans, able to be fed and petted. But there's one that's stayed. It's red and male, skittish, frightened, hard to feed and, as a result, to keep alive. A shame."

Ed gave a little half-smile, a wince really, either in reaction to the sad events or to his—they must have been by now—aching arms, shoulder, and hands, or both. Then, because Faye wasn't responding, he turned toward the path to his own building.

Faye was silent because she was shocked, to put it mildly. She couldn't imagine anyone being so cavalier about other living things, especially those that had trusted Ronnie and didn't have the mental capacity to understand the shift in their circumstances.

"Well," she finally blurted out, stopping Ed at the last second, "couldn't someone take him in? Couldn't *you*—"

"I already have three cats," he said softly, but with the first small hint of an edge to his voice. "So I don't think that would be feasible. Besides, some have attempted it, and it's impossible."

"Well, what about just feeding him, what's—"

"I and others have tried that, too. But, as I've said, he's too frightened to even come close. But you're, you know, perfectly free to try."

He said it as if it were a project doomed to failure but one he found touching, endearing even, for her to attempt. Then, since this prompted no reply from Faye, who was still chewing over and trying to digest the nauseating account Ed had offered her, he disappeared inside with his bag of Dry Friskies.

"Funny," he said, or at least she could have sworn he said for he was halfway through the door. "You're the only one who's ever heard him cry."

Faye knew that she identified with the cat, the scared one who couldn't come close. She assumed this was who—what—had been crying, or *was* it crying? Begging. And the fact that she alone heard it—and she convinced herself that Ed had said so—confirmed their bond. She didn't go any further with this idea; her interest in psychology, especially her own, was small and tended to be self-aggrandizing, engaged in only to make her feel better. Faye had been hurt by men, all of whom had been unfaithful to her, or just as good as, often eyeing other women or renting certain movies with certain female stars in them—they didn't have to do that more than once or twice, and she was out of there!—and she didn't much feel like being hurt anymore. She waited tables at Coco's, the local bar, and her interaction with the male customers tended to be flirtatious—and was certainly more profitable in tips when it was—and this for the time being satisfied her in that regard (the way someone tells himself he's worked out for the day by walking two or three blocks to the store instead of, say, actually going to the gym). There was a younger female bartender who was obviously and aggressively interested in her, and Faye wasn't entirely against the idea, but Rita, the woman, seemed just about as bad as any man, hitting on lots of women. So why would it be any better with *her*? Maybe it would be more tender, she didn't know. (Rita had posed sucking a straw for a sexy highway billboard ad for Coco's, and the owners thought it was funny that male drivers ogled the picture when Rita would never have given them a second glance. Faye just thought the whole thing was stupid, maybe because she was mad and hurt *she* hadn't been asked to pose. Faye looked almost child-like—shorter, flatter, and slighter than the curvy and half-Spanish Rita—and still had acne scars.) Still, she never even thought of the word "lonely" and certainly would never have said it to anyone else.

Maybe that was why the cat sound plagued her—and the next time she heard it, it was even worse: a kind of loud, bitter cat shouting, if that were possible. It seemed someone else's utterance of what *she* was feeling, like a lyric in a song that puts into words what you can't express. Except these weren't even words, just cries that sort of sounded like words.

That night, Faye stood at the open glass back door of her apartment, looking out into the darkness of fields that were abbreviated by backyards but still retained to her a wildness, a sadness, and a sense of secrecy and threat. She had decided to follow Ed Koch's example and put food out, to see if she alone could lure the cat to nourishment, as she alone could hear him speak. She had bought the same brand as Ed, though a smaller bag for she was a smaller person.

When she got back from her shift after midnight, which was why *she* had been home during the day—*she* wasn't retired, no sir, and the way things were going she might never be—she poured the dry pellet-like food out onto the small asphalt square that the landlord pretended was her "patio" but which really looked more like a short stone continuation of her living room floor. Tonight, she felt that the floor passed through a dimension or a membrane—the glass door—and became somewhere else, some other world. When she opened the door, *she* entered it; by pouring the food, she was asking to be accepted, as if her actions were an offering. Faye was usually exhausted when she came home and yet so keyed up that she sometimes—often—always!—smoked pot, and even then remained so restless that she'd stay up until two or three watching TV. Tonight, though, she watched the show outside, finding the darkness more fascinating than any old movie or infomercial, because they, after all, were other people's worlds, worlds others had made up, and this one was both real and invented by her. It was hard to explain, the pot made her fuzzy. At any rate, she sat up and waited for the cat to be beckoned by her and be saved.

No one—nothing—came. This hurt and disappointed Faye, especially because when she finally dozed off, she could swear she heard the cat crying again, louder than ever (or was it a dream?) and now felt he might be wilfully and self-destructively avoiding the very thing that could save him. (Anorexics did this too; it was infuriating to others when they refused food placed—pushed!—in front of them. Faye had done it as a teenager and had moved away from home, which made it harder to get back to a normal weight.) But these feelings reminded her of hopelessness, so she pretended to simply feel frustrated by Ed Koch, not only because she disliked negative people but also because she didn't want him to be right.

"Sorry," he shrugged when he heard—why did she tell him? It was stupid—as their paths crossed again, she driving out of the parking lot, he carrying a bag of trash to the communal dumpster. "You did your best."

Since he owned cats, Faye figured he was probably a warm person, but he sounded so brusque and fatalistic that he appeared kind of cold. And didn't he ever *go* anywhere? Still, she always ran into him, so what did that say about her and her travels? (Besides going to work, she meant, and even now she was just going to get some paper towels, a carton of OJ, and some ant traps at the Buy 'n' Fly and come right back.) So she put up her car window and, without another word, drove away.

That night, she tried again, tried harder, went farther. She stepped outside, stoned again (though she'd only had enough for one joint and the rolling paper was so old it crumbled in her hand, leaving a lot of the pot in her lap), wearing her PJ bottoms and T-shirt, and stood without shoes or socks on the cold asphalt, the food at her feet like small stones in a sacrificial ceremony. This time, she called the cat, made a welcoming sound, sent kisses out into the air. But just as when she used to playfully kiss over and over again the necks of boys in high school and they would squirm away (what was the matter with men?), the cat kept his distance.

Faye fell asleep on the living room floor, inches away from the door she hadn't remembered closing. She hadn't pulled the drapes and the rising sun woke her up, heating and almost hurting her face. When she squinted to see outside, she had to stare to make sure. But it was true: most of the food was gone. The cat had come, eaten it, stayed alive. A fat little blue jay stood pecking at the few pellets left.

"It was probably just birds or squirrels." She bet that's what Ed Koch would have said, so she didn't tell him. She sped right past him early the next evening when she saw him exiting his building at the exact same moment she was driving away from hers, their schedules again bizarrely coinciding. (And *she* had actually called a co-worker she hardly knew and was going to see the sequel to a movie she hadn't even liked, *that's* how socially active *she* was; Ed was just planting a little tree in the complex's garden area.)

After the movie, Rita the bartender at Coco's—for this was whom she had called—stopped her car at a light on the highway going home.

"I'd like to go over there with you," Rita said softly, pointing with her head. "I think that'd be really nice."

She had indicated a dark, as yet undeveloped field to their left, off the road, covered in tall, waving, camouflaging grass. (A sign nearby announced that condo building would start soon but hadn't yet.) Rita had spoken mischievously, not menacingly. She reached over and touched the back of Faye's head, drifting a few fingers under her hair onto her neck, with as gentle a touch as could be imagined. Faye felt a bubbling begin in her breast; she saw water starting to boil on a stove or something; it was a new feeling, she didn't have the words. But at the same moment, a cloud moved away from the moon and it lit up a small muscle in Rita's right arm, which had tensed with the effort of moving her hand. It was as if nature, the world itself, was warning Faye, and she felt afraid.

"I think I'd just like to turn in," she said, shaking her head, and ended it.

When she got home, Faye poured more food than ever on the cement, hoping perhaps foolishly that it would be an incentive—"More of the same thing at the exact same low price!" like a strange supermarket sale—especially since the cat had clearly liked what he had consumed. She again made the sounds of love into the night, though her mouth was dry from all the soda she'd had at the movie and the joint she'd just finished. (Rita had agreed to give her some of her own before letting her off. Faye had offered to pay and Rita had seemed offended, for some reason. She could still taste the chocolate that had been on Rita's tongue when she had kissed Faye goodnight, holding her chin still with surprisingly strong fingers and inserting it forcefully between Faye's firmly closed lips before giving up. It had been from Milk Duds at the movies, Faye figured, and her memory of it faded along with the taste.)

This time, she dozed off on the patio, in a plastic lawn chair that had already been there when she moved in and which she hadn't removed. Before she did and thought she might, she considered what the neighbours would think (and had she locked the glass door when she closed it? Could she not get back in? It would be almost funny to be stranded out there in her free Coco's T-shirt and gym shorts—almost). But it was a warm August night, easy to get lost in, and soon she dreamed of someone, some*thing*, standing over her, a big paternal tree like the one in, what, *The Wizard of Oz*, with a knot for a mouth and crazy fat branches for arms.

She was awakened by the sound of a scraping across the stone. She squinted and saw the base of a steel table also left by the last tenant, without its glass top so it always looked to her nude or just strange, like a planet with its sky unscrewed and stolen. It now stood at an angle, had been shifted a little, just enough for her to notice. When Faye fully opened and focused her eyes, she saw what had done it, what had obviously sprung onto the patio and accidentally slapped it to the side.

The cat was there, eating the food. He was red, as Ed had said he would be, though she was surprised and alarmed by the dinginess of his colour and the patches of fur that were missing from his coat—from fighting, she guessed. He was thin, almost but not quite bony, and he had a long, handsome head with an equine—no, that was for horses, like hay—with whatever word meant an impressive snout. He ate diligently and carefully, too proud to gobble and reveal his hunger, she thought. He did not seem to notice she was there.

Faye sat up in her chair, trying not to make a noise. She failed: the backs of her thighs had stuck to the plastic seat as she slept and now they made a little popping fart sound as she ever so slightly raised herself. The cat turned, suddenly. He stared at her with eyes at once wary and not hostile—inquisitive. He did not seem rattled. Maybe he was only sorry he had awakened her.

This projection of personality was as if she had added a sheer layer upon him, the way a soul "escapes" from a dying person in a movie, only with the film going backwards. To Faye, he now seemed coated by this extra protective impression, glowed with it even. It allowed her to approach him without fear.

Faye moved slowly on her knees across the cold stone to where he was. The second she came within reach, he sprang. He didn't scratch her, didn't hurt her in the least. Instead, he placed his two front arms—legs? Paws?—around her neck and hugged her, his mouth at her ear, softly and wetly whispering things that only she could hear but would never understand (as it had been when she heard him cry): the words, or whatever they were, for thanks.

—∾—

"Well, that's very nice," Ed said—she couldn't help herself, she had had to tell him. Leaving her apartment the next morning, which was Friday, she had seen him wheeling a cart of clothes to the laundry room. She had immediately rushed back inside—figuring she'd buy mouthwash, a candy bar, and a box of tampons at the new Drugall's later—gotten her own laundry and followed.

Luckily, Ed was alone there, leafing through an old seventies romance novel someone had left on the "Take a Book—Leave a Book" shelf.

"Nice?!" she said. She couldn't keep shock and even anger from her voice. It was such a condescending word, what you called a boy in high school you wouldn't even consider kissing, or a meal cooked by a friend the effort of which you wanted to praise but which you never wanted to eat again. Ed didn't even look up when he said it; then he moved from skimming the book to a washer, where he started pouring in bleach.

"Yes. That certainly is very nice."

Faye hadn't even started cleaning the clothes she brought in; they still sat overflowing from a bag in the corner. Now she forgot all about them and the supposed "coincidence" of running into him. She followed Ed back to the bookcase from the washer as she had followed him there in the first place, and she didn't care if he knew why she had come.

"No, it was more than *nice*. It was . . ." But how could she describe it? It was so intense—not just how glad it had made her feel to summon and help the cat, but how proud she had been to be the only one who could. The physical sensation of his arms (legs? Paws?) around her neck and that helpless, moist, and mysterious communication in her ear. It had felt better than being with a baby, the times she had held and heard one—even her baby sister the first time she no longer hated her as a child. It was certainly better than it had ever felt with a man, the times with their tongues tickling at and then actually *in* her ear; whoever said *that* was so hot must have been a comedian, because it was like a bad joke! How could she tell Ed, who now looked at her with an expression of being-happy-for-her so benign and bloodless it made her furious not to know the words for how wonderful—unforgettable—it had been?

"I only meant, you have a lot to be proud of," he said, trying to ramp up his praise, but by his obvious insincerity making it worse.

Faye turned to go; she wouldn't wash her clothes. Let him laugh at her; let him tell all his friends—if he had any, which he obviously didn't. And it was about time Ed washed his clothes—she could smell the checked shirt he had on halfway across the room, that indescribable musty aroma that always meant lonely old loser. She started dragging her laundry bag, which was so stuffed that a pair of underpants fell out (which she noticed with horror had its own slight musty tang). She was bending to embarrassedly pick it up when he said, quietly, not calling but as if he were still standing right next to her, "But don't expect too much from him. I'd hate to see you get hurt."

Faye turned, slowly, still bent over, shoving the panties viciously back into the bag the way she had once seen a French farmer on TV force-feed a duck before slaughter. "What?"

"He's a stray now, you know. He always will be."

Faye took her time reaching her full height again. Now she understood. Ed wasn't being judgmental or superior or even indifferent. He had a much more basic reason for trying to dismiss her accomplishment, for trying to deny her the first—and she suddenly understood what it was and was shocked even to *think* that it was this—feeling of love she had ever experienced.

"You left food out for him, too."

"I'm sorry?"

"You're just jealous."

"I don't understand."

"You're jealous that it was me and not you."

—

That night in bed, Faye remembered with pleasure the shocked look on Ed's face—or maybe the look she imagined him having, for she had turned away and walked out right after speaking. Let him chew on *that*, she thought. The food idea was meaningful because wasn't that what this was all about? She had provided crucial nourishment to someone, some*thing*, and received sustenance in return, and he had not. Her mind was especially sharp tonight for she hadn't smoked—didn't have any left to smoke, actually, but would not have if she did, she was totally sure.

(She had hoped Rita might cough up some at work, but while Faye had smiled at her several times, the bartender had only winked back at her once, strangely, camera-like—even made a little clicking sound with the side of her mouth as if to officially record and forget her, and then ignored her entirely.)

After her new routine—pouring the food and puckering and puckering—Faye was determined to stay up and wait for the cat's return. But in case she fell asleep, she set the alarm for three. Before she did indeed pass out, she could have sworn she heard the cry again, but only once and from far away. It might have been a fantasy or the whistle of a train, passing through and going away for good.

The sound faded into the beep of the cheap travel alarm clock on the floor by her bed. Faye slammed her hand down, missed, knocked it over, and kept chopping down blindly until she broke it and it stopped. She rolled from bed, totally naked, for the sunset hadn't caused any cooling and she had feared the air conditioner racket might make her deaf to the cat's coming back. Squatting, lean, almost hairless and baby animal-like herself in the dark living room, Faye drew the drapes. Eyes shone back at her from the patio.

But they were not her cat's eyes. They were eyes surrounded by what children and TV commentators always call a mask, as in a burglar's mask—and that's what the raccoon seemed to her tonight, a thief. Faye banged on the window to scare him off, yelling at him through the glass, though she knew it was pointless. The animal only looked up once, indifferently, and then went back to eating, using its paws in an efficient, human-like way.

The next night was even hotter, so she kept all the windows open and lay waiting nude above the covers. She watched a drop of sweat roll like a pinball from behind her ear (where the cat had held her), slip milkily from her nipples, fall down between her breasts, over her small flat belly and into her navel where it pooled. As more balls emerged, she imagined herself a pinball *machine*—they had one at work—and shifted and squirmed ever so slightly to direct the sweat to the shallow hole, her behind tensing and sticking a little to the sheet as she did. Moving in this way—causing a fair amount of friction between her legs—began to make her dizzy, and soon Faye fell asleep to escape the feeling that was approaching, her last sight her own twitching hand poised to move from the side of her bare thigh.

She slowly came to, alerted not by a sound but by a smell. At first she thought it was gas—the stove? No, stupid, it was electric. And wasn't there (didn't there have to be) a carbon monoxide thing, monitor, alarm—and besides, didn't that *have* no smell? She slowly understood that it was not a chemical odour or anything man-made, not something human even. It was coming from an animal yet it wasn't like the smells one perceives in passing on the road. It was different, lasted longer, was more piercing—probably because it was closer, coming right through the screen on the window to her left. It could only be from a skunk, warning another animal away from food it saw and wanted.

Faye ran to the glass door again. She crouched small, nude, and sticky—a dewy faun—and looked out. She saw, to her dismay, that all the food was gone, the cat nowhere in sight.

—∾—

Who else was there to tell? As much as she had hated—and the word was not too strong—the way Ed Koch reacted to her experiences, he was the only one who knew of them. The next late afternoon, which was Sunday, fearing the night that was ahead and what would and wouldn't happen, Faye found herself in the vestibule of the building from which he always emerged, checking the names on the mailboxes and then banging desperately on his door.

It turned out that he, too, lived on the first floor, one door over from hers, a few buildings down. It reminded her of those pink and blue man-and-woman towels hanging side by side in bathrooms in old movies, and she didn't like the idea at all.

"Well . . . Well . . ." This time, he didn't know what to say, wasn't so fast with the condescending retort, was he? Of course, to be fair, Faye realized that first he had to accept the idea of her being in his apartment and on the verge of tears, so what she said might take some time to sink in.

Ed was in a bathrobe at five P.M. (though it was over his clothes—the same kind of clothes as ever), and his musty smell was indistinguishable from the one all over his apartment: this was where he got the smell. There were also the extra odours of cigarette smoke and—coming from Ed's surprised open mouth—red wine. They were especially strong on the couch where he put Faye; she breathed through her lips.

"I'm afraid that something's happened to the cat," she said, blubbering now; she couldn't help it, it was so embarrassing. "Like he was hurt in a fight or, or—something worse." She couldn't say killed.

She looked up from her hands, which were joining and separating in her lap, and saw where she was. It was a living room filled with books, papers, and magazines. There was an old framed photo on a bookcase of a woman with an infant; it could have been from ten or twenty or fifty years before. The place was decorated so darkly Ed's overhead light and standing lamps were defeated in their efforts to illuminate it. The best they could manage was a dim, exploratory glow, like lanterns shining in a cave—and yes, this was how Ed's apartment felt to Faye, a lair. The air conditioning was on so high it was as cold as a refuge lost climbers find in rock formations, where sensation soon ceases.

"Oh," Ed said, sitting beside her on the too-soft pillow. "I see. Well, that's possible. I'm afraid that's always been a—possibility."

His voice, his tone, they were again so unsentimental, so cavalierly accepting of life's cruelty—even appreciative of it—that she hated them. Why had she come? And why couldn't she stop talking, which would only make her hear them more?

"I hope it's only temporary," she said. "If he doesn't come back, I—I don't know what I'll do. If he had never come, it would have been one thing; I would have forgotten. But now that he has, it—it hurts so much."

There was silence for a time before Ed spoke again. "I know, I know. And I'm sorry."

It took Faye a second to realize that Ed's tone had changed. There was the tiniest bit of tenderness in it now; it was the tone he might have taken with a child.

Faye wasn't sure how it made her feel. Before she could decide, Ed's arm had wrapped gently around her shoulders. He began whispering to her, his words slurred and unintelligible, maybe meant to comfort, maybe not. It was an awful parody of the gesture and sound that had meant so much. Faye felt strangled and then frozen: her heart seemed to stop, not beat faster.

At the exact same moment, one of Ed's cats—he had three, she remembered now—climbed out of a pile of dirty clothing, made an awful effort to do so for it was obviously emerging from hell, which she now knew was cold and not hot. It hissed at her, its eyes fried, and Faye couldn't stop screaming.

Nights followed with no more sign of her cat. Faye kept putting out food, but slowly it began to resemble another ritual, like lighting candles for the dead, one that conjures nothing and just commemorates. She began to avoid most travel, except to work and home again, began even to shop in bulk so she could emerge from her apartment less. (Though this was the way most sensible people shopped in town, doing so in short spurts had been a way to remind others of her existence and her of theirs—a way to say, here's one more chance to know each other—so she had stopped.)

She didn't mind, because Doug, the new waiter at work, had provided her with pills that were even better than pot (or made pot better when they were added to it). He had begun by *giving* them to her, but soon she realized he expected an exchange of services, so to speak, and that wasn't going to happen, no way. So he started charging, and now she had to take on extra shifts if she wanted more of them, and she did.

They were sedatives, not stimulants. Doug explained the most effective order in which to take them (or pieces of them, to be frugal): first, the Klonopin, then the Xanax, then Valium. Faye quickly forgot the names and went by their colours alone—first the blue, then the white, then the red; they were a mixed-up and ass-backwards America, Doug said, profoundly—going by simple signs, almost by instinct. If she could have just sniffed them before swallowing, she would have. And in this way, she could finally relax at night, expect nothing, and sleep.

One night in early October, the seasons seemed to finally hint they were changing, as much as they ever did these days. Faye turned off the air conditioning, which she now used for the express purpose of drowning out sound. As she lay in bed wearing only a T-shirt that wore its own layer of dust and smoke, she marvelled at the quiet. It seemed strangely vital and interesting, though existing dimly, as if in another dimension, or like a (silent) song from a neighbour's apartment. In her new state, everything felt like this, far away yet compelling, and the quiet was just one more thing.

Soon, strangely, it was interrupted. A cry was cutting through it. It was familiar yet brand-new—it sounded like a cat, but also the bay of a wolf, a baby, and an old man—all ages through the evolution of need. It drew Faye like a—what did they always call it, and what did it mean?—siren song from her bed. She didn't walk but floated to the glass door, a vague memory of something she wanted propelling her.

Setting down again, Faye opened the door. She looked at the patio. There she saw, on all fours, Ed Koch, stuffing pellets of dry food into his mouth and spitting out the ones he could not fit. At the same time, impossibly, he was wailing in a language that was universal but that no one could ever understand.

THE UNEXPECTED GUEST

He had never buried anything before, not even in childhood, when kids put cats or turtles or hamsters under headstones in backyards. He had no idea how far down to dig, had always had poor spatial judgment, and couldn't tell by sight or any other sense two feet from six. He was working, in other words, by an instinct he didn't possess, the same way he cooked: "Add a little salt," someone better in the kitchen—all right, his wife—would tell him; he'd reply, testily, "Just tell me *how much* to put in," knowing his anger was really embarrassment, for he hated feeling incapable and hadn't really wanted to cook in the first place, had only offered to be accommodating (always a mistake), and the whole thing would invariably end in a resentful fight.

Tonight, of course, he had had no choice but to start digging, yet he still found himself veering mentally off-subject (which was again how far down to go): worrying about his health, whether he might have a heart attack after he ended his exertion and moved from the cold air of the woods back to his warmer car, the way millions of middle-aged men drop dead after shovelling snow and then entering a heated house. And he knew this was true—there was the maître d' from Formaggi, the Italian place in town, remember?

He decided to take rests after one or two swings of the shovel, then realized at that pace he'd be at it all night (and Michelle would wonder where he was or maybe even call the cops—the worst case scenario), so instead he thought he'd finish it all up in one shot. He was amazed at how exhausting it was to work so fast and finally figured he'd split the difference and settled on using leaves as a cover for what he could not conceal with the dirt.

Before he stopped, he remembered an episode of an anthology horror show he'd seen as a teenager in the seventies. John Carradine played an old farmer who told kids to dig in a field and they'd get a "surprise." After they'd spent all night at the job, reaching, it seemed, the bottom of the world, they found a coffin. When they opened it, inside impossibly was Carradine, who said, "surprise!" Joe was unnerved at how, decades later, working in a dark wood in which he seemed the only living human inhabitant, the story still scared him.

Joe had watched and ragged on the show, he remembered, with his friend, George, who had been his and Michelle's dinner guest that evening. He and George had grown up around the corner from each other in the suburbs and stayed in touch, even while attending separate colleges and graduating and getting jobs. In more recent years, Joe had married Michelle and moved ninety miles north of the city, where they had their son, Tad, now eight. Joe had opened one, then two, then three independent bookstores in the area, all called Left Brain—no mean feat in a country ruled by chain stores and conglomerates. George, for his part, had stayed single and in the city.

They had had George to dinner because Joe had not actually seen him for two years, the longest such gap in their lives. George had never been to the house; they had stayed in touch only by phone or by email, and Joe didn't want to lose touch with him entirely. He was aware that people with kids tended only to see other people with kids, and he was alarmed to learn that he had fallen into this pattern and become this cliché. Still, he was surprised at how hard it had been to arrange the dinner. George, who owned no car, had acted as if leaving the city and travelling ninety miles by train was the most difficult thing he had ever done, agreeing to and then cancelling date after date, and needing Joe to read him the train schedule very slowly over the phone and then writing down where to transfer so painstakingly he seemed to be struggling to communicate in a second language. (There was no question, of course, about Joe and Michelle going down to see *him*; that would have been impossible.)

Michelle and he had fixed up the guest room, more than happy to have George sleep over. Joe had even looked forward to staying up late alone with him, shooting the bull and maybe even watching and mocking old science fiction and horror shows on TV, as they had growing up. There were whole stations now showing this stuff, in some cases the same exact shows they'd seen as kids—like the Carradine one, what was it on, the new

Night Gallery or something, or one of those endless resurrections of *The Twilight Zone* with Rod Serling, colourized like a painted corpse in an open casket. That was what George had said, Joe remembered, while passing a joint they almost enjoyed dreading Joe's mother (and it had been in his house, he was almost positive) would come down and discover. Joe had even scoured the TV listings to see what was on, to set the whole evening up.

But George had sounded as if sleeping over was like agreeing to live at the bottom of the sea, or taking up residence in a space station—the most complex and wrenching decision a man could ever make—and after what seemed a half an hour of going back and forth with so many pros and cons that Joe began filling out tax forms he had been avoiding while George was talking, he came to the conclusion that no, thanks, it would be better if he took the train back that night; well, maybe, now what if I, no, no, it would be better, but thanks, anyway, no, really, thanks.

Joe was so hurt by his attitude—that George considered the offer so exotic, and also by his over-courteous consideration of it—that he threw out the TV section he had circled. Michelle wondered where it went and Joe lied and said she must have lost it, and then he changed the subject.

When Joe picked up George at the station, his guest described his experience on the train in amazed and extensive detail, as if he had been on the Orient Express during WWI and not on Amtrak. Joe blocked out his commentary, but he was distracted anyway by how George looked. It *had* been a while since he'd seen him: the rings beneath George's eyes had become crevice-like and put Joe in mind of Storrow Lane in town, where the snowstorms this winter had worn semi-circles in the street that were yet to be re-paved (and that should be an issue in this year's council election, Joe believed, for he followed such things, and had even thought of running himself before he chickened out).

But it wasn't that George looked bad—in fact he looked *great*, at least for someone his—their—age: as thin as a whippet, with actual definition in his chest and arms. Getting older had given him gravitas in his face, too, which had always been a little beaky and, well, bird-like in appearance. His hair may have gone grey but in that salt-and-pepper way, and it was still there, seemed not to have thinned or fallen out at all, and was set off by a haircut that looked cutting-edge without being a transparent attempt to imitate youth. He wore a sweater over a T-shirt and jeans above an attractive leather blend of sneaker and shoe. The look was relaxed yet not sloppy; if clothes could seem confident, his did. Not arrogant—there was a difference. In short, George looked *handsome*, not a word Joe or anyone else would ever have applied to him earlier in their lives, and one, which Joe had to admit, he himself did not deserve to this day.

Not that Joe looked bad exactly—but glancing at himself in the rear-view mirror, he acknowledged that he just looked *normal*. He had lost most of his hair and in the worst way possible, starting from the front and shedding it up his scalp, as if baldness was a lawnmower and his forehead a hill. Excess weight had settled below his belt, so that it—again, predictably—almost obscured his crotch. He had to peek over the flab to see it, as if he was taking a photo of a tiny town way down below from a mountaintop that was slippery and slide-y in the mud. Even his teeth—and he bared them now in a sudden "smile" that looked leonine or maybe just demented—were yellow, no matter how much he brushed and flossed, while George's were purely white, as if never stained by food or drink. They seemed even whiter than the last time they met, for, after all, Joe had not noticed them then. As for Joe's clothes, he wore his usual plaid button-down shirt over belted pleated pants hiked up, he knew now, too high, for he had heard the high school girls who worked the registers in his first flagship store giggling about his pants one day when he walked in.

The point was, he was a normal man and time had taken a typical toll on him, set upon and beaten him up a little bit each day, and he hadn't resisted, had accepted its thrashings and their cumulative effects on his head, gut, and gums, grateful to at least be let to live, as if this disfigurement was the price he paid for going forward. George, on the other hand, seemed to have—and he liked this analogy, so he continued it—one day stayed the hand of his attacker, maybe even bent its arm back until it agreed to if not reverse at least not continue these assaults, leaving him looking appealingly "aging" without actually aging at all anymore.

It was, in a word, unnatural, that's what it was, and Joe today found himself both envying and resenting his old friend. It was the first time he had ever had either of these feelings about him.

"Thanks so much for picking me up," George said, passionately, as if Joe had driven across the country over broken glass to get there.

"It's no problem," Joe said, trying not to be annoyed. "It's only a mile and a half away."

George shrugged broadly, smiling and implying that rural directions and distances were all mysterious and arcane to him. "Anything to do with cars . . ."

Joe tried to show how quick and convenient the journey could be by driving home at a high speed, intending to shave time off the only ten-minute trip; however, he hit a patch of ice that sent his car skidding across the narrow, two-lane, two-way road and forcing a frightened "Jesus!" from George before he withdrew into wordless, quickened, and audible breathing for the rest of the—now twenty-minute—ride.

When they entered Joe's house, George responded to the place so emotionally—wow-ing and whoa-ing over everything from a rocking chair to a dog door to a refrigerator magnet—that he sounded like a parent hearing his child's first witty remark, or a senile relative's rare correct recollection.

"It's just a house," Joe said, again trying to laugh away irritation, but he couldn't help it—it *was* just a house.

"I can't imagine living in such a place," George said. "If I lived in a place like this, half the rooms would be unfurnished. There'd be a chair in one room, a table in another, a bookshelf in a third. It would be like my one-bedroom apartment spread out over three floors, the way a starving man makes one meal last a month."

First George had overreacted to the house; now he had turned it into a little monologue about himself, one filled with imagery more palatable on a page than coming from a man's mouth. George was a poet, one who—beating all the odds in human existence—actually supported himself in a field as dead in America (as far as the paying public was concerned) as a Civil War soldier or a suffragette or a crusty old cowboy. In his bookstores, Joe even split the "Poetry" section with the "Drama" (another long-embalmed art, if sales were any indication) and George's books had become, in the past two years, among the few that appealed to anyone. Joe had neglected to stock the books at first, until his high school girl helpers, who carried copies of them in their bags and backpacks, asked innocently, "Hey, where's sexy Rabelman?" which was George's last name. (Had Joe neglected him on purpose? Had he even invited him tonight so as not to be forgotten by him now that, in their time apart, George had grown famous? These questions flickered across and then faded from his mind like lightning in a storm that never happens.)

George was continuing to reflect on the contents of his imaginary house—which would of course pale in comparison to this one, which was so quaint and beautifully designed: "Just look at those wet boots lined up on the mat, like in a fantastic still life"—when Michelle came up from the basement, carrying a bottle of the wine they kept down there.

It was hard to say what riveted George more now, the "fantastic" red or the "incredible" Michelle herself. He linked one subject to the other, contrasting favourably the choice of wine with the appearance of the woman, even reciting a poem Joe assumed was one of his own before (to his embarrassment and grateful he'd kept quiet) George identified it, off-handedly, as "obviously, you know, Yeats."

They went into the living room, where Michelle had placed cheese and crackers on a plate. Joe turned on music to drown out George's effusive tribute to the plate, the design of which seemed to him "so utterly American," but which really just had a pattern so ugly the set had been sold for nearly nothing at the Buy 'n' Fly. Adoring the plate led George back to praising the woman who'd chosen it. Joe couldn't deny that Michelle seemed to be enjoying George's compliments, nearly beaming at him, wiping cracker crumbs much more delicately from her mouth than usual. She accepted George's refill of the "luscious" wine with a girlish nod—a new gesture for her, or maybe an old one, unused since youth. It maddened Joe to see this, not because he was jealous but because he had no cause to be: it was obvious that George's attentions to her were sexless. His one and only glance below Michelle's neck resulted in a secret (he thought) and appreciative recoil, as if he were watching a walrus emerge—and keep emerging and keep emerging—from an ocean. Wow, he seemed to be thinking, what a walrus. Joe knew that Michelle had put on weight, just as he had—put on even more weight, become by any measure (and use any word you want, be nice or not—it didn't matter, she was his wife) fat. But that was no reason for George not to flirt with her, to instead treat her as he had their unremarkable home, to marvel at her and, since marvelling was not merited, to put in relief her mediocrity. He did it again when she said she sold real estate—and successfully; this was a booming area, getting bought up. George listened with open-mouthed wonder then repeated, quietly, "Real estate," as if she'd said "sword swallowing," and then he had, too.

In earlier days, Michelle had dismissed George as an amiable dork, whose company she endured because he was Joe's old friend. Now she seemed to actually like this new George, one who, as Joe saw it, had stopped physical time and, during its suspension, become an accomplished person who had kept living while everyone else was doing the normal thing and passing away.

George didn't stop during dinner—which was an okay pot roast and potatoes; Michelle made no claims of being a great cook—reacting with giddy disbelief that they still ate red meat, a choice he thought "brave" and "bold" given all the evidence against it. The whole time he served himself only one thin fat-free sliver of the main course while filling up on salad, vegetables, and (unbuttered) bread.

George sat next to young Tad, whose plate held food in exactly opposite proportions: 80 percent meat versus 20 percent (heavily buttered) baked potato and (even more heavily buttered) bread. While it had taken Joe and Michelle twenty years to officially join the fat club, Tad had done so in a mere eight years, seeming to start energetically applying right after birth, with no tactic by his parents—discouragement, admonishment, encouragement, threats, doctors' visits, strategically placed diet books, sports playing (with Joe pulling every muscle he had after throwing and catching a football for the first time in his life), love—succeeding in slowing him down. Add to that his difficulties reading, writing, making friends, or even having any actual relationships with people not imaginary and existing only in a video game, and Tad was a large and obvious next target for George's enthusiastic applause. Busy eating his low-calorie meal, however, their guest restricted himself just to giving him glances, complete with approving head nods and smiles.

Joe saw all this through a new haze, one caused by his fourth glass of wine, which effectively emptied the bottle. Although no one asked for more, Joe volunteered to get a new one from the basement, secretly vowing he'd make it one of the cheaper kind since George obviously refused to go beyond the medical community's recommended one glass a day (for a healthy heart). He had actually held his hand over his glass when Joe offered him a refill, like a virgin pushing a hand off her knee (Joe thought, red-faced and unsteadily weaving now down the cellar stairs).

Before he reached the bottom, he lost his balance and skidded down the last few steps, then was forced into a painful sit-down on the final one in order to avoid pitching left shoulder and neck first onto the floor. Now he added right buttock to the areas on his body that—after yet another pointless ball toss with Tad yesterday—ached with fiery pain.

(Who was George to so condescend to and have such contempt for him, his life, and his family? Who was George, anyway, but—)

"Joe?"

A voice startled him. He realized he had—even in this uncomfortable position and in agony—fallen asleep. He turned and saw the shadow of a man above him in the basement doorway, looming weirdly large though speaking in the familiar—though not as familiar, he allowed, as it once had been, now slightly affected—tones of George.

"Joe? You all right?"

Joe made to wave but was so weak that his guest began to climb with concern in his direction, his shape refracted by the kitchen light behind him, shifting bigger then smaller then bigger as it came closer. Joe couldn't help it, he felt his heart beat faster as he was about to be reached by someone he'd known all his life yet whose distorted form he no longer recognized and even sort of feared.

"We were all worried. You've been gone so long," George said when he got there. "Can I help you up?"

"No, I'm fine," Joe mumbled, more than a little annoyed by George's solicitousness. What was he, an old blind dog who'd wandered out a door someone had left open (like their own dog, Clowny, recently had, and who tonight had only one milky eye opened from her usual place under a living room chair to acknowledge George's head pat—the evidence of which was immediately removed by George with a squirt of his hand sanitizer before he proclaimed her "a remarkable beast")?

"I'm fine!" Joe called up to Michelle, whose faint voice replied "Okay" with so little urgency that Joe knew George had been the only one worried, and only at being left alone for so long with Joe's wife and son.

George shrugged, apparently eager to spend more time with his old friend—or just not return so soon to his old friend's family. He sat one step above Joe on the chilly cellar stairs, and his leather blend of shoe and sneaker—now an annoying symbol of either pleasing everyone or committing to nothing—bobbed in Joe's face when he crossed his legs.

"Wow. A ping-pong table," George said, checking out the items near them on the floor. "And what's that? A boiler."

"Almost sounds like a new poem," Joe said, smirking. "You want a pad of paper, or can you keep it all up here?" He pointed to his bald head, miscalculated the distance and jabbed his finger uncomfortably close to his eye.

George stared at him, as if literally not understanding what Joe had just said—or what, more accurately, he'd just done: ranked him out, as he and Joe had called it in their youth on the uncountable occasions when one said something comically snotty to the other, an event apparently unknown to George now with all his acolytes. Then understanding appeared like a flashlight beam on George's face and he smiled, as if once again seeing a new sight, though this one was less entrancing than the others, was even a little annoying.

"Oh, right," he said, "right."

"Hey—remember the summer we both worked in that insurance office, which was in that guy's house, and you spilled soda on his files and we threw them away and never came back to work until he told our parents, and then they forced us to go back and work for him for nothing the entire rest of the summer? And my Dad always called us 'the two dumbkopfs' after that?"

George's smile of recognition briefly appeared, grew, then shrank, then grew again, then disappeared altogether. It was as if he were a computer trying to retrieve information it had erased, and after briefly succeeding, completely failing. George didn't answer at all, as if even acknowledging the question was impossible since Joe's password to their shared past had been removed and so denied. Then he simply looked around the dusty basement with the same nod of admiration he had shown to everything else all night.

"Yep," he said. "Some place. Some place you've—"

"Look!" Joe said, and he didn't care how loud he got—the basement was sound-proofed enough that they'd stuck an expensive drum set down there to divert Tad, which he used so rarely they soon donated it as nearly new to the high school's music department. "I've had just about enough of this! I know what you're doing! Why don't you just stop it and say what you really think! You hate all of this! You think it's awful! It's okay, this is me!" And he was surprised to discover that he had meant the last three words not to encourage intimacy with George but to establish that he and his environment were the same—or he would have done had Joe really said it instead of just imagining he said it, since he was now afraid to say anything of the kind to his old friend.

"Thanks," was what he said instead, and even that was slurred by his intoxication. "Thanks, Gor," and he couldn't get out his whole first name intelligibly.

George shrugged, confusedly—why thank him? He should be thanking Joe—and then let out a long, refreshed and refreshing sigh.

"It's just such a joy, I don't mind telling you," he said, "to know oneself—to be oneself. Finally, finally, like meeting someone I've always heard about and who everyone else was so sure that I would like. To be able to admit that I care nothing for respectable things—family, kids, career—that all I care about is my work, about—pretentious or not, call it what you want—creating beauty. And that I can say this out loud to you—it's such a risk, to you of all people, my old pal—is so freeing, like saying, I don't know, I'm gay, or something other people are so often ashamed of. It allows me not to mock anyone else anymore, and what they are and how they live, which I always did when I couldn't say what I wanted out of life—what I loved, that's really the word. And if it's mawkish not to judge others anymore, to merely appreciate them because they don't reflect on me or me on them—as if we're from separate planets or in different galaxies or however far away we'd have to be not to reflect on each other—then it's mawkish. I'll accept any characterization of myself because I finally know who I am, so I don't care when people say what I'm supposed to be and know that I'm not."

George stopped talking then and suddenly burst into tears, his face hidden by his hands, his shoulders shaking in the showy style of actors in old or even silent films. Yet when he revealed himself again, he looked shocked and exposed and real water dripped off of him, as if from a snowball assault that leaves your face wet and red and secretly hurting much more than you let on when you're little.

Joe—who was supposed to have been helped up the stairs by him—now offered his own hobbling assist to George, supporting him emotionally at least with a hand on his back until they emerged from underground. Then the two quickly and abashedly separated, George making for a nearby bathroom on the ground floor, Joe heading up to another on the second. He caught a quick glimpse in the kitchen of Michelle, who was already doing dishes like a hypnotized woman unable to alter her nightly routine of eating, cleaning up, and going to bed early. Tad was already in front of the TV, his mouth brutally set in an expression he only had when doing this: making menacing little movements with his thumbs against onscreen characters who fled from his bullets as if stuck in his dreams of aggression.

In the bathroom, which was unofficially his own, Joe thought about his guest. George had dug deeper and deeper until he found himself buried alive—"surprise!"—like those kids and that actor, whose name now escaped him, on that scary old TV show. He wanted to be accepted by Joe as his true self, which was sincere and sensual and secretive and not the goofy boy Joe had known. He didn't feel superior, felt no animosity, nothing negative—felt nothing at all in fact about Joe and his family and his life. New depths had been revealed to George, and Joe hid all his reactions to them beneath being "impressed," which was neutral, neither positive nor negative.

Then he quickly locked the bathroom door and went into a Dopp kit designed for travel that sat in a wicker basket, not conspicuous yet not concealed, that he had intended would require a special amount of suspicion and an extra commitment to investigating for Michelle to open. From it, he took three small bottles of prescription pills, which he considered half-empty and not half-full given how much he depended on and needed them, which interacted unpredictably with alcohol, and which had blurred and distorted his perceptions all day, not to mention helped him to skid his car on the way home from the station.

Joe was on an anti-depressant, and to it he often added (in addition to large amounts of red wine) a pain killer he'd gotten after another father-and-son football game and a sleeping pill which, given his usual state of anxiety, served merely as a mild sedative and didn't even begin to induce sleep. He'd become adept at re-filling prescriptions numerous times, using tools from Wite-Out and an old typewriter to the Internet, with its access to pharmacies as far away as Canada and New Zealand. He'd forgotten how many of any pills he'd already had today and so decided he'd had none and simply started his own self-determined daily dosages from scratch, and then doubled them.

The new pills mixed with the old ones already inside him, creating an even larger family of contrasting half-siblings, some amenable to teamwork in doing their job of easing or emptying his mind, others openly opposed.

The back-and-forth effects caused Joe to dizzily hold onto the sides of the sink, staring at his own reflection, then seeing George when he closed his eyes, then himself with eyes open, then George, et cetera. Resisting a swoon and sitting on the closed toilet, he began to create a new interpretation of his friend's behaviour and blurted-out confession that was more creative, comforting, and easy to accept.

How was it possible for someone to feel nothing about, well, about a way of life humans had willingly adopted—and not by instinct, but by *choice*—ever since they evolved from lower forms? They'd even picked lice off their loved ones when they were apes, right? Trying to stand, then deciding to delay that move until his sight of things stopped spinning, Joe leaned back more authoritatively on the closed commode, ignoring the scatter of glass as the back of his head hit and tipped over bottles of Michelle's makeup on the shelf behind him as well as a paperback book which fled and fell, spread-eagled, onto the floor.

It wasn't possible—to feel nothing, that is—about a little baby, a cute little baby, not if you yourself were human. It meant you had recused yourself from the human race, or had never been a member in the first place. To only feel affection or allegiance or whatever George had said he felt toward something abstract, like art or whatever, and not toward a little baby—and look at that cute little baby now, the one flying in the air by Joe right there in the bathroom, look at his little feet, and goodbye, baby, he waved, as the infant flew away on obvious strings and headed to someone else's hallucination—well, it was unnatural and everything else that word implied.

When Joe thought more—squinting to do it, for it took an enormous effort to concentrate in this condition; he strained and looked like someone having specific physical and not philosophical difficulties, given where he sat—he remembered George's own words and used them to incriminate him. (And not unfairly—maybe George wanted his words to be used in this way, for he needed to be known as himself, didn't he, wasn't that what he said: "We'd have to be from separate planets or in different galaxies or however far away you'd have to be not to reflect on each other"—right, wasn't that it?)

Images from old sci-fi TV shows the two boys had seen and spoofed whirled around his face—actors in cheap comic costumes to play characters in the cosmos—like holograms seeming no less real than things that *were* real. Then he shielded his eyes from what looked like blinding bright lights directed down at him, which heralded the arrival of a vehicle with an ear-splitting engine roar and cold and powerful winds from landing gear that blew any object in its path (toothpaste, hair dryer, towel) from its perch.

Joe's own remaining hair was whipped away in a frenzy and stuck out like swinging saloon doors from the sides of his head.

Then the cataclysm passed and silence and warmth returned to the bathroom. Joe was left with new knowledge; it had just been dropped off to him, as if from a helicopter hovering above a catastrophe site—though this had been no helicopter or something that made only stops upon the Earth; this had been at least the idea of a spaceship, the one that had brought George to this planet, for he was an alien from "elsewhere," George number-for-name, or however he really was known.

It made perfect sense. He was here to destroy it all. Joe's only question was: how long had George been here like that? He hadn't seemed distant and detached as a kid, so had he been abducted later, snatched and then returned, with some crucial part of him gone? Were the two years they had lost touch the time when the transformation took place? Or had he actually been exchanged entirely for another creature (one thinner, better dressed, famous, and of course, with inhuman priorities)? Or had George-not-George been there all along, playing the "person" he had been and preparing to strike, a one-man sleeper cell from outer space? There were so many questions.

There were more questions than he had answers—or pills, for that matter, for Joe now saw he was running even lower than he thought, and he could have no more answers (or come to any more of these kinds of conclusions) without them. But he felt this knowledge demanded action, and he was the only one who could take it, since he was the only one who knew.

When he came shakily downstairs, George was already by the door, blinking a bit more than usual and moving side to side in a restless style that suggested impatience. In his hand was a train schedule he had obviously ripped from the kitchen cabinet, for tape was still stuck to its edges. He no longer had trouble deciphering it, had instead become an instant expert.

"It's 8:55," he said. "If we miss the 9:16, there's nothing again until midnight."

Joe was nearly amused by George's opportunistic sense and non-sense of such things as a train schedule; obviously he could have any ability, be any character he wanted, was adaptable as no one on Earth was. Too bad he had given himself away by his coldness. Too bad Joe had deduced the truth!

Yet Joe concealed his own cleverness with a clueless "Sure, sure, let's go," fighting to form the words with both his lips going every which way at once for reasons he attributed only to fatigue, the fact of the pills evaded shamefacedly since he had never admitted to a soul he took so many—not even to himself.

George tried to quickly say goodbye to Michelle and Tad, his earlier admiration for them now replaced by a single-minded desire to leave. Yet he had to agree, with a grimace, to be pulled close and hugged by Michelle, who held him as if embracing for a final time any appreciation of her as a person. George appeared to get no pleasure from her fleshy press against him, more evidence of his alien-ness: who didn't enjoy a little feel of a friend's full-breasted wife? Joe endured whole dinner parties for them, and he didn't begrudge Michelle the same small treat for herself, sometimes even pimped her out for it, especially if it meant he could avoid having sex with her himself later (though, to be honest, between the two of them whose indifference was greater in this regard was hard to figure out). For his part, Tad only looked away once from the TV, with a small yet terrifying smile, his thumbs still shooting with deadly accuracy independent of him, seeming to consider the day when he could kill George, too, and everyone else on earth.

"We've only got sixteen minutes," George said as they came outside, so eager he only carried and didn't wear his coat in the nippy air.

"No problem," Joe replied, gunning the car. "We've got six minutes to spare, if we don't hit traffic. I'm going to take a different way from the way we came."

Joe knew this would do little to assure George; he wanted to watch him squirm. George's determination to go was exhibit B (or C? Or D?) against him, this feverish need to flee normality as if he feared being infected by it. (Or had he already laid his eggs and so completed his mission? Or left behind his slow-ticking, invisible-to-the-human eye, made-of-other-planet-particles bomb? Or would he at a certain hour turn back into a giant snake, his slick, dripping skin bursting through his sweater, jeans, and leather sneaker-shoe?)

"You sure you're okay to drive?" George asked nervously as Joe backed screeching out of the driveway, knocking over a trash can as he hit the street.

"Sure. Don't worry so much," Joe said, pronouncing it "woolly" and so being of course a comfort only to someone as obsessed with exiting (and willing to absurdly accept such an answer) as George.

"Okay, good," George said.

After his initial burst of speed, Joe purposely dropped down to a pace below the limit on the passing signs. He noticed George's foot pressing on the passenger side of the floor, as if willing Joe to pick it up, after sneaking a peek at the watch beneath his glove.

"Think we'll make it?" George asked with desperate hope.

"I haven't missed one yet," Joe replied; then to remove any relief, added, "Of course I've never cut it this close."

"You haven't?" George's voice was shrill.

"No, but there's a first time for everything."

Beyond the slowing of his speed, Joe was also swerving wildly around the roads. This was no ploy but a defensive reaction to seeing supernatural cars and caravans—some with wings, others with huge, twice-tractor-size wheels—coming at, then racing right through his car.

"That was a close one," Joe said, after a near miss.

"What was?"

"Nothing." Why tip his hand? If Joe could see such oncoming "traffic," he could see through George as well, and he wanted to ease slowly into this revelation.

"Oops," he said, starting to do just that. "Did you hear that?"

"Hear what?"

"That thump. Like a flat tire. Oops. There it goes again."

"I haven't heard a thing."

"Really? Jeez, let me pull over for a second and see."

"*What*? But, no, we can't—"

Not signalling—there were rarely real cars on the near-black back road, the reason he had chosen it—Joe pulled over to where a shoulder should have been but was instead just grass bordering the woods beyond. Then he killed the lights, turned off the engine, and got out.

George was too stunned to say anything besides a beseeching "The time—." The words echoed in the empty area and seemed to refer meaningfully to their pasts, the changes they had made in themselves, and a world they could no longer recreate. Or was it the start of an explanation for his years-long masquerade—or sudden subterfuge—or however long it had taken him to alter himself, that Joe didn't stay for him to complete?

His breath visible, stumbling not on ice but from drug-caused clumsiness, Joe pulled on the gloves he had removed to drive. Then he knelt and made to "inspect" the back tires. After a long enough pause, he called, "Just what I thought!" knowing that George's closed windows limited how much he could make out.

"What'd you say?" George asked predictably, emerging to learn the answer—and then stopping, suddenly, when he saw that Joe had popped the trunk.

"Hey, we don't have time to—" he said, advancing. "Can't we just drive on the tire until we get there? I never heard anything myself anyway."

George's voice had returned to one rougher, less recent and more recognizable than the one made soft and feathery by the lofty thoughts it had to convey. George more resembled his old self, too, looked goofier, less the grand man of letters. Were these reversals caused by panic? Joe's imagination? Or was George purposely shape-shifting to put Joe at ease and off the track? Joe had no time to choose an answer; he was too busy searching in the trunk for the implement he wanted.

"This'll only take a minute," he said.

He saw it immediately, but scrambled more for show. Then saying "Got it!" he turned and looked up. George was right beside him, his expression one of total confusion and complete understanding, if that made sense, which it did to Joe, the way many strange things did now. Then George said, as if realizing something crucial in his life had ended and would never again begin, "I've missed the train."

"Have you?"

"Yes." Now it was resignation—though not exactly acceptance, which meant there was also the quiet start of rage.

To forestall it growing—for who knew what monster this emotion would turn George into, and how many heads and grabbing hands he would have—Joe revealed what he had found in the trunk. It wasn't what he assumed George assumed it to be, a jack. It was instead a shovel Joe had bought as a gift for Michelle, for her to start digging that garden she always said (past the point of tedium) she wanted. He had hoped that her creating one would occupy her for hours on end each day, without ever needing his company. But he had (out of pure indolence) forgotten to give it to her, and the tool still had a price tag like a cardboard noose tied around its neck. He stared, deciding whether to peel it off, for appearances sake.

"What's going on? Are you drunk?" George asked, his anger growing, though luckily waiting until it had all the information it needed to explode.

Then Joe thought he had no time to lose, there was a world to save. So he lifted the shovel and smacked George square in the face with it.

George staggered back, slightly, his hands out to signal stop, his nose and lower brow caving in. Before he could escape, Joe hit him again, this time on the side of his head, harder than he'd ever hit anything in his life. He dented George's skull right above his left ear. After George went down, standing over him Joe finished him off with a final smash—like a last hammer blow to nail—that flattened the rest of his face. Then he stood there, panting, before deciding he better drag his body into the woods.

He dragged George by the foot, the leather half-shoe coming off in his hand and making him cry out as if he held the foot itself. The journey was arduous in ways he hadn't imagined, and he felt new aches in his lower back and wrists as he finally got the one hundred and sixty-pound corpse (if only he did as many push-ups every day as George obviously had!) to a forested area suitably remote from the road—plus he had the shovel to contend with, which he pulled along with one pinky hooked into the hole of its handle, the price tag still stupidly shaking against his skin.

The woods where he was were obviously part of a hiking trail, for the moon revealed paint marks on trees, which tipped travellers on which way to turn. For a second, Joe was sure he saw a troop of boy scouts wearing uniforms from Depression-era Norman Rockwell paintings parade past, but they disappeared as quickly as he had made them come.

Then he was left with just the digging and burying and the worrying about his health—and finally the cutting of corners by covering with leaves the parts of the body he could not submerge. At last, he approved of the job he'd done, a public service for the human race that would forever go unknown.

Dragging the shovel behind him, Joe found his way back to the car, necessity giving him a better sense of direction than he'd ever had. (His lack of it was a sore point with Michelle on quarrelsome family car trips full of cranky U-turns, reluctant asking of directions, and silent miles with front seats full of angry Mommy and Daddy, while in the backseat, with his thumbs, Tad destroyed more helpless people on a portable, lap-sized death machine.)

Joe waited a second before re-entering the car—but how many cooling-off minutes would discourage a coronary? (It had always been an hour between swimming and eating, but that was cramps and who had an hour?) Then, deciding if he died he died and the car must be kind of cold anyway, he began to get in.

The second his key was inserted, the car started screaming, as if telling everyone what was happening on the dark, abandoned road. To his horror, Joe realized he had pressed with his palm the red security thing on the key chain (something which he had once done to devastating effect in front of the town's Farmers' Market, setting off what sounded like a siren and briefly ruining his local reputation). Now, knowing only that closing and re-opening the door would stop the Subaru's shrieking, he frantically, hands shaking, tried to make this happen. Only after a too-loud second slamming of the door did the alarm, with a final infuriated croak, actually end.

Sweating uncomfortably, Joe stood near the silent road, waiting for the authorities or anyone else who had something against him to appear, but no one did. So he entered the car, immediately locking the door, fearing retaliation from George's interplanetary partners once they'd learned of their (if this was what he was) leader's demise.

Before he turned on the motor, he looked down and saw grim proof of his suspicions: blood that had obviously spurted from George as he was dying now stained the front of Joe's big down jacket. Yet it wasn't red or frankly any colour he recognized, but a kind of sick-making amalgam of all colours, with white the dominant shade in its weird little rainbow:

confirmation that George had come from (and now perhaps returned to) another universe. Joe would have to hide the jacket—or maybe secretly keep it, in case he had to appear in an intergalactic court. Then he drove home fairly competently and facing no traffic.

He assumed no one would be the wiser or none the wiser or whatever the expression was; he was home free, in other words. He pulled into his driveway, wondering who'd knocked over his trash can—probably that nasty kid from next door, hyperactive Billy. Then he got out, went in, and walked right into Michelle, who was wearing her nightgown, had been worried that he'd been gone so long, and immediately said to him, "My God, why is there so much blood on your coat?"

In the harsh light of the hall, Joe saw that his jacket had indeed been colour-corrected, the liquid now truly red—or the dark brown blood becomes when it starts to dry. Discombobulated, yet with an even faithful married man's mastery of lying (about everything from how he doesn't watch internet porn to how he didn't gamble away his paycheque to why he *was* just paying attention), Joe immediately began improvising a story, one about a dark highway, a deer, and its accidental death by their car. It was so convoluted that Michelle interrupted, as he planned, with, "Okay, okay, as long you and George are all right. Let's just get that jacket off."

After she had stuffed the coat into the hamper, Joe chug-a-lugged a nearly full Brita pitcher of water, said, "I really need a shower," which was true, and then ran up the stairs to the second bathroom. There he found, to his shock, that the sedative bottle was in fact empty and the others had only a few last pills rattling around in them like forgotten patients roaming an asylum shut down by the state. He swallowed the ones that remained.

Joe sat on the toilet and nearly fell in; he cursed and laughed, closed the lid, and sat down again. He thought about his coat and considered what had happened: he might have made a big mistake about George. Possible? Yes. Probable? Not really. Still, if it was true, Michelle now knew that *something* had occurred and would know more once George's body was found by hikers, or those Depression-era boy scouts, or when it was half-eaten by coyotes which now prowled the area because they'd been displaced from their habitat by developers—he'd read an article about it and even thought he'd once seen a white one running frightened across the highway at sunset; it had been too big to be a dog.

Joe looked down at the carving knife he'd just swiped from the kitchen while drinking the water, which he had hidden inside his plaid shirt and which had scraped his stomach a little when the handle was hit by his arm, which had been knocked by his rising knee as he came up the stairs. As he gripped the knife, last used to slice meat from a Christmas ham for late-night snacks, new images trickled down before his eyes as if they had burst the banks of his brain and overflowed, like rainwater spilling from the gutters of his roof. He saw his wife and son slaughtered from behind, their throats slit with no time to scream, his secret safe. Then, dropping the blade, he sat forward, his eyes closing, his hands patting them as if to dry up the pictures and keep them from ever coming back.

Perhaps one pill, like a single, fertilizing sperm, had completed its mission and for a second brought him clarity, dying and dissolving as it did. It was he, not George, he, not George ("surprise!") who didn't care, who was completely cold to his wife and son, who loved nothing—unlike his old friend—who was actually already in a crucial way dead. But before he could completely ingest this information, other medications muscled in to adjust his understanding of it.

Now he saw something strange upon the tiles at his feet: drops of blood were falling from the slight gash in his skin caused by the knife, skiing from his stomach over his belt and jumping between his pleated knees to the floor. To his terrible relief, they merged with the grey-white that was down there, were almost as clear as tears, were not, in other words, in any way human—*he* was not human, for the blood had come from him, and so he did not have to face his future or look back upon his past.

He, not George, had arrived on Earth—and by accident, not with the diabolical designs he had accused his friend of having. It had all been a mistake, and so now he needed to get out and go back to where he belonged.

Patching his cut gut with a little circle bandage, which was not big enough but the last one left in the box, Joe stood up. He hadn't showered but felt oddly cool, perhaps from a special inner air conditioning system he now secretly had, or maybe just because his realization had relaxed him. For whatever reason, his "body" was climate-controlled, and so he didn't feel he needed the jacket Michelle had put into the wash when he tip-toed down the stairs and ran out the front door. His wife's quizzical cry of "Joe!" followed him out, as faint as he knew now his connection to that name, this home, and her had always been.

"Joe" got back into the car and saw the shovel stupidly not hidden, just sitting there on the passenger seat, reminding him for a second of what he'd done and not very well, and shouldn't have in the first place. He threw it onto the backseat to remove it from his sight, and its knife-sharp edge barely missed slicing open his mouth.

Then he drove. He drove for hours, past the part of the world he recognized, crossing over into places he'd never been before. At last, at dawn (at the start of what day?), his gas tank empty, he left the car in the middle of a road in a place in America he couldn't name. Then he ran down the highway, laughing and screaming, because he was so happy that he would soon see the large and welcoming lights of his mother ship.

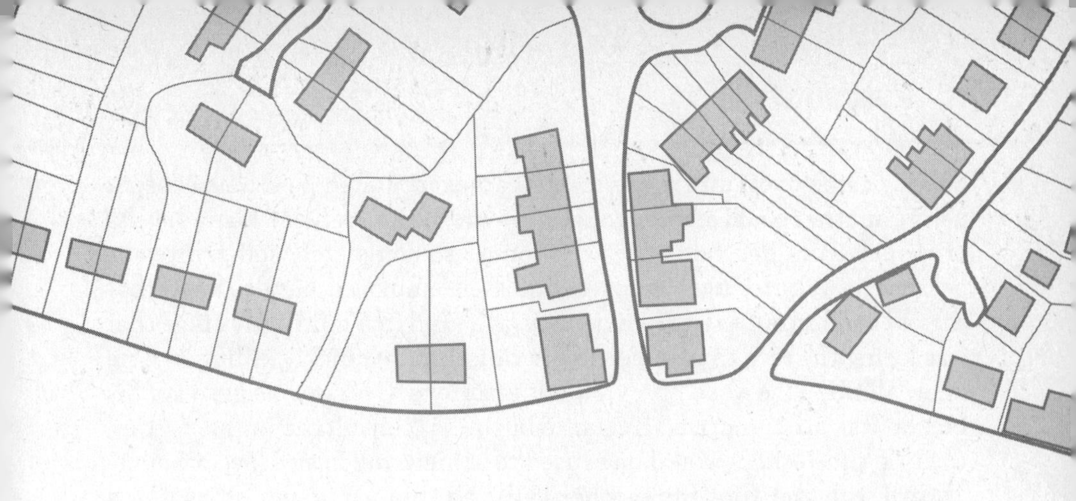

LONG STORY SHORT

Rick thought if she told him the story again, he would kill her. It was an irrational decision, since she was near death and if he merely practiced patience, the event would occur without his committing a crime. But the anecdote—which she had repeated heedlessly for the third time today? Fourth?—was as inciting an offence to him as infidelity might be to a married man.

"It was at a restaurant in Paris forty years ago," his mother said, as if sharing a delicious secret. "Jean Calot was suddenly seated at the table beside your father and myself. I'd always loved him in the movies—'belle laide,' ugly beautiful, I called him," as if she had made up the movie star's generally accepted nickname and needed to—once again—translate the common foreign phrase. "He had a little dog with him, which appalled your father—it seemed so unclean and against the restaurant's rules, unusual for France. But I took that dog—a Pekingese, I think it was—hid it on my lap for the entire meal, and fed it scraps. Jean Calot whispered thanks to me at the end. 'Merci, Mademoiselle,' he said. Mademoiselle! And I was over forty!"

And clearly married—and borderline humiliating her husband, Rick's father, by flirting with the film star. But that wasn't really what infuriated Rick about the story—it was his mother's obvious delight in all its shallow details: the fancy restaurant, the trip to France, the purebred pedigreed dog. They reflected what she relished in the world, what she *respected*, even worse.

Rick knew that his mother's considerable wealth would come to him once she died: he was her only relation and now her kind-of companion (though he only came over once a day to spell an exasperated paid housekeeper before another could arrive). In recent years, he had refused loans or gifts of money from her, but he was no longer so completely self-righteous, because he was no longer so successfully self-employed. He also knew that the old woman suffered from dementia, a kind in a mild early stage that was losing the race to ruin her to the cancer more quickly killing her. He knew all this—he wasn't proud of his emotions. (Nor was he proud of his life: he was an unmarried freelance business "consultant" in his forties, wasting time others would have used to achieve much and love others.)

Still, the fact that his mother clung to this particular story like a shipwreck survivor does a last piece of wood in the water—that this was what was keeping her afloat, that its (what was the word politicians always used?) *values* were still accessible in her brain long after most others had been washed away—repelled him. If this was what she prized—and if she lived more in movie fantasies than in life—what did it say about him? His fists primed to pummel her only relaxed when the last words of the tale rolled out of his mother's mouth, and they were always the same—she was as practiced and perfect in her part as a Broadway star in a long-running play: "Mademoiselle! And I was over forty!"

Rick exhaled and rose, hearing the knock that was obviously the night nurse.

~

An option beside matricide, of course, had always been available to him, but it had seemed too creepy and even cruel. Now, with his mother lingering longer in life than he had anticipated, it was imperative that he stop the story. And if the best he could do was simply change it to another, so be it.

He'd always heard rumours and hearsay about the service, but now trolled the Internet for actual information, which he found. He was tipped off to a storefront on 23rd and Third that had once played host to a hockshop, in the days when people still sold only things and not ideas. It had no official website or phone number; it wasn't actually illegal but unsavoury enough to have to be discreet about itself. Some court would rule on it eventually. Until then, it was hidden in the back of the small shoe repair store, one so inexpensive and old-fashioned that it—ironically enough—attracted beat cops as clientele. They either suspected nothing or used the clandestine business themselves, the way they did whorehouses, providing "protection."

When he arrived, Rick had a peculiar sense of having been there before, but he dismissed it as déjà vu or a wistful regret he hadn't shown up sooner. The paunchy and sixty-something shoe repairman put out a "Closed" sign and took him into the back when he said what his need was. The man closed the door of a cluttered storage space. Half hidden by boxes of shoes was a cabinet that looked not unlike an old card catalogue used before libraries went completely to computers. (Maybe he'd even bought one at auction, Rick thought.) A crude scrawl on an index card taped to the front said simply "Anecdotes."

"Buying or selling?" the man asked, getting right down to work. He had the kind of accent one didn't hear much anymore.

Rick was caught off-guard by the lack of formalities but quickly recovered.

"I—buying."

"Category?"

"Well . . . edifying, I guess. Is that a category?"

"Sorry," the man said, flatly and with a touch of impatience. "The closest I can get to that is probably Inspirational."

"Religious, you mean? No, that wouldn't be right."

"Well, there's two sub-cats: Inspirational-slash-Religious and Inspirational-slash-Secular."

Rick felt he wasn't being given time to think. (Or to reconsider?) Maybe it was better this way. "The second one."

"Okay. Good." Then the man said, as if to himself, "That's Lot Number Twenty-Five."

Rick waited for him to approach the cabinet and offer up some choices, but that wasn't the way it worked. First he was asked for whom he was buying—presumably people bought for themselves as well as others—and then with gruff tact what "the situation" was. Rick explained compassionately yet directly, and the man nodded once, immediately understanding (there were only so many reasons to replace the expression of experiences) and, after calculating silently, said, "Two days."

"But—don't I get to hear—"

"We choose for you. That's our service. That's what you're paying us for."

The last line was Rick's blunt cue to cough it up, cash only, and he did. There was no handshake—Rick awkwardly offered one before withdrawing—just a receipt stamped "Bought" and pulled from a pad not unlike a policeman's ticket book. Maybe the man had gotten it from one of those friendly cops. (And who would want more than a cop to have other anecdotes than his own painful ones, Rick wondered?)

"Thanks," he said, but it was unnecessary. Still stupidly trying to ingratiate himself, he bought some shoelaces on the way out.

—ɯ—

Two days later, the little envelope arrived. It contained a packet filled with solution and a sort of syringe. A tiny booklet of directions—in English and in Chinese—was the only other item. Dutifully following the instructions—and looking at the surprisingly elegant, crosshatched illustrations—he performed the procedure. (He had stayed after the night nurse arrived, and while she read a magazine in the living room, he entered his mother's dark bedroom. As the old woman slept, he gently rolled the nightgown sleeve up her scrawny arm. The vein was easily found and pierced beneath her wafer-like skin.) The booklet said to give it twelve hours to work, not so much for the new story to take hold but for the old to be subsumed. It was like colouring your hair, Rick thought, remembering concealing the grey in his own, though it took longer.

—~—

The next day, he heard with trepidation his mother twice begin the usual story—"It was at a restaurant in Paris"—and each time get no further than the first line (the second time, no further than "restaurant"). Finally, on the third try, he heard her say:

"I was on a crowded subway about twenty years ago. It was in February, around Valentine's Day. A girl in her twenties came on and sat down next to me. She had a half-flat balloon decorated with hearts tied around her wrist. She had obviously come from an office party and was very drunk and not used to being so. As soon as the car took off, she got a distressed look on her face. Then she vomited all over the floor. People scrambled into each other running to avoid her and it. But I unfolded a page of the newspaper I was reading and carefully laid it down upon the sick. Then I put my arm around the ill—and clearly mortified—girl, and rode with her like that until her stop."

Afterwards, his mother's face had the same self-satisfied expression she always wore after the Paris tale (as her voice had been just as smug during the telling). It was as if she had been dubbed by someone else's voice in a foreign film, or had her lines changed and censored for a TV showing: her essential performance was still the same.

Yet it didn't matter, not to Rick. As he heard her story—and heard it again and again, for his mother's memory hadn't been improved nor her repetitiveness decreased, only the specifics of what she said replaced—he was moved. He was more than moved, he found himself feeling something he hadn't felt for his mother in years, not since the days when he was young, his father still alive, and her acquisitiveness and shallowness were not so intractably in place—when she could still surprise him with a sudden show of warmth and kindness. He felt love.

It was a lucky and last-minute love. As he helped her into bed that night, he sensed her slip beneath the silk sheets with finality: hers was like a body poured from a ship under the waves. She disappeared inside their liquid flutter, and before she fell asleep, she died.

—~—

In the days ahead, as he cleaned out her apartment, Rick could not stop his tears. Inevitably now, when he thought of his mother, he thought of the one event—his mother and the sick girl on the subway—the one that was easiest to entertain, that had been worth every penny to place inside her.

He inherited her money. He paid his considerable credit card debt with it and bought an apartment, an actual investment as opposed to his current worthless rental. As a tribute to his mother, the first thing he ordered for the place was a box set of the classic films of Jean Calot, called *Ugly/Beautiful*.

His attachment to her grew; her selflessness soon made him feel unworthy of the legacy she had left him. It made him wait to unpack, as if he did not deserve to put his things in a home that she had made possible for him to own. The closed boxes, brought in by professional packers and movers, became symbols of his inadequacies—his laziness, selfishness, and hostility, some of which had been directed at his mother—all the flaws he had to hide.

At last, if only to get a glass to fill with obliterating wine, he opened up a box. He pulled out a long-stemmed flute and hastily tore away the newspaper in which it was wrapped. As he was casting aside the yellowing page—from his home, he assumed, and sports, he noticed—he saw its date.

It was, strangely, from around the time of his mother's inspiring story, twenty years before. He saw that a corner of it was encrusted with a dot of dried-up liquid-solid mix.

Rick sat on the floor, though a chair and couch were available; he didn't even think to have that wine. It had been he who had placed the paper on the subway floor and saved a page as keepsake, he who had helped the sickened stranger.

He scrambled to open another box, and then another, until he found his folder of meticulously kept bills and receipts. In the middle was a familiar looking, shabby ticket from the shoe store, dated from two years before and stamped "Sold."

He had dealt the anecdote when he was strapped for funds—when he was poor and yet still principled enough to turn down his mother's cash. The selling—a reverse procedure, an incision and withdrawal performed under vaguely unsanitary conditions in the store's back room—was meant to take away his memory not only of the incident but its removal. This was why the shoe store had seemed familiar. It had been a faulty process, and left him with a shard of knowledge.

Had the shoe repairman remembered his face and returned the story to him? Was that what he had really been "paying us for"? And how many other such incidents of charity had he hocked?

Rick didn't know. He only knew that it was his own good will he should have been celebrating. Whether he inherited her wealth or not, he was as far away from his mother as the living were from the dead. With new tears—the "cry for happy" kind he'd heard so much about—he began to unpack for real, to fill the empty space with the things of himself, those of a man who could show love to others and so was worthy of receiving it.

—ɷ—

It took several weeks until the rooms were fully furnished. In that time, he took two steps to truly right his life: made inquiries about starting a foundation for the poor with his inheritance and asked out a bright, attractive woman who worked in the city agency he had approached.

"It's been a while since I've been on a date," said this Sandra, who was a saucy type. "I'm rusty. I'll have to remember all my charming anecdotes."

"I'm looking forward," Rick said, "to hearing them."

He was to meet her for dinner that night. It was *his* first date in months as well, too many months for him to count: he felt nervous and excited.

To calm himself, in the half hour before he left, he surfed TV. Then he saw something sitting beside the set: the unopened box of Jean Calot's old films.

It seemed amusing and appropriate to pop one in. He chose the best known of the actor's many hits, a film considered classic that he was convinced he'd never seen: *La Derniere Histoire*, made forty years before.

The black-and-white print was pristine. Even though Rick had neglected to turn on the subtitles, the story started simply. In Paris, a young and handsome, mug-faced Calot was commuting home from his labourer's job. When he boarded a train, the good-natured hero saw a pretty girl seated opposite him. She wore a balloon on her wrist and a pleasant but queasy expression. As she suddenly and unsteadily rose, her face grew grim and her eyes wide. Rick saw the newspaper folded beneath Calot's arm. He rushed to hit the stop but hit the pause instead and, before it could occur, froze the incident forever.

Rick sank to his knees and covered his face to escape the truth. The newspaper had belonged to the movers; its stain was food from some forgotten meal. He had never behaved—never cared enough about another person to behave—in such a way. He had been touched and inspired by an incident from someone else's mind, sold a story from a story, lived in other people's glossy dreams. And if he had marketed other such instances, they had been similarly purloined.

He was a creature from his mother's lap, the little dog that she fed scraps. It was the story, the only story, of his life.

—ɷ—

NOTE: Anecdote currently available. Ask for Lot #731. Categories: Family/Values; Funny/Sad; Ugly/Beautiful.

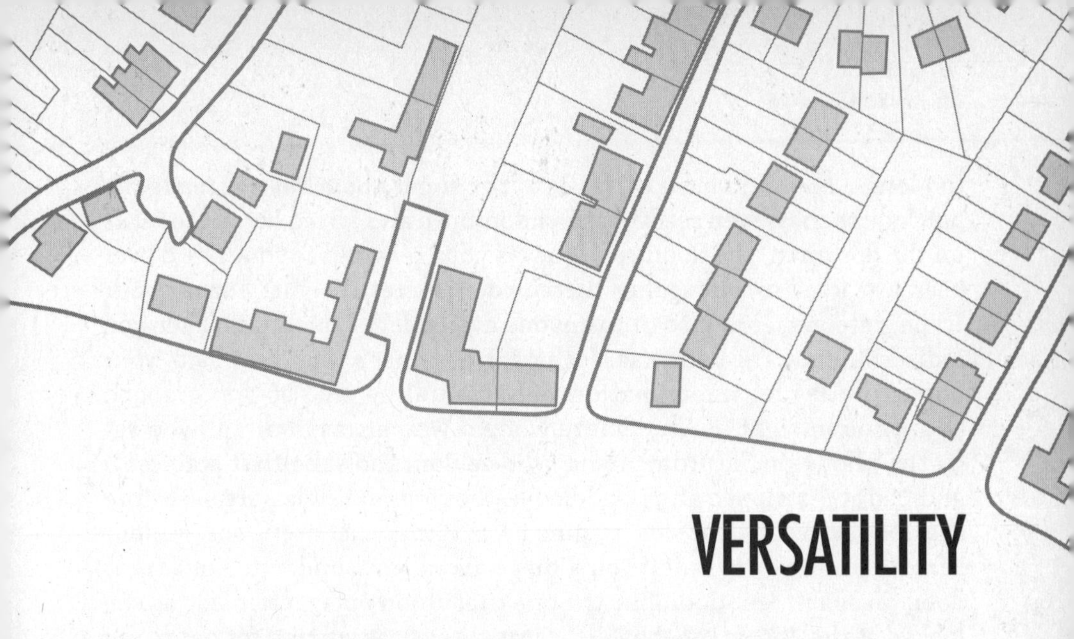

VERSATILITY

She heard a bang, a clap, a spank—something—from outside in the hall. Her eyes opened and she rose from where she was, reclining on the couch. Then Lee opened the door.

The doorman was there, the new one, the young one, the one all the girls made excuses to hang around. He was delivering the mail in the old-fashioned way it was still done in her pre-war building, by dropping it before each door.

He looked at her, a pile of mail held in his arms, cradled, with seeming kindness. Yet he had just dropped a big piece of it—a magazine? A catalogue? Something heavy enough to make a sound—so he was capable of being callous, too. He was a combination of both, was soft *and* sadistic: she'd heard that that was sexy, imagined it would be, like, what was his name, Martin Brando in the old movies, though this kid could have been Brando's baby brother. In truth, he didn't look like Brando at all, but maybe he would be better than Brando who had ended up so fat.

"Did I scare you?" he asked.

"You woke me up," she said.

The exchange was insinuating, suggestive, and—despite their being in a northern city—southern-seeming, as in *The Streetcar Driver*, or whatever the movie with Brando was called. Each knew what the other slyly meant, neither was in the dark—though the boy actually stood in the dim, beneath a blown-out ceiling bulb that had been unattended for too long. Lee would have to speak to the super about that; it made the hall look shabby, even seedy—and she stopped and forced herself to focus on the doorman, the door*boy*, who was younger than anyone she'd ever been attracted to, but ageing altered your interests, right? Turned your "type" into someone else (into anyone available?). Loneliness made you indiscriminate; the door was closing for her, that's what they said, your opportunities for impregnation were dwindling, and so you grabbed at anyone in sight. Even demure women who always waited, who sat by the phone on Saturday night, who seldom took the first step, now grabbed at—stripped and straddled!—the first plausible partner before the door closed, a door she imagined was like an electronic garage door that could cut you in half if you didn't roll out from under it. Not a front door, an apartment door, like the one that stood open at her side as she looked at the doorman—boy—she was aware was waiting for her to say something else, something after, "You woke me up," which she had said spontaneously, for it was true, and which had sounded sexy and clever but had really been unintentional. She begged herself to focus, and tried to, but she had been sedated and was so thrown, made so nervous by him that the most she could manage was to take her mail and give him a little nondescript smile before she quickly shut the door.

In truth, Lee was not menopausal or even middle-aged; her anxieties made her feel older than her (thirty-three) years, made her identify with those whom age had slowed down, made demented or otherwise kept from normal social intercourse. The fact that she was even home today, at noon, was a measure of how much agoraphobia had reduced her normal way into the world (and pills and talking therapy and hypnosis had done little to ease it), how much it had thrown roadblocks, so to speak, onto entrances to heavily traversed highways and away from her own lonely road.

It was travel that had finally waylaid Lee and forced her behind closed doors—and not even long distance travel but local travel, on mass transit and even between floors in her building. It was a final ordeal a few months back inside a subway car, one not even crowded but stuck between stations, that had sent her gasping for air above ground and to the nearest bus, which, moving at a snail's pace, seemed again suffocating and shot her out onto the street where she walked for thirty blocks in a pitiless rainstorm toward her home. Even there, the elevator kept threatening to stop—it was going so slow—and she had suddenly pressed the button for "10," surprising the one woman with whom she rode (and she had waited for a nearly empty elevator before getting on as she had let even moderately filled subways pass before taking one, turning a typically thirty-minute commute into a ninety-minute marathon), and then went on foot, wet and panting, the twelve remaining flights to reach her flat.

The experience had ended Lee's ability to work every day and she was now on unemployment (and maybe soon on disability). In fact, she hoped a check from the agency was among the pieces of mail the young doorman had just handed her, his eyebrows raising a little as he looked into her eyes, an intimacy she had very much enjoyed but allowed only briefly.

Indeed the letter was there—but apparently it had been somewhere else first. Lee saw that the envelope had been torn open and taped shut, the words "Sorry—opened by accident" a jagged surgery scar on its white paper belly. She felt furious, but more she was mortified that someone had seen—knew about—her condition: how she had been stranded alone in her apartment (a rental she had once shared with and inherited from her parents), or at best in the lobby or nearby neighbourhood. Someone knew what woman her troubled mind had made her into and had been both cavalier about knowing and too cowardly to put a name to the confession.

Since the envelope had been in the doorman's bundle—his package, his pile; after she saw him everything had become an innuendo (like bang, clap, spank, she realized), everything was naughty or nasty, she noted with amusement; she had been alone a long time, everything was something else—he was the one she decided to confront. Luckily, she would have to go no farther than the lobby.

"What's up with this?" she asked, holding the envelope, realizing she had meant to say, "What's the meaning of this?" but (her identification with those older suddenly irksome and unwanted) she had replaced it unconsciously with a younger, hipper person's expression.

"What do you mean?" He was alone at the front desk; she had waited unseen around the corner near the elevator until he *was* alone, until a UPS man had left after what seemed like interminable obscene male banter between the two.

"This. This. Who opened my letter?"

He looked at the envelope (she had already taken out the cheque) with utter incomprehension. As he strained to think, he squished together his face, forced his forehead forward, altered his—perfectly pleasing and symmetrical—features, gave himself a sort of simian cast, which since it wasn't permanent and his face immediately returned to normal, since it was just a split-second shift, like the skull superimposed on Anthony Pearlman's face at the end of Hitchcock's—what was it called? Her pills had made off with her memory—it was kind of exciting, cruelty and kindness again combining in him, and wasn't that what you wanted? Well, as long as there was occasionally kindness, right? Lee was so inexperienced, well, not entirely, but almost, and wondered—as she stared at the doorman, tried to discipline her disobedient thoughts again: the ripped envelope, remember?—did he take her stare as interest? She couldn't tell.

"I mis-delivered it the other day," he said defensively. "One of your neighbours gave it back to me. I'm sorry."

He seemed concerned that she might blame him, report him, even try to have him dismissed. But then he sighed, as if to say—she was almost sure—listen to me; why am I so weak? What the hell am I so worried about? His eyes closed and reopened, and to her his long lashes seemed like stage curtains, which ended one scene and then began another with a new character, which was strange since he then said, "Look, I'm not really a doorman. I'm an actor."

Lee was interested; it made sense, his being so young, good-looking, and incompetent. Yet she didn't want to lose the upper hand or her authority or whatever it was she might have gained by grilling him. So she asked, as if only politely or even condescendingly inquiring, "And might I have seen you in anything?"

"I wouldn't think so," he said honestly. "I'm just starting out. So I'm acting all the time in real life. Right now, I'm playing the part of a doorman, if you know what I mean. And not too well, apparently."

She only allowed herself to smile and just for a second, though she was legitimately and mightily amused. Why was he telling her this? Because he was so stupid—or so indifferent to his job—that he didn't care about the consequences? Could he tell she was crazy and homebound (she hadn't combed her hair or put on any makeup) and that no one would ever believe what she said (as if he'd opened up for laughs to a lunatic screaming curse words in the street)? Or was he so sensitive, being an actor and all, that he could see that they were kindred spirits, both made to play parts they did not want, for which they had not auditioned, and from which they longed to be released? She wanted to believe the latter.

"I know what you mean," she said. Then, to young it up: "I hear you."

"Good. So, again, I'm sorry. I'll try to, you know, do the delivery bit better next time."

He said "bit" as if, yes, it was just part of a performance, one for which he had (somewhat unfairly, he thought) been criticized and which he would begrudgingly and half-heartedly work to improve.

He looked into her eyes, held the look longer this time—or maybe she just let him linger—and, unless she was crazy (which she knew she kind of was), she thought he meant to do more than just deliver her mail: he would, by knowing her, free them both.

—w—

The next day, Lee learned he was on mail duty again (she had called down to the desk on a pretext, heard his voice in the background as he coarsely kibitzed this time with a house painter). She listened for the sound of the mail landing before her neighbours' doors, the placement of the letters today tender and not tough, as gentle as a touch to someone's cheek or to a forehead to take a temperature. When she heard the feathery brush of a bill—probably—down near her welcome mat, Lee whipped her door open grandly, as if indeed making an entrance on that stage the doorman said he always stood upon, whether employed as an actor or not.

"Yes?" he said.

Oddly, he didn't seem to recognize her or was only being courteous—and confused, for his eyes glanced at the number on her door to confirm that it was hers.

Should she be hurt, she wondered? She'd make sure this time that her hair was settled, her pale skin covered by foundation; did she look *that* different, had she looked *that* much worse the other day?

"Hi," he said, pleasant and impersonal. "How's it going?"

Then Lee's eyes moved as well, to a mirror on the wall in her vestibule. She saw the cause of his perplexity and felt the start and swift growth of her own.

In the glass, there was another woman, one a few years older—pretty, freckled, heavy, not in an unattractive way, her hair bright red, dressed in a provocative manner, her shiny blouse cut low, her spangled jeans tight. She was very different from the woman Lee had seen reflected earlier, who had been slight, pretty if you paid attention (her mother's words), her hair dirty blonde or mousy brown (if you were trying to be nice or not), her clothes a shapeless T-shirt she'd kept since college over sweatpants: herself, in other words.

Yet this *was* her, too, now: she certainly saw *out* from this new woman as she might from a Halloween mask, the way she sometimes viewed the world from her usual self when she was feeling most distant and detached, when she felt like a floating consciousness contained in somebody but connected to nothing. This feeling today was less hopeless, especially since she saw how the doorman reacted—purely physically checking her out, as the saying went, as he never had before.

"I'm—" She thought she ought to introduce herself, since that's what he obviously wanted. Her voice was whispery in that Marilyn Monroe way. She remembered the actress' name—her memory had improved, was more vibrant, like her hair, a contrast to Lee's usual low, downbeat, almost miserable teenage boy-sounding tones. "I'm Lee's sister . . . Angelique."

The name just came to her: it sounded like a model or an actress, or a—it sounded like a perfume, that's what, and no wonder: Lee could smell her own strong scent, different from the, okay, the nothing that she usually wore.

"Well," he said, meaning, well, well, well, who *do* we have here? And "Hello," this word a welcome for a new and wonderful opportunity.

She asked him in—this was what Angelique would do—and he accepted, after a surreptitious glance down the hall and then down at the letters still in his hand, which he a moment later had placed not very carefully on her front hall bookcase as she shut the door, some poor person's postcard dropping and sliding forever beneath her standing lamp.

"Are you from out of town?" he asked.

She made up something: yes, from Chicago, a city that seemed as hearty and instinctive as Angelique. They engaged in other small talk, much smaller than anything she as Lee and he had made. The doorman seemed particularly suave and adept at this ("Chicago—now *there's* a city") and Lee realized that he, too, was playing a new part now: he was no longer a doorman or even an aspiring actor, but a dapper, lupine lover who thought nothing of interrupting his afternoon in such a way with such a woman. Angelique was his distaff edition, his partner in crime, or better yet, his co-star.

"Want some wine?" she improvised and he, of course, said, "Yes."

The small talk and the drinking continued until at a certain point she stopped them both. Suddenly, his mouth looked to her like a beautiful red and white seashell: would she hear the ocean if she put her ear to it? She wished to find out.

Lee as Angelique knew exactly what to do, for she had done it many times before: the way to wetly probe his tongue with hers, then push it until it pushed back—or didn't (his did); how to intertwine their tongues, as if her initial action had been intended to inspire camaraderie (the way one playfully smacks someone else's shoulder until the smackee either gets enraged or becomes aware that it's a joke, an aggressive greeting to mask genuine affection, and wraps his arm around the other); then to bite lightly at his tongue, as if to say, don't trust me entirely, I'm no softie, no matter how soft I may have seemed a second earlier.

That led again without any awkwardness—expertly—to the rest of it: her undoing his uniform and everything else, even her—for she was more experienced than he, imagine that—touching and kissing, picking up and placing his parts (his hand and his penis) onto and inside her.

It came as easily as other things, doing the dishes, driving—not to make it sound casual or inconsiderate, but they were all things she had learned to do when younger and now needed no more help to do, had been okay doing by herself for years.

When he had opened her clothes—or she had opened them for him, or had helped him open them—there was so much more of her to see now. He had the reaction she hoped he would—"So much, so gorgeous"; he didn't stay silent in a way that meant he wasn't pleased by her appearance and was too polite and too prideful to lie. In fact, he seemed pleasantly—excitedly—surprised, and she understood, for she was surprised to see herself, too.

In bed, she controlled him, sent signals from beneath him, supervised him in a sense with her hips, hands, and sex—once more with confidence. (Lee remembered an article she'd read once that said women always really make the first move—not men—by the way they sit or look or speak to someone. It gave her a new way to understand aggression, and now she knew that this power went beyond just inviting someone's attentions all the way to controlling the actual event once things moved along—though she soon learned the limits of her new power as, shaking and shouting out, he finished immediately, no matter how much she tried to impose order. She accepted this with her new worldliness: it was their first time together and he was young, after all.)

He fell beside her ("Thank God," he whispered; she didn't want to know why), and she watched him now as she had the whole time: partly from outside her new self, her older sister (why had she said that, for God's sake; she was an only child), and partly from within the experience.

"You're a woman," he said appreciatively, meaning, she guessed, a real one, and what a one.

"I am," she said, imitating his grateful tone.

"That's a gift. That's rare."

"Thanks. I'm—I had nothing to do with it." And this was true—it wasn't a joke, though that's how he took it.

"Right," he said and laughed. "Right."

(She wondered: should she be upset at how quickly he had commingled with her sister after showing a slightly more nuanced interest in her? Then she remembered: she was, if anything, cheating on *herself* with him.)

"I better go," he said, kissing her—seriously freckled, look at all of them—shoulder.

Lee didn't join him at the door, just lay undressed above the covers in bed. She heard him fumbling with the mail again and opening the door.

"Bye," she called quietly, affectionately, and thought she heard him answer. Then she fell into a sleep from which she eventually awoke as

Lee, her body lighter, an hour and a half late for her afternoon pill. She luxuriated in the bed, secretly celebrating the freeing of herself from her stale and painful character, the expanding of her repertoire.

—ʌʌ—

The next time she saw the doorman was two days later, after being awakened by the sound of a package being propped up and then crashing onto the floor in the hall, followed by a whispered but still audible curse. Lee cracked open her door and peeked out: she saw another door had opened across the way and a female neighbour was catching the doorman red-handed, carefully placing the (perhaps destroyed) package against the wall.

"Sorry," Lee heard him say.

She was afraid he would go into his explanation—his only acting the part of doorman, a confidence she hoped had been reserved for her—and was relieved that he did not.

Still, he stayed at the door, 22F, for longer than an apology, speaking in low enough tones to be inaudible by Lee. (Was he playing the lover part again, an even worse infraction?) When Lee saw him leave, he did so with a smile and a discernible—what was the expression?—spring in his step.

Lee stood at her own open door long after her neighbour's had been closed. She knew who this tenant was: an attractive young woman in her twenties who had recently moved in, seemingly anti-social or simply spoiled, who (obsessed with her iPod or speaking into a cell phone) never said hello or even smiled when Lee passed her while taking out the trash; who upon moving in had left her empty boxes in the hall for someone else to toss instead of walking the few steps to reach the garbage; whose parties had been loud, crowded, and filled with blaring music made by famous bands the names of which, to her frustration, her synapses blurred, Lee couldn't recall.

Lee had resented the girl but now she hated her—not just for her youth, which of course accented her own retreat to an earlier generation (she was super-aware of her real age now, had pulled definitively away from identifying with those older), and not just because the doorman had flirted with the girl after probably breaking what she'd had delivered, but for a reason that had only just occurred to Lee right now, a crime of which she realized 22F was guilty.

In a second Lee found that she was walking on clomping feet across the hall. She didn't stop banging on the other door until it opened.

"Yes?" Her neighbour already seemed impatient, though no words had been addressed to her (and were her tank top and short shorts the outfit she'd worn to greet the doorman? No wonder he'd gone away skipping).

"What's the meaning of this?" Lee had no compunction about using the older person's expression now; as she revealed her damaged pay envelope, the sound of her own voice, the deep and crackly aspect of it, stunned her.

"I don't know what you're talking about." The girl shifted uneasily onto one hip.

"Oh, I think you do, honey."

Now 22F seemed a little rattled. "Look, sir—what's the—please, who are you, anyway?"

Lee was made silent by the strange form of address. She glanced down at her own frame, caught sight of a paunchy male gut that jutted out in wide-fit jeans over feet wearing flip-flops. Trying to seem casual, she ran fingers through her hair—and found what little was left pushed forward, Caesar-style, to hide her baldness.

"I'm—" Lee became more aware of her voice, which cigarettes had turned raspy, though she'd only ever tried half of a friend's Pall Mall in high school and only ever smoked dope twice. Swiftly, she spoke lines. "I'm . . . Roddy, the brother-in-law of Lee, down the hall." She tapped contemptuously on the envelope's address, half-hidden by the words "by accident." "Though I bet you don't even know her name, your own neighbour, do you, sweetheart?"

"Well—" The girl now seemed even younger, unprotected. "So what if I don't? And so what if I opened that?" With a shaking hand, she gestured at the letter. "I gave it to the doorman and wrote that I was sorry, didn't I?"

Lee had to admit it was true and so had no retort. She saw the girl back slightly away, to escape breath Lee smelled on herself was dipped in beer. She plunged ahead with the bellicosity that was apparently the stock in trade of Angelique's blustery (and, she now knew, constantly cuckolded) husband, whom Lee had impulsively named after a wrestler she heard of once on TV.

"Well—just be more careful next time, *okay*?"

Deeply frightened, the girl closed the door. Lee stomped back down the hall to her home.

When she was safely locked inside, she glanced in the mirror—and saw her old female self, which looked if possible even less prepossessing than usual, in a purple sweatshirt painted with a puffin that she'd bought a decade earlier for ten dollars in Maine.

Eased by meds, Lee slept for much of the afternoon, exhausted by the thrill of changing shape, feeling the fatigue some patients experience after surgery to impose or remove things from inside them. Hours (or minutes, or days) later, she was revived by a buzzer or a bell, which in her groggy state she imagined was from an oven to declare her dinner done. Soon she realized it was her door.

After stumbling toward it, Lee paused to understand who might be calling. If it was the doorman, she was now only herself and not her sister—she smelled and didn't even need to see it—and would that be a problem?

"Did I scare you?"

"You woke me up."

Would they say those words again and—like "sim salla bim"—what would it start now?

It wasn't him. It was her super, Martin Raveech. He was lean, middle-aged, and strangely hysterical, unlike others in his field Lee had known who were tough and even physically threatening.

"Look," he said, as always glass-half-empty, "we've got a problem."

Lee didn't let him in, just let him continue, realizing that her pills had made her mouth too dry for her to do much more than lick her lips.

"You know the rules," he said.

He referred to Lee's long history in the building, in which she'd been raised—indeed she'd seen many supers come and go before Raveech. Her mouth still parched, she only shrugged, remaining noncommittal before knowing what he meant.

"I mean," he said, "your sister and brother-in-law. You know they can't be living here without being on the lease."

Lee now nodded—not just because she was aware of the rules of apartment habitation, but because she knew that Raveech had been tipped off and intimidated by her girl neighbour, and then had quizzed the young doorman who had admitted what he knew, endearingly innocent of (or indifferent to) the results.

"Hold on," Lee rasped and let the door half-close.

When, after a long moment, it opened completely again, Raveech had to look down at the person who was—with an effort—still holding onto the knob.

"Hey," he said and couldn't help but smile. "Who do we have here?"

"I'm Aunt Lee's niece." And now Raveech saw the six-year-old pause as if—adorably—trying to remember her own name. "Glinda."

(Indeed with her head full of red curly hair, she very much resembled her mother, Angelique.)

"Well, Glinda," he said, imitating her childish voice, "where's your Aunt?"

"She's not feeling well." Glinda put on a frowny face, which made the super squint and chuckle cloyingly.

"I'm sorry to hear that. Tell me—" and here Raveech revealed he was not above trying to pressure and mislead a less capable companion, even seemed glad to have the opportunity, "are you and your Mommy and Daddy living here? We'd love to welcome you to our great big building."

"No. We're just visiting."

"Really? Was that something a grown-up told you to say?"

"No."

"Oh. Well, that's a relief. Tell me—do you know what a super does?"

"I'm not allowed to talk to strangers. Goodbye."

"But—"

With her tiny hands, the newest member of Lee's family pushed the door definitively shut. The little girl waited until she had stopped shaking, unnerved by having faced down and defied an adult. Then slowly she realized that the doorknob was no longer at eye level, was in fact at her waist, and the spyhole—which had been completely out of reach—could be accessed with just a brief lean forward. (Raveech was gone.)

"Wow," Lee said, and heard her own deep timbre return. She didn't even bother with the nearby mirror, knew that she was once again herself now that another self had done what needed doing, and that, like TV shows about law firms or crime units or hospitals, she employed a whole ensemble.

~

The next day, Lee didn't need to keep an ear out for the mail. Dozing without pills, and so only really resting like a dead fish on the watery surface of sleep, she was caught and jerked into consciousness by the sound of paper sliding. She rose stiffly and saw that a note had been pushed beneath the door. It had no stamp or envelope, had just been torn out of a memo pad and folded. She stooped to pick it up.

"Meet me," it said, at a popular bar, twenty blocks uptown, at eight on that night. And then there was a name she should have known but had never even asked to know—"Bobby"—who was she assumed, hoped (it had to be! Who else?), the doorman.

The prospect of leaving her apartment suddenly didn't frighten or upset her. Today it seemed both a wonderful challenge and a relief. Lee took the elevator—she could have used the stairs—and was untroubled by the slow pace of the car and the proximity of two other riders. She looked nice but not nicer than she had ever looked: hadn't done more than comb (and pin, all right, and pin) her hair.

Outside, she approached the subway entrance without her usual racing heart or the slow start of sweat upon her back. She took if not the first then the second car that came, which was full enough that she felt the touch of someone's sleeve against her arm and didn't panic. The knowledge that she could whip out another woman, man, or child was now her concealed weapon; it had replaced the pills in her pocket that had been her usual—ineffective—reassurance.

And then she was there—in half an hour, a straight shot, travelling like anyone else—at Tadley's, the after-work bar that Bobby chose. (Because it was closer to his own home, which was farther uptown? She had never considered where he went after work—she'd been too tied up in her own troubles like the rest of the not-well. Well, not anymore!) And then there he was, at a table, out of uniform.

It was a startling sight—not like seeing him nude, which she already had; it was like catching him in costume, and one from a cheap, second-rate show: a checked shirt with both sleeves buttoned self-protectively, jeans not so distressed as to be stylish, and red-rimmed glasses, someone's odd idea of "edgy." His hair, which she had felt as thick and boyishly unruly when she stuck—when Angelique had stuck—her fingers in it was now combed conventionally, parted politely, and thinning prematurely. Or was it doing it on time? In her building, Bobby had looked twenty-five; in the bar, he was thirty-two or thirty-three, his face a little fallen, his eyes hammocked by dark rings.

"I'm glad you came," he said, and sounded genuinely relieved—it wasn't a formality.

"Me too," she said quietly.

"How do you like the place?"

"It's—" She looked at the raised TV, the paper placemats and framed pennants. "You know, it's fine." The drink seemed watered, but what did she know? Her medications had made her a teetotaler too long.

"Yep—my brother's got me washing dishes for now, but he says there's plenty of room for advancement."

"Wait a minute—" She leaned forward and the overhanging light exposed her own brow wrinkles and light facial down. "You work here?"

"Yeah. Didn't I tell you? Raveech couldn't stand me screwing up so much, so I got canned. I haven't been there since Monday. I left you that note on my way out."

"Oh." In fact—this was Wednesday—she now realized she hadn't seen him in days but hadn't thought much of it, had taken him for granted, been complacent—or unconscious?

"There was always a standing offer here," he said, "so I took it. It's nights for now, but that can change."

"And it leaves you time for auditions."

"Well—maybe. But that's not my focus now. I mean, who was I fooling with that anyway? I wasn't making headway. Who was I, Heath Ledger? And look what happened to him. No, that's not for me. There's a realistic future here. That's what my brother says, and I believe him."

With that, he looked more openly at her, and lights from the mirrored bar opposite made his eyes shine with hopefulness.

"I'm also, you know . . ." he said. "The doc has put me on anti-depressants."

Bobby continued to stare, awaiting if not her approval her understanding. She understood. This was why he had asked to see her here, on his new turf: to link the man he felt he was with the woman he thought her to be—someone mentally damaged and of limited potential. To end for them, in other words, all other options. She felt hot and pushed away her drink, pretending it had been the cause despite the little alcohol it contained.

"Excuse me," she said. "I'm not used to—"

Lee walked unsteadily to the ladies' room where she punched her face with water, her eyes closed. She didn't prepare a thing to say, kept her mind clear, hoped irrationally he would be gone when she returned. When she came out, she hadn't noticed that a stray red hair had fallen in the sink.

Her journey back to Bobby was slow and halting, for she walked on higher heels. The look on the face of the doorman—no, the dishwasher, and maybe one day the waiter—told her what had happened.

"Jeez," Bobby said, standing, stunned. "I didn't know *you'd* be here."

"I like to look after my little sister," Lee said—or whispered, in the Angelique way.

They took their seats and she immediately leaned forward, her breasts book-marked, and picked up and threw back the vodka Lee hadn't finished. Bobby made to order her another. When he brought his hand down, she took it between her own and rubbed it determinedly.

"It's warm," she said.

Maybe she moved her fingers too swiftly on his skin, implied too obviously that she wished to cast a spell, as if he were Aladdin's lamp, so that he'd change shape as she had done. For whatever reason, having to make an effort, he pried his hand out of her grip.

"Where is she?" he asked impatiently. "Where's Lee?"

The use of her normal name jarred her; she had never told it to him, had kept that line blank, waiting to be filled in. Silly, she thought: he had read it on her mail and known it all along.

"I'll see what's keeping her," she said, defeated.

Angelique rose, knowing he missed the seriousness—the sickness—of her sister and was in no mood for her. She didn't bother to hide that she was hurt. She fought through the pre-commuting crowd, which was young, loud, and jungle deep.

As she did, she suddenly felt weary, being squeezed from all sides, and utterly out of place. The others looked at her with a mix of snobbery and amusement.

"What's up with *him*?" one asked.

"Is he here to fix the toilet?"

"Be careful. He might be with the mafia."

"Get the hell out of my way, jerk," Lee found herself saying—growling, then coughing with a smoker's choke, her ruddy, red, and hairy fist at her own mouth.

Ruddy and Roddy—well, that made sense, she thought, for here he was, a silver cross she had not even known he wore around his neck being accidentally yanked by the customers in his effort to get out. He was a working stiff out of water, or whatever the expression was, just as his wife—looking for love, apart from him, as usual—had been misplaced, unwelcomed, and wronged.

Roddy managed to push his way to the door and then the street, snotty asides showered on him like beer at a ball game. Outside, his legs spread, and he swung his arms like an ape—on purpose, as a warning, to regain *some* power. Then he reached and descended the subway stairs.

But once the train came—and it was even nearly empty—he went back to being weak, became even weaker. Again he was lost, and unconscionably, criminally, it was illegal to be there by himself—the incredulous stares of other riders told him so. He held onto the centre pole with both hands, feeling abandoned, trying not to cry.

"What's happened, honey?" one solicitous old lady—maybe twenty-five—asked, half-kneeling near her, her hand clasped as well around the pole. "Where's your Mommy or Daddy?"

Glinda couldn't answer—she was too scared. This was not the warmth of her aunt's apartment, with her folks somewhere around. This was a wilderness, one shaking and swiftly moving like a spaceship toward—what, another world? Who knew?

"I-I-I don't know!" she cried, the sound covered by the subway brakes—which was to her a witch's scream—as the train came to a stop.

The little girl ran out, followed by expressions of dismay from the good Samaritans and busybodies left behind. It was not her station—she had many left to go—but she ran by instinct in the direction of her Aunt Lee's house.

The second she set foot in the safety of the lobby, not even looking at the new—older—doorman, and sprinted toward the stairs, there was no more little girl and she was Lee again.

Lee slammed her door behind her. Then she was shocked to see that she had company.

In fact, her apartment—which was always silent except for electronic voices from images on TV, which even the super had only ever truly entered once or twice to free a drain or fix a phone jack—was packed.

A merry party was taking place—gossip was being spread, canned music played, and old-fashioned appetizers (pigs in blankets, shrimp toast) gobbled up. There were so many guests that Lee could hardly get beyond the vestibule to enter.

Once the visitors became aware that she was home, they slowly stopped their celebration—then found new cause for it in her arrival.

"Hey!"

"There she is!"

"We've been waiting for you!"

Lee's back was patted, her cheek pinched. She was pushed farther in and nearly passed around like a new hors d'oeuvre fresh out of the oven.

"Don't be shy!"

"Don't be a stranger!"

"Come on in!"

As if by magic, the group began to grow. She realized that it was made up of her family: cousins, uncles, even one old granddad who wasn't dead. They had come to surprise her—no, it hadn't been their choice, they had been summoned, like people in old movies in which a mysterious letter leads a group of strangers to a house and they find out—by telling tales—that they are linked. No, that wasn't it, either. They'd never met each other; she'd never met them, either, but being related, how could that be?

Lee was growing dizzy, being traded from each embrace. Then she was airborne, lifted, as in a raucous rock concert—a mess kit, a mesh pit, a mosh! Her memory was being shredded as she dropped and, hugged and crushed, her clothes were being torn.

She knew now she had released them—her "relatives" had gotten loose from inside her and couldn't ever be re-integrated. There were suddenly more and more of them—of her: some old, one infant, one ugly, another violent—they were multiplying like mice or like cancer cells that kill off the original host. Soon, as she screamed, they closed upon her, engulfed and erased her—none of them remained—and no one would be there to do the dishes or turn off the lights or set the alarm for the morning.

—~—

Lee heard a bang, a clap, a spank. This time, awakening, she kept her eyes closed. Was she all right, insane, or dead? Had the noise been made by a doorman, a paramedic, or an angel? (Was it true? Would they really exist?) Had it all already happened or was it ready to begin? Would she and someone say, "Did I scare you," and "You woke me up"?

All she had to do was open her eyes. But suddenly she was aware she wouldn't know the answers even if she did.

MODERN SIGN

He turned the steering wheel hard to the right, changing lanes without having signalled. The driver of the car behind him, whom he had just cut off, blared his horn then tailgated him, bitterly, before moving left. The other man drove parallel for a while, giving him the finger, before hitting the gas and whizzing away.

Get a life, Bill Chubbuck thought. Then, forgetting the other man immediately, he thought: I hate that expression. I wonder who made it up: probably some poor dumb bastard like me. Now, through no fault of his own, it's become part of the language, polluting it, one more cancer degrading the English tongue until it destroys it completely. And you've got men like me and whoever invented that goddamn "Get a life" to thank for it.

Bill had had a few drinks after spending a long Saturday at work. There he had been harangued, then pressured, and at last mildly praised. He had done his job for too long not to know that this mild praise—faint praise, that's what the expression was—meant that he had done marvellously well, saved his job, that of his superiors, and even those above them. But giving him more than faint praise might mean he would want something in return—a raise or a promotion or even a better job—and that could not be.

"Damned with faint praise," he thought and liked the expression, sensing that it was invented at a time when people were still creative and not yoked, lashed like galley slaves as all were now, no matter what age, race, or sex, to some kind of corporation.

The expression made sense: if you were damned with faint praise, well, you weren't condescended to exactly, but, anyway, it was worse than getting no praise at all, right? So even if the expression didn't quite apply to him today—he had been *under*-praised, intentionally—he still approved of its clarity and wit, qualities that he associated with this earlier, freer age in America, and he knew that the separate parts of the sentence did in fact apply: "faint praise," as he had already mentioned to himself, and, frankly, "damned."

Bill cut right, again without signalling, but this time there was no need—no one was behind him. He was entering a narrow, two-lane highway that grew more dark and deserted as it moved farther north from New York City. It was six o'clock, the sun had already set, and there wasn't even the occasional weekday commuter to impede his speed, which was just about to reach seventy-five.

Bill wasn't seventy-five, he was forty-two, but he thought he looked seventy-five as he glanced in the rear-view and saw the crow's feet beneath his eyes, wrinkles which made other men look distinguished and only made him look ill and exhausted. "Crow's feet"—he approved of the expression. Its origin might even have been archaic: it was descriptive, precise, and unsparing, and he felt like cruelly sparing himself nothing today, on a day when he had succeeded, a day when other men might have felt exhilarated.

But these other men, he thought, his speed now at eighty, weren't working for two corporations, which were, in turn, working for two other corporations. Olly Olly Advertising, his employer, had recently been bought by—"merged with"—September, October, & Terwilliger Advertising, and was now handling the account of Cedar Ribbon Investments, which had recently been bought by—"folded into"—High Landing Financial Enterprises, which had been born during the depression as Pennywise, Inc.

Bill had survived the inevitable Olly Olly firings that came with the "merger"—firings all employees had of course been assured would not happen—because he was a gifted copywriter, the best they had, though not one apparently deserving of the praise that might give him ideas of his own worth and ambition to be elsewhere. (And where else could he go now, anyway? September October? Olly Olly *was* September October now—it was Olly-September, that was the new name!)

Even when he was given the Cedar account, it was bestowed on him with the veiled threat—"veiled": cliché, he hated it!—that he had to deliver, because, remember, they weren't just Cedar anymore. They were Cedar-High Landing now—they were 35 percent of the U.S. investment business now, wrapped up in one, demanding, ever-unsatisfied client. So don't blow it, he was told, instead of, Do your best! We know you can nail it! You're the best guy we've got!

A raccoon raced across the road a few feet from being crushed by Bill's car, just missing joining the ever-growing collection of roadkill (deer, coyote, woodchuck) that smeared the shoulder—there was no shoulder, the side of the road. "Roadkill," "shoulder"—these expressions were . . . all right, Bill thought, there was nothing wrong with them. And in this strange, sudden calm moment in his overexcited mind, his foot eased off the accelerator as he neared ninety.

He passed a billboard on the darkened road. Annoyed by the presence of an ad in what should by all rights have been a wilderness, he tried to avoid it, looked only at the logo of the billboard company at the bottom: Modern Sign. Then, helplessly tempted, he glanced back up.

It was an ad for a local bar with a sleazy joke—"Get a Margarita. And she'll go down easy"—next to a picture of a pliant, Spanish-seeming woman suggestively sucking on a straw. It was a double-entendre about getting a Latina girl drunk and getting oral sex—right out in the open where kids could see it. Was there no decency anywhere? What the hell was happening?!

Bill's foot slowly started to push down again. The ad was probably done by some small upstate agency. There was no money for a New York firm at Coco's or whatever the hell the bar was called—it wasn't part of any chain. Maybe an employee had come up with it—maybe there had been a contest and the bartender won!

Still, Coco's played by the same rules as Olly-September did now, as everyone did: cut through the clutter, grab the attention, and whatever you do, don't get caught advertising! People are too sophisticated to be sold to, so blur the lines between other kinds of expression and an ad: sneak the ad into (in the case of Coco's) a dirty joke or a beautiful image or a heartfelt notion. Further pollute the language with ads hidden like terrorist cells inside words that make you laugh or cry or consider an idea. Then just put the product logo at the bottom, subtly and insidiously. Nothing was safe from it—everything was imperilled!

Bill took a turn now at a treacherously high speed. Cedar—sorry, Cedar-High Landing—hadn't wanted an ad, they had wanted (and here someone in the office—Bill didn't remember who, he had blocked it out—had actually touched his heart before saying) "truth." Not "you can trust our investment counsellors," or "please invest your money with us," but *feel* something when you think of Cedar-High Landing, *believe*. Your money isn't a commodity, it's an emotion; we don't want your wallets, put those wallets away, we want your tears, your hopes, your souls.

Make it "profound," Bill was told—and implicitly threatened instead of encouraged, because they were all scared. Everyone at Olly-September was scared of Cedar-High Landing; one corporation was scared of displeasing another, as if they were robots with insecurity installed. Make it—and here the growing meaninglessness of all words made Bill blink, dizzily, as his car flew up the empty highway as if acting on its own volition—"real."

And what had been Bill's response? Revulsion? Indignation? Even a small, appropriate amount of anger? No, he had obeyed, because not only was he good (oh, don't ruin that word, too, he thought, he wasn't good, he was glib: glibness was both his gift and his downfall; it allowed him to make a living and buy a house ninety miles north of New York City *and* it had ruined his serious writing career *and* it had driven his wife away, for he excelled at a facile, talented imitation of truth, the kind of thing that ruins novels and ends marriages but makes one a—albeit under-praised—star in advertising) not only was he good (glib) but he was scared. His superiors always succeeded in scaring him, even though he knew better: he always feared for his future even as he knew they were faking; he was the best, he had nothing—or as close to nothing as anyone working for two (no, four) corporations could have—to fear.

He was scared because he wanted their approval, because he was weak and so he obeyed and so he was glib and so he did brilliantly, even as he hated himself for being scared and weak and glib and doing brilliantly and thereby saving a job that wasn't in jeopardy in the first place and then feeling—for a fleeting, disgraceful moment, before he got in his car to go home—proud of how he'd done!

The world on his right, off the road, was pitch-black now—"pitch": cliché!—and he knew this was where it all fell away, where the highway began to climb a mountain; he could feel his ears pop. For a second, deafened—before he mimed a yawn and cleared his head—Bill heard only the scream of his own thoughts, which were the words of the campaign that he had written.

They had wanted truth, profundity, reality, and he had given them those things. On a white background, the ad said, "You only get out of it what you put into it." Then, in a different, lighter, ghostly type-face, three words, "Save," "Your," and "Life," floated, as if at once disconnected and connected to each other, at once self-sufficient and dependent on each other for meaning. Finally, in the lower corner, centred, minding its own business, merely playing host to these words but not, of course, benefiting from them (if letters could say, "Who, me?" that was how he conceived it), the logo for Cedar-High Landing was placed: CHL.

Bill was a clever boots, all right! It had a little bit of mystery and, above all, meaning. The ad was a truism both for living and investing: "Save Your Life" referred both to putting your money where it would grow and remaining existent, pulling yourself back from the brink. Remember, it said—he, Bill, said, for he was responsible—without your contribution nothing can occur, whether you're living in the world or putting your money in a high-yield IRA or secure government bond or whatever the hell Cedar-High Landing (CHL) was offering.

This was what he had written and he knew from the minute he wrote it that it would succeed, that it would be exactly the new kind of non-ad they desired—that it would fulfil every shallow, underhanded need four corporations had to insinuate themselves completely into people's lives, to co-opt and befoul their language in the process, to replace their art, their philosophy, even their religion. Bill had been their handmaiden, their henchman in this, and for it he was both rewarded (with a hearty handshake and the implied promise that he would not be fired—for now—though the look of sweaty sweet relief on his frightened superior's face was transparent) and damned.

At the highest point of the highway, his headlights the only illumination, he started his descent in the direction of the exit that would lead to his home. Then his eyelids began to droop. The drinks fogging his mind, Bill turned his wheel toward the flimsy guardrail that would be insufficiently strong to keep him from bursting through and crashing to his death down miles of mountain onto the black earth below.

Suddenly, he opened his eyes and turned the wheel the other way. Right before it hit the rail, he brought the car back from the edge, back onto the deserted road. Shaking, sweat streaming from his face, pits, and back, he managed to keep the vehicle steady and stay in lane. Soon his breath slowed, his heart rate eased; he even hit the brights to see his way ahead. Then, fearful of falling asleep again, he turned on the radio to keep him alert through the rest of the ride.

It had been nuts to drink so much after work—he had never done it before. But then Tony Hooker had never been laid off before, left high and dry by a liquor store that was being replaced by a chain store, a Drugall's. If a man couldn't get a little tight then, well, when could he? Still, look what had happened—or almost happened. Had he even *wished* it to happen? That was crazy, wasn't it?

It was worse than crazy—cowardly. What would Connie and the kids have done without him? Still, strange to say, he wasn't slowly being revived now by thoughts of them. It was something else that was sobering him up.

As he climbed the highway—the fastest, most familiar, and at night most death-defying way home—Tony passed the same old billboard he always did. Only this time, it wasn't that hot Spanish chick from Coco's who had been there for so many months. (He doubted any girl who looked like that would ever go to that crappy dump, and he'd long since grown tired of that dumb joke once his boy, Baylor, twelve, had explained it to him.)

No, tonight there was a new sign.

The sign was white, which got his attention right away. Pure white, as white as—well, as the driven snow, what else, he was no wordsmith! And it said, "You only get out of it what you put into it." Then he saw the words "Save Your Life." They weren't put together, they were set apart; he had to be clever to connect them, and he had been.

It was no ad. It was a message, it had meaning, one that he understood. It was all up to him, this life, and without his effort there would be nothing. Though Tony knew someone must have written those words, they seemed to just exist without having been invented by anyone—to have been formed naturally, like a rock face or a river—and he saw something in them the way people see meaning in those shapes in nature and never forget.

Die? Those words made him want to live! As he got closer to home, now driving at a normal speed, Tony felt empowered by them, as if the future—no matter what he had hopelessly thought an hour before—was not out of his control.

He was strong; he was himself. He felt it physically now as his big hands gripped the wheel: it was what the sign made him feel. He couldn't blame his store now; blame was for weaklings. He was sure they had their reasons, and they had to make money—if he was at their level, maybe he would have done the same thing. If? He *would* be at their level one day—he was going to be past it, goddamnit! That was what the sign made him feel, too.

Tony took the exit that led him home. He remembered one more thing from the billboard, right at the bottom: the logo CHL. He knew it represented the people responsible for those words. As he pulled into his driveway with a deep sense of gratitude and relief, he vowed that the first chance he got, he would find out what it meant, who they were, and what else they might be able to do for him.

THE HAPPY HOUR

This was the worst part, waiting for the sentence. The trial had been excruciating enough—all of Bruce's unhappiness hung like underwear behind his house—but the spectacle of it had diverted him, as funeral services do survivors of the dead, before the solitude and silence of interment brings the truth and their tears. Now the eulogies (evidence) and songs (cross-examinations) and prayers (something else? the verdict? whatever) were over, and he was about to be buried: the judge might as well have carried a shovel with him back into the courtroom. How far down he planned to plant Bruce was the only question left: would it be under one layer of earth so a wind would reveal him? Or so far down it would take a rope and pulley to bring him up again? What difference did it make? Either way, he would be dead.

"All rise."

As Bruce stood, he suddenly felt light-headed, as if he had pushed up through clouds, past planes and even planets, and could see another place. Not heaven, if it existed—he would not be going there—but somewhere just as unattainable: his past.

In fact, the past was slapping him in the face, hard enough to get his attention. Soon it was his wife, Cora, who was putting her palm against his cheek, pulling her punch at the last minute but landing enough of a blow to let him know that, if she wished, she could really haul off and hit him; she had the strength but lacked the nerve.

"What am I going to do with you?" she had said, as she often did.

Cora paid their rent, running a successful business that catered to companies on the verge of collapse, advising them on staying solvent, increasing assets—he didn't know the details, couldn't stay focused on what she did; his mind would always wander, as he had physically his entire life before they married. He knew she'd been attracted to him because he was emotionally on the edge of oblivion, and she'd been inspired to save him. He also knew he'd been her most unsuccessful client, unwilling to heed her advice, never able to recover. Instead of quitting, she had always hunkered down harder, providing him with more plans, drawing up more blueprints. And when he still lingered as it were near liquidation, she sometimes lashed out, with the back of her hand or, on this particular day, her palm.

"What am I going to *do*?" The question was not an expression of despair but a way for her to begin imagining more options, to jump-start more great ideas. Since Cora couldn't stop and he lacked the will to wander again—he had settled into this routine as he had the one of restlessness—they internally and silently accepted that they would repeat their pattern forever.

Tonight, though, for the first time, Cora had grazed his face with the edge of her first finger nail. The slight sting of pain—and the drawing of a drop of blood beneath his right eye—had shocked them both, causing Cora to cry out, "Sorry, Bruce!" in a cracking voice and Bruce, holding a stanching napkin against his face, to leave their house, get in their car (which was under Cora's name), and drive.

The wound healed almost instantly—though was briefly opened again when, trying to scrape free a piece of napkin stuck to it, he pushed his own nail in. Looking in the mirror to do so, Bruce lost sight of the road and swerved his car to avoid one oncoming. Panting, he pulled over to the curb of the suburban street and stopped outside a bar, the name of which he hadn't noticed.

He had driven farther than he expected. Had he actually been leaving forever and looking for a highway? His intention had been unconscious, yet maybe he *had* reached the end of his rope (as maybe Cora had done by cutting him—he was open to considering that, was clear-eyed, almost unemotional about it). Whatever he had really wanted, Bruce had ended up on the slightly shady side of their expensive town, on the few blocks that appealed to appetites unsated by foreign furniture outlets and frozen yogurt shops. The bar before him—and he saw the name now, dim in blown-out neon: The Happy Hour—was such a place.

He had heard of it, of course: it was whispered about at local barbecues and black-tie benefits that Cora dragged him to. Sometimes a daring and drunken guest—almost always male—would even brag that he had been there, though he'd be conspicuously short on the details.

Bruce had never shown great interest or even casual curiosity in the place; however, maybe he'd been intrigued by it all along and his unconscious had caused him to come. He turned off his headlights so that the only illumination on the empty block was what little light escaped the bar's closed curtains.

As he entered, Bruce couldn't help it, he checked behind and around him—though he suspected that few who knew him would be surprised to see him "slumming": those in Cora's circle secretly dismissed him as a deadbeat, her failed and private project, her problem.

A burly bartender glanced up as he walked in, but didn't linger looking at him and went back to pouring shots. There was a small crowd, maybe twenty people, equal amounts of men and women, talking loudly on wooden barstools or cracked red leather banquettes. It could have been any shabby suburban bar near a highway exit; they could have been any customers. He knew it was irrational to have expected different, yet he had. Was he relieved or disappointed? Maybe a bit of both.

The door squeaked shut and Bruce felt sealed inside, though whether to be entombed or kept viable he didn't yet know.

"What'll it be?"

Bruce was about to order his usual red wine, then blurted out, "A vodka, straight up, please." The kind of hard drink Cora complained about him having. He suddenly felt free and weirdly welcomed, though he had yet to make eye contact with any member of the cast-off, maligned minority around him.

Then he turned and saw her. She was about ten years younger, small, slight even, dressed—wrapped—in a tight black leotard, her eyes the biggest things about her. Her crude and close-cropped hair gave her a feral look—no, furtive, like a woman shaved as a collaborator in a faraway war and hiding out. Yet she seemed cheerful. Was her haircut an ironic comment on the prejudice against her group? Or just a current style? He had never paid much attention to fashion.

"New in town?" she asked.

"No. I mean—"

"But you've never been here before."

"If you already know that, why should I answer?"

"Good point."

He knew he sounded hostile, but her aggression had unnerved him—perhaps because he enjoyed it? She took no offence and spun around on her barstool, snapping her fingers to music from a flat-screen TV that Bruce could barely hear above the laughing chatter of her kind.

"Well, maybe we could celebrate your showing up then," she said. And with that she revealed a tiny phone and took his picture, the taciturn barkeep suddenly waving two fingers foolishly behind his head.

"You want to dance?" she asked.

Bruce didn't, hadn't for years; it would have required bestirring himself. Yet before he could reply, she had pulled him to his feet. Immediately, she moved dreamily, somehow finding an actual melody in the shard of song still floating in the talk-polluted air. (Was this a special gift that she and others like her had? No, Bruce told himself, stop it; that was silly.) He managed a few tentative steps but soon they weren't needed: the woman was in his arms, clutching him as if he were a stone monument that anchored her in a storm.

"I'm Jane," she said.

Even her name was normal. "I'm Bruce," he answered and drew his arms about her like a cloak. He saw a few patrons shoot them a glance and smile: was it always Jane's way to wrap herself around a stranger? Probably. Yet there was a tradition to their kind of chemistry—between the skittish and the solid—and if Jane had announced it instantly rather than after an acceptable period of time, what difference did it make? Life was short.

Bruce smiled sadly to himself. Life was only short for Jane and the others in the bar; only they would die, not Bruce or Cora or the vast majority of others on the Earth. He knew now he had been lured to their hangout by a feeling of kinship with them, a sense that he himself was dying, was living as if he were. He held her tighter, swaying to a tune he now swore he could hear as well.

"Come home with me," she whispered, and he agreed after he had kissed her, the music rising, the bar becoming black as he closed his eyes, burying them both.

"Be seated."

Bruce turned his attention to the judge now sinking into his chair, fussing with his robes like a small girl wearing her first fancy dress. He was stunned at how few seconds had elapsed since he'd started to remember, how many things had happened in his past. He wondered how much more he could recall before his sentence was passed down. It would have to be accomplished quickly, a race—a real one—against time.

The phrase had occurred to him as he had gently picked a piece of pillow feather from Jane's brow as she slept later that night. It had been stuck there by sweat, for she had made love as if every moment counted, which, of course, for her, it did. How different, Bruce thought, from his and Cora's cavalier encounters—on the rare occasions they deigned to have them: why move so much, after all, when you'll always be around? Jane's eyes were squeezed shut and her lips moving slightly as she deeply experienced a dream. It was Bruce who couldn't sleep, the one with all the time in the world.

He wandered to reach the balcony of her small apartment, which faced a shabby street a few blocks from the bar. No one was out and the bulbs in the street lamps had blown and never been replaced; it was as if everyone was already dead. Bruce's eyes adjusted quickly to the total darkness. He felt at home, and that made him look suddenly at his watch. Cora would be concerned—or maybe not. Either way, he wanted to stay as long as he could.

"Get out."

Bruce turned quickly. Jane was standing there, agitatedly, already in a T-shirt and shorts, her right hand rolled into a fist. With her crew cut and jaw jutted out, she looked like an angry seventeen-year-old boy. Her appearance was endearing, yet she was clearly beyond angry and poked the thumb of her left hand behind her, toward the front door.

"I said—"

She didn't have to repeat herself. Bruce saw where she was staring: at his own right hand, the fingers of which held a cigarette. The smoke had drifted back into the bedroom, awakening—and informing—her.

"What," she said, "this was just a way to get your kicks? To tell your friends what it was like with one of us? Can you be *that* bored?"

She was right: who else would smoke except someone who would never suffer its ill effects, never die of a disease but only by force, from his own or someone else's hand? Had he been lazy or complacent lighting up? No: he had just been at ease, and that, he was aware, was always risky.

"Please," he said. "I can explain."

Moving toward her, then trying to hold her still, he offered his explanation, his sense of their sameness. It was a fancy and theoretical notion, and he feared Jane exposing it as rarefied and easy. After all, hadn't the bar's name referred to its patrons' pain, advertising a brief respite from their agonizing about mortality? He had no such problems; all *his* problems were in his head. How would she respond now that she knew what she had thought to be solidity in him was just inertia?

Slowly, Jane stopped struggling and her arms fell limply around his neck. She could not end a connection as quickly as it had been formed: how many more chances at one would she ever get? At least that's what Bruce assumed she meant by embracing him; she didn't specifically say.

The only thing she uttered, peculiarly, was what Cora had said—a question that for Jane was rhetorical and referred to her helplessness in the face of what seemed like love:

"What am I going to do with you?"

Bruce didn't return home until dusk the next day. Cora was at work, the house was empty, and, in the aftermath of his affair, it looked different to him. Always spic and span, now it seemed uninhabited: a model home in a development shown to buyers. Feeling suffocated by it, he rushed out to the patio and was inhaling deeply the chlorinated air rising from the swimming pool, when the front door opened.

Bruce wheeled around. Cora was coming in, dressed in her best business suit, carrying a computer case. Watery light shot shadows on his face, concealing his expression (apprehension), but living room lamps exposed what Cora felt: relief and sorrow, immediately covered by rage.

"Where the *hell* have you been?"

"Driving around." Bruce flicked his cigarette far into the backyard, sure that it would start no blaze on their fire-resistant lawn. Then he closed the sliding door, caught his fingers for a second and cursed, as if preparing himself for greater pain that was to come.

"And that's all you've got to say?"

"Yes."

"I think I'm entitled to more of an explanation. I mean—all night!"

"I don't feel like talking about it right now."

"Really? Well, maybe that's not good enough."

And on they predictably went, as if repeating dialogue from a marital argument program they had downloaded online. Yet if their voices had been muted, an astute observer would have seen in their faces what they meant: they were guilty about what they'd done over the years and afraid of what lay ahead.

"Don't turn your back on me, Bruce. You're not a child!"

"Well, don't give me orders, Cora. You're not at work!"

Bruce walked past Cora toward the stairs, noticing with curiosity that she didn't follow; she was instead staring at the coffee table on which he had dropped his keys. Turning away, he caught a last glimpse of his wife reaching down to pick something up from it.

Bruce was halfway to the second floor when he heard her steps behind him. Running in bare feet, her heels left near the front door, Cora caught up and clawed at his shoulder to turn him around.

"Is this where you went?" she said, her voice more shrill than he had ever heard it. "Is it?"

Bruce turned: her hand was so close to his face that he had to recoil to identify the object she was holding and read the title on its front. Then she flung the bar matchbook down to the floor from which they'd risen.

"I hope you're proud of yourself!" she screamed. "Bringing filth like that into our home!"

Bruce suddenly felt like having no secrets. There was no point in lying (I only had a drink; nothing untoward happened; you sound crazy, you know that?). He knew that if he promised to give up Jane, Cora would forgive him; they would continue in the same cycle of encouragement and failure literally until the world ceased to spin. Suddenly, he wished to know something better for a shorter period of time, even if it would end in great sorrow, and soon.

"Not proud," he said, "but not ashamed."

Cora's hand, now empty, came back to his face—again, she didn't quite hit him but this time grabbed at his skin, as if trying to mould him into what she could not make him be. All of her nails, not just one, dug into him and hurt; he pushed back. She lost her balance, and he encircled her with his arms to save her. Like that, they rolled down the stairs together, turning over and over like boulders in an avalanche that moves a mountain undisturbed for centuries. It had only been chance that Cora's head hit the floor so hard and not his.

~

". . . this is the sentencing phase of . . ."

Now the crucial phrase snapped Bruce back—forward—in time. But instead of watching the person with authority to decide his fate—who still wiggled in his seat, as if uncomfortable with the responsibility—he glanced around the courtroom.

It was crowded; these types of trials always were, since violence was a rare and avoidable end to unending lives. A plea of accidental death had not convinced the jury, not after an unwilling witness had been called to the stand. From a passing car, one of Cora's clients had seen Bruce leave the bar with a huddling Jane. On the stand, she had had no strategic sense and simply admitted that, yes, she might love him; stranger things had happened.

Now Bruce stopped his pan of the spectators, seeing her. Jane wore a wig—the media had made much of her near-baldness—but its bright blonde colour seemed either defiant or indifferent. She stared back at him and her red eyes seemed to ask, "Why is the world the way it is?" Since he didn't know, all Bruce could do was smile.

He turned back to hear the judge explain his "reasoning process": how he had taken into account Cora's financial position and Bruce's passivity, how the jury believed he had attempted to make an accident of a murder that let him enjoy his wife's riches with a new mistress—a low-caste mortal woman, disdain for whom the judge could not keep from his sneering face. How long would he keep the two apart? Fiddling the most ever that morning in his chair, the judge seemed to enjoy the irony as he sentenced the defendant.

"Life imprisonment." He brought the gavel down.

Bruce didn't hear it; the room was suddenly as silent as something dropped down a hole that has no earth at its end. He realized—though he would not remember it—that this was what it meant to faint dead away.

—·—

There were not many others in jails: Bruce had his own comfortable cell, which he didn't bother to decorate. For the first few years, he simply stared at its white walls and thought he could see something in their emptiness; then he stopped deceiving himself. He who had once chosen stasis now had it forced upon him. Mostly, he just waited for the weekly visitors' day.

Jane would always arrive on time, or a few minutes early, though the guards were never lenient. The two had exactly sixty minutes to say what they had to say—for her to say and for him to listen, for he was doing nothing, not even the little he would have been able to do inside. He realized that, as she had once made him feel as if he were dying, too, now Jane was the thing that made him feel alive.

"This is *my* happy hour," he said.

Seeing her so often should have masked the signs of her ageing, yet he saw them anyway. When Jane let her hair grow, at first she didn't conceal the flecks of grey; after it threatened to take over, she splashed her head with red. Her features were framed differently by the style, and he noticed anew the fine feline structure of her features, as well as the start of slackening skin and lines around her eyes.

"When I was young," she said, over the phone, through the glass, "I used to believe that ageing made people more beautiful. But that's because I was young. And, I guess, afraid."

"You're still beautiful," he said and meant it.

Jane began waitressing at the bar and eventually took over its management. A rock was thrown once through the window, which was expensive to replace; otherwise, things went smoothly. Soon Bruce realized that Jane had passed him in age, his own metabolism moving so differently from hers.

One day, she was strangely silent, which made Bruce fill the gap, self-consciously, with stories of prison life—most of them made up. At last, she interrupted.

"Look," she said, "I'm getting married."

She spoke in a rush, as if escaping what she had done and how it might hurt him. "He's like me, of course. He's our sous-chef, and about the same age. He's a nice guy. But I want you to know that I'll never stop coming, no matter what."

Bruce thought he was okay with it; what sense would it make not to be? Yet he did have one evening of irrational weeping and banging his fist upon his bunk, until another prisoner yelled for him to "Shut the hell up!" One of the few times he had ever heard from anybody else on his cellblock. He swore that he would kill himself if Jane stopped coming, and he began sharpening a toothpick that had fallen from a guard's pocket for this purpose.

But Jane kept her word. Eventually, she showed him pictures of a baby she named Bruce and then of a little boy. Her weight began to rise and her hair, which she had once kept intentionally close to her head, now began to thin on its own.

Bruce initially recorded the years on the wall of his cell, in little armies of vertical and horizontal lines. After a while, he stopped seeing the point and gave up, or maybe he saw the point too well. At any rate, one week, Jane didn't arrive, and she had always come even when ill, overworked, or when there had been a storm.

A week later, someone else showed up. It was a young man of about seventeen, gawky but with the beginning of a lank handsomeness. He spoke nervously, clearly trying to fulfil an adult responsibility that had been pressed upon him.

"It was my mother's last wish," he said, "that I keep coming."

Bruce felt all the air fall out of him and he inhaled sharply, as if to keep at least some of it from escaping. He closed his eyes, afraid that he might faint for the first time since his trial. He told himself he could not bear it, that he would bash his brains out as he had accidentally bashed Cora's.

Then he found the courage to look at his visitor. The younger Bruce had his own spiky hair, probably a tribute to his late mother. It made him look like a wholly masculine version of the youthful hoyden Jane.

"She showed me your pictures," Bruce said.

Then the two sat there, saying nothing (it would be two weeks before their exchanges grew longer and more relaxed). The younger fidgeted, the elder was still; the time was frozen, one man an example of urgency and expectation, the other of languor and squandered opportunity; one of the temporary, the other the eternal, a moment preserved forever—as Bruce himself was—inside the prison walls.

ALERT

Hands, so many hands of other travellers were hanging beside her own, lined up like winter coats in a closet or fish in a school under the sea—or like trains themselves, waiting to take off, trains stopped in their tracks, that was it. Except one hand, his hand, more disobedient than the rest, moving up her thigh then gently beneath her skirt, the fingers cool and slightly chapped even though it was summer.

Allie was trembling but so was everyone else: trembling and rocking back and forth and sometimes lurching forward as if pushed from behind. Allie was aware that her reaction to riding the subway was like someone's in 1904—the year the system started, an overhead sign informed her—but she was, after all, innocent of the experience, never having done it before.

And it was twice as terrifying today, she knew, despite the unclean conditions then, the—she could only guess—cholera and diphtheria and the TB, that was the other one, at the turn of the century. It was so much more treacherous today that she never would have agreed to come if not for—and now she thought of nothing other than his hand, because his fingers had found and were touching the little raised flower stitched on her underwear between her legs. His was like a blind man's hand and so she closed her eyes to be like him and only know what it was like to feel and never see, never in a crucial way to know anything but what you felt. Doing this—only feeling, in the dark—she went into a new tunnel, one that led back to the blackness of her sleep that morning, a tunnel she had exited by opening her eyes.

Allie had been angry those few hours earlier; she was a punitive girl, punishing, which was surprising, for she was short and blonde and pale and pretty, and others in their shallowness assumed that she was sweet. She'd been angry because she had not wanted to come, had spent eighteen perfectly pleasant years without going down to the city, which was ninety miles south of the town where she was and had been born. Why should she add to her "experience" in such an arbitrary way, like those people who fly private planes without expertise or jump into gorilla cages just for the "rush" and end up in frozen pieces on foggy mountaintops or as bloody stumps in fake zoo streams, their last startled sense being pain, their final feeling regret (or who were so drunk that they were dead already before being blown or torn to bits). She had no sympathy for these people who asked for what they got—and since she was unlike them, was sensible and not stupid and heedless, she was angriest with herself for agreeing to go. She had been weak—being guilty was a way of being weak—and that especially irked her.

But Dan Stabler was an old family friend and had offered her a job in his store for the summer, right after she graduated from high school. Loafin' was the town's most popular bakery and café, and while Allie hated the store's stupid name and having to wear the apron with the smiling slice of bread on it—a logo other people liked, apparently, though how many over the age of four Allie couldn't imagine—she had accepted. Allie hadn't gotten into Picard, the local college, and so would have to wait to apply again next year. She didn't want to go any farther from home—and why should she when there was a perfectly good school within driving distance? She could even keep her old room; it was pretentious and phony to want to "see the world"—wasn't this the world right here? Of course it was.

Her parents hadn't been as happy as she thought they'd be when she said that she'd be staying put, had never really understood her only applying to one place, and had gone behind her back to ask Dan if he had something—anything—for her to do. When he came up with the job, invented it out of thin air by adding another counterman, woman, or whatever, her parents made it plain there would be no saying no.

Allie thought they'd be glad to still have her around, but the job seemed like a punishment for what they felt was her bad idea. (Allie's scolding sensibility was a direct inheritance from them, but she didn't make the connection, for she always felt totally justified in her harsh and severe judgments of others.) So how could she refuse when Dan asked her to do more, to work the stand in the Farmers' Market down in the city that day, because someone else had gotten sick?

That meant getting up at five to take the trip, sitting beside Dan on the lumpy front seat of his bread truck while he listened to the radio repeat the same exact weather report (sunny and hot, sunny and hot—what did he expect, it was summer?!), depressing news stories from overseas (we're here, aren't we? We're here, we're not there!) and songs from the seventies, a time when apparently all people had lank and dirty hair, took too many drugs, and sang songs that made absolutely no sense at all (well, why don't you give your horse a name? Then your horse would have a name!).

Dan, who still looked like someone from that era, actually remembered the words well enough to repeat them in a flat, horrible voice that sounded like the world's worst walrus singer. Allie had never had an opinion of Dan—he was like a hundred years old and so hardly even alive to her—but today she disliked how he dwelled on the radio's news reports about the city, the threats to the city, and actually turned it up to catch every last disgusting detail.

This was, of course, another reason Allie had not wanted to go and for her to condemn anyone reckless enough to live there. She had no doubt the threats were real and that the government people communicating them were sincere. This was just the sort of thing you'd expect to happen in such a place, and what was wrong with warning people? She herself would want to be warned (which wouldn't be necessary, because she wouldn't be living there) and she would heed those warnings. Even now, as Dan changed channels to hear the same information from a different source, she said, "Maybe we should just turn around and go back."

The remark unnerved Dan enough to make him snap off the radio altogether. He considered being concerned enough to lose a day's profit, and it was clear it was a new idea and not one he was at ease with.

"It'll be okay," was the best he could come up with; then, after additional thought, "Why let our enemies win? It's our country."

Stymied, Allie didn't say anything, just looked out the window at the highway, increasingly crowded and unclean as it approached New York. Roadkill was being replaced by potholes, as if nature itself had ceased to exist and great gaps were now appearing as evidence of a new nightmare world, and all would soon collapse as a result. She bet Dan thought that worry would protect him, when turning back (or not even going) was the only action that made sense. But that would take guts, and Dan was too greedy.

"I had a piece of the walnut loaf this morning," she said petulantly, to punish him. "I almost broke a tooth."

Dan didn't answer right away, then said, quietly, "Then you should talk to your parents about orthodontia."

Referring to her parents had the desired effect—she felt young and diminished and guilty again about her aimless summer, which she had been sure her Mom and Dad would want to share with her, and why hadn't they?—and took the focus off his bread, which truth to tell, wasn't bad, and she had never even tried the walnut. Dan seemed to be getting sneakier as they hit the bridge that brought them into town, as if he were absorbing a big city character through the automatic traffic pass Velcroed to his windshield that let him be billed later. (And that was another modern idea she couldn't abide: you ought to pay then and there.) Allie pulled upon her chest the sweater her mother had insisted she bring, as if it were a lead apron to prevent her being filled with the same flaws now entering Dan. Then she saw him peel off the pass and place it in the glove compartment, which he locked; he never had to do those things at home.

Allie looked at the big buildings, the suffocating crowds, the water that surrounded it all—everything made vulnerable to attack because of its decadence, irresponsibility, and excess. She found herself getting angrier and angrier, the way she always did when—and her parents knew this even if she didn't and she absolutely did not—she was utterly, unbearably, and to her unforgivably afraid.

The Farmers' Market was held at Union Square, on what looked to Allie like a big concrete slab that probably used to be a parking lot. It scalded in the morning sun, and not even the stand's awning provided any relief. Allie started sweating the minute she left the truck, and large dark rings appeared on her white track team T-shirt that looked like those potholes in the road. Now she was marked, damaged, too, by "progress."

A never-ending parade of people filed by, some obviously on their way to work, looking self-important yet also stifled and suffering in overpriced suits, others obviously wasting their lives riding rollerblades on the way to nowhere. The people who bought bread from her were stingy young executives who forfeited fifty cents for tiny raisin buns not big enough to feed a baby or demanding yuppie mothers who acted entitled to stop traffic with their strollers and didn't say "thank you" when Allie handed them their loaves. She felt like a hick serving at the pleasure of sophisticates, and she bet she was better read than any of them. (Who had gotten through the whole *Dune* cycle last summer? Certainly not that young business boy whose hair goop couldn't hide his hair loss and who bought a tiny bun.)

Throughout the morning, Dan acted pleasant and didn't even seem to feel the heat. He told her, "Acting surly never sold a scone," but she pretended not to hear and walked disgustedly back to the truck for more bread.

Dan had parked in an allotted area behind their stand, right near a rope that cordoned off the lot. She thought it looked like a carnie van in a circus convoy she'd seen once in a movie: at day's end, they'd pull up stakes and go someplace else where people made fun of freaks. She was carrying out a new supply of *miche*—and leave it to New Yorkers to buy the bread with the phony Frenchiest name—when she was stopped by someone's voice.

"Hey."

Allie looked up and over the rope that separated the market from the rest of the metropolis, the only thing that lay between her and its awfulness—a protective ring she hadn't realized was a comfort until she looked up and over. A skinny boy her own age was resting on the rope, oblivious it appeared to cars flying by, hardly making the effort not to hit him.

His face was dark, darker than any in her own town—he was Spanish or Italian or Jewish, it was all the same to Allie—and his hair wasn't even brown but so black it seemed to have been coloured, but it couldn't have been, could it, he was a boy. Still, it was a pleasant face, the face of an orphan in a bombed-out Italian town during World War II (she'd seen in a documentary once in school), and his voice had the innocence of a child when he asked, above the street sounds, "What's it, bread?"

Allie, of course, had been taught not to speak to strangers, so she didn't respond right away. But the question was so open, direct, and benign—and the questioner so seemingly guileless—that after a second she said, with much less hostility than she'd intended, which surprised her, "Well, what does it look like?"

The boy took the question as he heard it—not as rhetorical or sarcastic but as sincere—and answered, "Bread."

Was he kidding, this kid? He didn't seem to be—and he wasn't flirting, either, not in the usual way, which is what Allie had figured at first. A weak wind made her belly feel cool and she remembered that her shirt was sweated through; he could clearly see the flower pattern on her bra, but the boy didn't look there, didn't direct one guilty glance, engaged her eyes the whole time, which was a first—since she was fifteen—with men and boys of any age. (Allie wasn't a virgin but her experience was limited to one encounter with an ex-boyfriend, which didn't even last as long as the commercial break on the TV not muted opposite them. Since then, she spoke in a worldly and dismissive way about men and love-making, unable to admit that hers was a subjective observation based on one unpleasant event and not an objective wisdom that put all others in the shade. In truth, she wished simply to put off doing it again for as long as possible.)

But that was not an issue here: the boy seemed as innocent as a sprite, like a spirit of the forest that had escaped to the city and gotten lost. Is that why he asked about bread, she wondered? Was he hungry?

"Here," she said, keeping her voice down, and then reached over the rope and handed him one and then two of the little raisin buns—let the yuppies buy something bigger.

Without looking again at him, she turned away with her bag of *miche* and started back to the stand. Behind her, she heard over car horns, sirens, and boring cell phone conversations, his small voice saying, "Thanks," with a surprise that convinced her he had not been angling for it but had only asked her something to be friendly, or maybe to make his own morning less monotonous, or maybe even because he thought she looked miserable and wanted to help. All of these possibilities—but especially the last one—made Allie turn around suddenly and less subtly than she'd wished to smile at him or do something, she wasn't sure what. But the boy was gone, his place taken by the traffic of which he had been so unafraid.

Allie returned to the stand where Dan was, and where he was impatiently wondering why she'd been gone so long. Apparently, it was the height of over-consumption and time-wasting hour; after nine, they'd merely be selling food to people who were hungry.

"I got lost," Allie said, aware she was being slightly too snotty, but it was too late.

As the day wore on, and she waited on more jaded or entitled people, she thought that seeing and feeding the boy by the truck would be the highlight of the day; everyone else had much uglier motives than he. She found herself checking out the crowd, craning for any sight of him, but soon felt it was silly: he didn't seem to have the same empty purpose or worthless destination that might make him one of them. His ambling was honourable, like sidling by a stream or sauntering down a dirt road, inviting adventure in its natural state; it was not his fault that he had wandered onto an artificial world.

It was a world where, for instance, there was no shade. More fat gobs of sweat dripped down her back to her waist, making the other side of her shirt sheer as well. Allie thought she heard a sizzling sound behind her; with a smirk, she supposed that something had been set ablaze by the sun, or was merely manifesting the burning hatred she was sending out. Then, slowly, she realized it was static from a transistor radio: Dan had been a few hours without upsetting updates, and that had been too long.

"Uh-oh," she heard him say, holding the radio close to his head. "Oh, no."

Allie was even more curious than annoyed, so she bent a little backwards to pick up what now worried him.

"Alert" was all she heard, because the radio was practically covered by Dan's hair. "Credible threat" and "subway."

For a second, sneering, Allie shook it off. How weird was Dan, cruising through stations until he found something to upset him—which he could then, what, disarm with his anxiety? What a nerd he was. But then she saw him spin the station again and then again, and each time the information was the same.

"Trusted source . . . Below ground . . . Possible bombs . . ."

Now the fact that every voice said the same thing seemed more disturbing than tedious; it was a bulletin, their obligation to report, a repetition for everyone's own good. Allie slowly felt the awful heat around her head replaced by a kind of cold, as if someone had rubbed an ice cube on her, the way her mother would in the summer when she was small. She missed her mother terribly now, and her father, too. Ninety miles north seemed the space from where she stood to a star in the sky. It would take her a thousand years to get home, and a different species would have evolved there by the time she arrived. She was trapped.

When Allie looked at the faces flying or trudging past, she couldn't help but add another element to their expressions: an awareness in their eyes that something awful was around them, a threat that loomed above like a giant bird from a bad horror movie, its massive wings spreading and obscuring the sun. (It was just a coincidence, but a convenient one, that a cloud—the first of the day—had just passed over.) She refused to feel compassion for them; indeed her contempt grew—or did it drop?—to a new degree. What did you expect, living here? Don't come crying to me! In other words, she placed her own panic and her hatred of it in herself on them.

She soon realized that the imagery wasn't exact: the threat—credible, corroborated, or whatever the hell they said—was from below, not above, in the subway, or would be once the bad people completed their plotting and gave the signal to begin. So it was more like a giant burrowing worm was underneath them all, another idea from an awful movie that soon would suck them under and obliterate them—and they would have gone down not by accident but of their own accord, entered by a simple staircase, even paid for the privilege of being killed.

She thought it only added to the anxiety they all must feel every day, entering the tunnels of a transportation system Allie would never in a million years want to take. Just thinking of the subway made her start to sweat more, and it wasn't the sun—it was no longer that strong. The idea of being crammed next to all those people, nose to nose, nose to neck, zooming into oblivion, was bad enough on a normal day: now it seemed inconceivable.

Slowly, she started to see the people passing without pigment, as pale as ghosts—like zombies, that was it, their skin sallow, their eyes scooped out, their steps scary because they were so slow, dogged, and steady. Allie felt faint, or what she imagined was faintness because it was the first time she'd felt it, and she nearly fell into one of the cheap foldout chairs Dan had set by the stand.

She thought she passed out for a while but she didn't; she just sat there with her eyes closed for a minute. When she opened them again, the crowd pushing past was bigger than before and going the other way: it was the evening journey home from work. This was the second "big sales" period; there were two more hours before they could leave. Allie glanced at Dan, but he was counting change for customers, the radio now barely audible. There would be no fleeing early while he could still earn.

Everyone was doomed, and Allie realized that she wasn't angry anymore: for the first time, she could admit it, she was afraid. But since she had to be angry with someone, she decided to denounce those who would judge and condemn her fear. Well, how else was she supposed to feel? What were they, crazy? This allowed her to cross over to this new emotion, as if using a rock in a river as her bridge to another bank.

When Allie focused on the crowd of the condemned again, to her surprise she recognized a face.

She was sure that the boy from before was standing across the square. Was she imagining it or was he smiling at her and even coming closer? If she waved at him, would she be making a mortifying mistake and have to turn her wave into a hair comb, like a comic she'd seen on TV?

She wasn't wrong: immediately, as if moving on an imaginary escalator, the boy was at her booth, standing right before her; they were no longer separated by a bungee cord or whatever wrapped around the fair. Each was on the inside now, and Allie felt safer just seeing him.

"So," he said, "how's business?"

Allie couldn't answer: she had no idea. It seemed fine, busy, lots of bread had been sold, so she only shrugged and saw it was the right reply—he didn't care, either, was just making conversation, needed an excuse to come back, and that made her smile at him with her biggest and maybe only real smile of the day.

"I'm Sonny," he said. Sorry? Ari? What had he said? It was obviously his name and she hadn't heard it, and within a second it would be too late to ask again, and then she never could—and there it was, it was too late, she'd never know.

Resigned to it, she said, "I'm Allie," and at least the name she imagined he had sounded a little like hers, so that was something.

"You, do you work here or—"

"I come from a little upstate." A little upstate? What did that mean? She couldn't even speak English, how appealing was that?

"Look, uh—you going back right away, or—"

Was she? She had no idea, was not in control of her life. She turned to check with Dan, and he was at once selling a chocolate croissant to a lady too fat to be buying one and speaking on a cell phone crushed ridiculously between his shoulder and his tilted head—probably to his wife, who had grey hair Allie thought was way too long for her age.

When she turned back, she was aware that the boy could have seen again through her soaked shirt, her bra straps through the crude track team stick figures—she was completely exposed to him everywhere, and her mom's sweater had long since fallen to the ground—but again his eyes were on hers and seemed never to have moved.

"I don't know," she said, and thought she sounded stupid, without a thought in her head—his worse image of someone from "a little upstate."

"Well, maybe I could show you around. We could take a walk or something—see the city—I mean, if you feel like it."

There was something in the way he said it—it went beyond his tentative quality, which was courteous, by the way, not clueless—that didn't mean mere tourism; he was offering himself up as a companion in an unstable world currently under siege. At least that's how she heard his idea, as a form of—not presumptuous or pushy but protective—partnership. If he'd intuited earlier that she was unhappy, now he knew that she was nervous; he was her link to something essential and real, not tricked-up like the city she believed they both were lost in. This made her agree to go and made Dan immediately a minor detail she could handle without really caring how.

"Let me just deal with this," she said.

Dan was now off the phone and customer-free, so unfortunately he had a clear head with which to hear Allie's request and in which to find a new cause for concern.

"But we're going back soon," he said, and then added something about Allie's parents, which this time she didn't let sway her, as if she were ignoring an insult, and then he even mentioned the "alert," which Allie couldn't say but sensed that she alone would now be safe from. Assuring him that she would soon return and knew his cell phone number—actually, just yelling this back to him as she ran away—Allie was gone, the boy behind and then right beside her, Sonny, or Ari, or whoever he was.

Enormously relieved, Allie found herself jabbering on to him—about her family, the whole college thing, her job, Dan, the city, the country, what she wanted from life—an explosion of honesty that was a working definition of trust, at least for her who was wary of almost everyone. The boy said nothing yet still seemed to hear—a plus given how other boys just listened long enough to learn when you'd stop and let them start talking—and the crowds, no longer of zombies or horror movie victims but merely hot and harried people, seemed to part for them and let them pass.

Allie was talking so much that she didn't notice where they were headed: across the pavement space of Union Square that led to, among other places, a park, a set of stores, and the wide thoroughfare of 14th Street.

None of them were where—with a brief but definitive touch of her arm—the boy signalled her to stop. When Allie looked up, people were no longer coming directly at them like rain on your windshield in a thunderstorm but were safely off to either side. She saw what they had reached: the entrance to the subway, the 4, 5, 6, N and R.

"What do you mean?" she asked as if he had said something instead of simply stopping, and then she even smiled a little at the absurdity of what she saw.

"What's the problem?" he said. "Haven't you ever been on it?"

"No," she said, "of course not." And how had he if he was just as innocent as she?

"Well, this is the day to do it," he said. "With this phony alert—this is when it'll be the most fun."

Phony? It was as if his words were in a foreign tongue—or words you've repeated so many times they're incoherent—and it took a while before Allie could turn them into words she knew. Suddenly, she understood: he was not like her, an alien visitor; he was the opposite: a native so steeped in this environment he knew its every corner, and so cynical he could distinguish a false alarm from a real emergency—and laugh about it—and then go right into the teeth of where it was supposedly least safe.

Allie instinctively felt the cell phone in the little fanny pack tied about her waist (which of course tagged her as from out of town) then turned back to see the stand where Dan was waiting. But it was lost behind New Yorkers, as if they had closed over and consumed it, an experienced army that kills with one shot an amateur naïve enough to intrude on its territory.

When she turned back, the boy was beckoning her, his face promising only pleasure—no, nothing that profound, just dumb fun, and amazed she wouldn't take the opportunity. How many would she ever have?

It was hard for Allie to go back to anger once she'd experienced fear—she'd left it on the other shore as it were, when she'd crossed over—and it was hard to feel fear once she'd experienced trust. She was young, younger than most people her age, and so insecure that she held onto every emotion fiercely until she could find a new reason all by herself to release it. With whom would she be safer, someone as ignorant as she or someone who knew the city better than anyone else? Of course—what were you, nuts?

So she let the boy guide her gently toward and down the stairs.

Immediately, it was like hell—so many steamy people on the narrow staircase you could take only tiny steps, orderly enough going up and down on either side until someone decided to breach the boundary and cross over and then all became chaos. The boy preceded her and, in the crush, her hand slipped from his and she grabbed onto the back of his belt—a gesture more intimate than she'd intended and one that made her fingers touch for a second the bare small of his back before she could loop them on the leather again. His skin was cool and covered in a thin down of hair as dark as everything else about him—except for his eyes, which she had only now noticed were blue-green and shone as bright as an animal's from its den when they're the only things you see. Soon they reached the floor of the station and the last sight of any sun vanished; there was no reversing course, at least not without her clawing through that crowd again and alone, for he was obviously committed to continuing.

"Come on," he said. "This way."

Holding her hand again, he weaved expertly through an onslaught of other people as if he was a white water rafter and they the waves, or some other image from "a little upstate" she clutched to keep calm. In truth, there was nothing from the natural world about what he did: he was more like a video game player entering and acing an invented environment, evading all enemies, and since she had never played before, what had been trust became total and utter dependence—she could not make a move without him.

They passed a table where police were opening and examining the bags of commuters, supposedly at random but really targeting young and attractive women. Allie heard her companion scoff, seeing this—saying "right" with a special spitting take on the "t"—before tugging her hand harder.

"Down here," he said, and they went—it was possible!—even lower.

Descending to the next level, Allie again held onto his belt, but this time she intentionally dipped her fingers over it and onto him, curling them so she'd rub against and feel his hair, scratching him a little when she did in a way that could have been deliberate or not, he'd never know. How could she not want to become closer to him when he was all she had and without him she was literally lost?

Soon they had no choice but be inseparable, for there was no room at the base of the stairs to edge apart. So many people waited for a train to come down the track that they milled in a giant mass, stuck together with sweat and the stink of themselves. Her front pressed against the boy's back, and since he wore a white T-shirt, too, it was as if she had partly disappeared into him, like the invisible man does into things in other, older movies.

If something exploded now, there would be no saving anyone; each person would be propelled into and annihilate his neighbour. But Sari knew it was nonsense and there was nothing to worry about. He remained almost dry on the damp platform; she noticed it when, with absolute ease, he brought her arm around him onto his stomach and held her hand there, and her heart beat so powerfully she was sure he must have felt it: they were so connected now her heart was pumping into his.

Then, from a distance, the track was illuminated. They all stirred, like refugees hit by a spotlight, their emotions ranging from anticipation to relief to fear. The ground started rumbling and Allie suddenly held the boy's hand tighter, her fingers wrapping around his palm.

"Here we go," he said.

The sound grew louder, the light became brighter; it seemed as if the station itself was about to erupt, no bombs were even needed. Then the rumble was joined by a shriek of gears that hurt her ears and what seemed a hysterical, high-pitched, mechanical scream from a new gizmo that could feel and express pain. Allie saw the "R" of the train cab come at and pass her, blowing up her hair, the letter seeming to stand for someplace mysterious, a final destination far in the future where there were only letters and no names. The train lasted forever before it finally stopped, the doors opened, and there was no turning back.

Allie saw that inside there was already no room. Each seat was filled and riders jammed the aisles, pressed together in brightly coloured summer clothes like the roasted peppers in that unopened jar in her mother's kitchen. Allie imagined it was impossible each had enough air, but what was there was cool and that was something, a seductive reason to get on and stay.

And they did get on, all of them—even if someone had wanted to walk away, he couldn't, there was no way out. Allie felt the new people must make the train bulge out from its sides, as in a cartoon—but, amazingly, it maintained its shape as they added to what could not be increased.

She and the boy managed to make it to—or merely were rammed toward—a middle pole, which Allie grabbed onto as if it were a floating relic of a shipwreck that kept her from being swept away. She wrapped herself around it and, from behind, the boy wrapped around her, and Allie felt this was the last place they would ever be—they could never leave and would have to live there.

They waited for what seemed an unbearably long time, the cool air slowly being diluted and polluted by the hot air from the platform, which seeped in like poison and threatened their survival. Then, after the almost comical ding-dong of a make-believe bell, the doors coughed and stuttered and finally closed.

Their savage peeling into the dark of the tunnel made her cry out, once, weakly, not sure she made a sound. But since Sari had promised, she was certain it was no longer death they were racing to find, and her freedom from fear was like discovering a second, braver self, and it was thrilling in a new and startling way.

As they left any recognizable place and were imprisoned at high speed in a tube, Allie's cries grew louder, became a kind of moan, and she scanned the signs overhead that told her of the system's origins, to centre herself somewhere, anywhere, in space.

It was then that she became aware of the hands at her side and felt one hand, his hand, moving slowly and determinedly beneath her short denim skirt with the sparkly studs she thought so cute until it reached the rose (was that what it was?) that bridged her thighs.

"I want to hold all your flowers," he whispered, and then his other hand moved to encircle and squeeze her right breast, the cup of the bra covered by its own bud. (He *had* seen her! How had it happened without his even sneaking a peek? Was it a bizarre gift all boys had or had he merely looked so cleverly he hadn't been caught?) Then he kissed gently at her neck and said, almost with sorrow, "I wish I had a hundred hands to hold all your flowers," and his fingers moved under her panties as if burrowing to the place from which the rose had grown.

He put one, then two, then three fingers inside her, and Allie was ashamed and grateful that she was growing wet. She moaned more and—never having done this before, darkness all around her, her death no longer imminent—moved her hand down amid all the other hands to press him in deeper. Then she got so wet his fingers fell in to their knuckles and he caught her nipple between the first and second fingers of his other hand, as if he were using a soft pair of scissors to snip it or something. She couldn't think straight; it was all connected—the flower—like she and the boy were connected, and she leaned her head back so her cheek was on his, and she came, which only ever happened to her when she was alone, using that old embroidered pillow her parents had given her as a tenth birthday gift.

"This stop is Times Square," someone who wasn't real announced.

It was every man for himself now—no more of one mind, some in the car struck out on their own, showing little concern for those who stayed behind, indeed using their arms and legs as springboards or stepladders to get out the door. Disentangling from each other, Allie and Sari were soon among this exiting and unsentimental group, though Allie whispered

"Excuse me" to a woman she practically jabbed unconscious with her elbow, a courtesy attributable to a country upbringing not yet as far behind her as Union Square.

"Let's go uptown," the boy said.

Soon there was a new platform and more new people—would she ever see the same face twice in New York, Allie wondered? (In her own town, even the guy at the gas station remembered she'd been a colicky child.) Well, of course you would: she had seen the boy again, as clear as if she'd conjured him; if she'd hadn't so desired, he would have disappeared. This was another truth about the city: you could work your will on it just as it did a job on you. If it called an alert, you could become awake in your own way; it was a contest of wills that anyone could enter, even Allie.

Now it was as if the boy and she were starting something over—was it their lives? As big as that?—because the new train they fought to board was numbered 1, the first of its kind. It was just as jammed, and they quickly laid claim to the same centre pole, the way an old couple always had the same seats in the movie theatre back home and resented you irrationally if you had the temerity to sit there.

This time, from behind, he hung his hands off the belt of her skirt, the sides of his thin arms brushing her breasts and even flexing a little, so she'd feel it. This time, as they took off, she felt the erection in his jeans up against her behind, half-exposed in her tilted and distorted panties, still not fully fixed from the last time. He used it to push open her cheeks the way he'd barrelled by people in the crowd; it felt fatter than the only other one she'd felt, the one of her ex-boyfriend—what was his name—and she tensed her ass around it, something she'd never done before and yet knew immediately how to do. He moved slowly up and down against her opening, and then suddenly he stopped moving and his arm wrapped tightly around her waist and he kissed into her hair and whispered, "Oh, no, not here." Allie felt sorry she had forced something from him, a promise or a story from his past, except she suspected he really was going to share it with her anyway, and only wanted her to think she'd convinced him to—she was that sophisticated now.

After standing there utterly unconscious, Allie looked up. For the first time, she was aware of someone watching her, from only inches away. It was a middle-aged man in a business suit with a ferrety face and five o'clock shadow. Allie was immediately prepared for his disapproval—and she couldn't look away, as if not allowed to not wait for it—but instead he stared back with a mixture of desire and disgust so strong that it startled her. She had never been aware of provoking such intense feelings in someone (though she had, in the very guy from the gas station who'd seen her grow up, though he never stood so close—that was another difference in the city). Allie stared back to confirm and then truly understand what she had inspired. But her comprehension was cut short by their arrival in a station she had not even known they were approaching.

"72nd Street," an unseen robot woman said.

They raced across the platform to the 2 train—child of the first, look what they had created!—and, as far as they were concerned now, the more crowded the better. For a change, they sat down, covered by a curtain of people, and he had one hand under her and the other around her. His feeling and fingering of her was so intense she felt it caused the train to blast by stations, as if the subway itself was staring at them and lost its place, as Allie herself had, so far from home. Then she noticed the word "Express" where the train's number was and knew that meant they had been matching its momentum and not it their own. To muffle her moans, she pushed her tongue into the boy's ear—another new experience—and it tasted nasty like everything adult did, she figured, before you learned to like it.

They got off at 125th Street, a stop actually and improbably outside. The crowds were sparser and the boy seemed in no more hurry to catch another ride. Instead, holding her hand as gently as a child, he guided her slowly to an escalator so long it looked like something out of that song "Stairway to Heaven" Dan had droned along with, except this one led oddly up to Earth, which turned out to be a street hiding shyly beneath an elevated track.

The boy brought her to a brownstone, the bottom floor of which held a Spanish restaurant. The tasty smell of cooked bananas followed them up the stairs until they climbed so high they lost it and stopped at the top.

His apartment had two or three rooms and, though they were alone in it, Allie could tell there were other inhabitants, that maybe he still lived with his family, too. She hoped so, for this would link them more.

In the kitchen, which had a bathtub, he gave her a glass of water but he was kissing her before she could finish it. His own room had just a bed and a TV and a few self-help books on shelves. He mumbled something about his mother having gone to work; it was around five and, if she had just gone and was not now coming home . . . but before she could ask or he offer anything else, he was on his knees, raising her skirt, kissing lightly between her legs then licking at the rose itself before, nearly begging her, he took off her underwear altogether.

It was different from how it had been on the trains—they were alone, obviously, and less hot because a breeze blew in from the window—yet she still had a sense of their subverting other people's desires, maybe just his mother's now and not the whole city's. And it was different from the other time for her—there were no TV ads in the background, no sounds at all except an occasional car horn passing or a car radio playing salsa—and it was not as fast as the first time: as he completely undressed and touched and kissed her all over, she felt everything he intended her to feel; when she reciprocated it was not out of resentful obligation as before but with a sense that getting and giving were now the same thing, a new idea she could not completely explain, even to herself.

She whispered "Wow" when she finally found him in her hand, almost unnerved by how much there was and how complicated it seemed. There were so many lines and streams and little dots like stars upon him, as if he had his own transportation system and was so big the map of it was magnified, she could find her way around it easily: she was surprised by how much more excited she was about this penis than the last one.

He fought a condom onto himself and she helped him do it, gingerly, not wanting to hurt him, but she did anyway, when the rubber got caught in the hairs at the base and he had to pull each one out individually, wincing the whole way.

Then, it was funny; both were wearing nothing but gold chains. Allie's said "Allie" and his said "Tony"—it was his real name at last; she read it the instant he entered her, as if she really only knew him then, and she said his name and kept saying it each time he pushed inside, expanding her knowledge of the world. He came a second *after* she did, he actually had that ability—it was incredible—and Allie thought (typically for her, for she was still the same girl) he was one of the very few and maybe the only person on Earth who did.

Then he turned her over on her belly and straddled her and whispered, as an apology, "I have to do this," as if it was a secret no one else could ever know. He didn't enter but only adorned her, and his sweat and other bodily liquids lacquered her, and she felt enjoyed to the last drop like that turkey on Thanksgiving everybody liked so much—so little had been left of it, and that's what she wanted, too: to disappear for his pleasure, leaving only bits of skin behind; he'd need a new one of her next year.

Afterwards, he considerately cleaned her off with a Kleenex then kissed her gently from her neck to her knees before she saw his pretty face again.

She slept for an unknown amount of time, anywhere from two minutes to twenty-four hours. When she woke up, not knowing where she was, she saw the boy too close to be in focus, stretched alongside her, staring right into her eyes and smiling, like a child waiting for a parent to get up.

They took a shower together, and they would have started up again—there was something about his being so wet and scrawny except for, well, you know where, and ready to go again; he *was* like the New York City subway, available at any hour—but through the tiny bathroom window, she saw that the sun had set, and she realized what time it must be and what trouble she was in.

Allie was surprised how different the kinds of disobedience could make her feel. This kind immediately eliminated any interest she had in more lovemaking and made dread an almost physical feeling, a form of nausea.

She quickly put her clammy clothes back on, which were soaked by shower water she had hardly wiped away, and her hair was so wet it dripped even more on her shirt and skirt and onto the floor, where it made an amazingly big puddle for someone with such a small head. It was helpful to concentrate on that and not on the dialling of Dan's cell phone on Tony's home phone, which was just about to end—oh, why weren't there more (a never-ending amount of) numbers to it?

To her relief, Dan was more frantic than furious, and his cell phone had such bad reception she only caught every other excoriation. His main points, however, were clear: he had trusted her and she had betrayed him, he hated but would have to tell her parents, this was no day to be running around wild in the city, he didn't know who this boy was anyway, and they had to leave now—not in half an hour but now.

Allie noticed that Dan could give full flower to his fears now that the day was over and there could be no more selling of *miche*. Nonetheless, she would have been mortified by his admonishments if Tony had not been standing beside her in his underwear, dripping wet as well, making screamingly funny faces to mock what he was sure Dan was saying. When he put his hands on his narrow hips and strutted around like a stupid idiot, then moved his lips as if Dan were a pissed-off pigeon or something, Allie had to lightly bite her cheeks not to laugh. She said, "I'll be there as fast as I can."

When Tony heard that, he got strangely serious. He pulled over a piece of old newspaper, then swiftly scribbled on its side margin and raised it for her to read: "Take the train. I want to see you off."

The certainty of the words impressed Allie, more than Dan was impressing her—after all, what had *he* done for her today? Tony knew where it all stood in the city—the truth about the threat. He was the wisest person she had ever met, and she felt closer to him than to anyone in the world. Egged on by Tony nodding over and over, pointing to his pencilled message—not aware *he* looked kind of funny now, because *he* was the one so serious—Allie obediently blurted out, "I'll take the train," then pressed the button and deserted Dan, a gesture nowhere near as satisfying as slamming down the phone but the best she could do and actually not so bad.

—∾—

They took the subway back downtown. By now, there were only a few passengers scattered through the cars, those who chose not those who needed. The tension—the terror—of commuting during a catastrophe had eased, and the people who remained were either resigned or indifferent to it, and too few for it to be fun or feasible to fool around in their midst. Besides, the urge had passed.

When they reached Penn Station, it seemed massive and clogged but not in a good way. Allie felt small and lost in its frankly grubby expanse—so many people were pushing valises on wheels with the sad faces of those travelling to funerals of friends—and she held onto Tony's arm tightly now, not wanting him to drift away an inch.

She noticed that he seemed impatient, glancing around, as if anticipating something. "All's clear here," he said, and sounded disappointed.

Then the two of them stopped, because they were forced to.

Three policemen in the near-distance were waving at them and everyone else. Not wasting time with courtesy, they yelled to "Go back" and "Get out." Soon other officers of all sizes and both sexes were crudely herding then virtually pushing them back the way they came.

Dozens of them were deposited outside, many obviously late for trips they had planned much longer than Allie had her own. Those who joined them were offended, annoyed, or—quietly but it was clear—made uneasy by having this happen. Allie heard someone say, "They found something," and someone else, "A suitcase," and finally, in a New York-accented voice trying hard to sound more inconvenienced than afraid, "Jesus Cwist." Then there was the approaching sound of sirens and car after car after car of cops pulled up.

When Allie looked to Tony for an explanation, she saw he was smirking in his by now signature style.

"Idiots," he said with certainty. "All of them."

Allie was comforted by his typical tone of voice, which seemed to restore and bring about calm. Yet she couldn't help recalling that he had said he'd see her off, yet had never mentioned seeing her again. And that he breathed a bit easier—and spoke with satisfied bitterness—now that the cops had found a bag.

"It's nothing," he said. "A fake. And they fell for it. They always will."

He lit a cigarette, something she had never seen him do, and exhaled smoke with indifference into the surrounding crowd. He appeared to enjoy the discomfort it caused and replied with a smiling obscenity when someone asked him to stop.

Allie couldn't help it, she saw more images from awful movies: Tony dissolving into a wolf or whatever villain the actor really was. Was there not a second he could be serious about such a thing? Was that how deep his disgust with the world went? And what did that say about how he felt about her? She was afraid to ask.

Slowly, she felt an alteration in herself as well. She felt her judgment of others returning: from fear of being tossed away by him, she was morphing like people in movies, too, back into a moralist.

"Well," she said. "I think it's awful."

"What?"

"That someone would do such a thing. Plant a bag."

They certainly would never have done it back home—a phony phone call was the worst kind of prank they pulled.

"Don't get on your high horse," he said.

"I'm not."

"You're going to buy into this now?"

"Well, why not? What would officials get out of faking it?"

"Lots of things. Keeping us controlled. Making us behave. And what do you mean, 'get out of it'? It's not like you did so badly by it."

The remark shook Allie like seeing a death notice in a newspaper of someone she knew. She imagined ringing in her ears like a kind of cash register, the daily exchange of services that went on where they were—that you would always hear as long as the city existed, no matter how many silent computers took their place to do the tally: the way of a world in which people lived too close to do anything decent with each other. Even in this new era—even if it was the end of the world—there were opportunities to make a deal, and she'd been smack in the middle of one and was mortified by it.

"Please get away from me," she said.

Allie fought through the new crowd—after those that had been so secret and stimulating, this one felt fit to suffocate her. Her need to escape was greater than the crowd's to gather and so soon she was free of it and him, the boy she hated now because she was vulnerable and he had made her ashamed.

"Help me, help me," she said to a female cop whom she crashed into and who—not very kindly—told her to please clear the area.

Allie hid a few blocks away in a chain coffee store, one not yet transplanted to her town. She checked out the window with false casualness, but she never saw Tony approaching. Did she want him to pursue her? Definitely not, which meant yes, though Allie was so rattled it was hard to imagine what he could have said to mollify her, and besides, he didn't come or couldn't find her.

Soon some of the people chased from the station had drifted as far as she had fled and were standing outside and smoking, philosophically. A few even joined her in the shop, shaking their heads at the modern world, and that's how she heard that the station was open again, the emergency was over, and the bag had been a bad joke.

She walked back in the dark, asking strangers for directions when she only had to retrace her stops, not wanting to know, to be at ease any longer in this environment. When she reached the station, she saw no one she recognized—he was not there waiting, in other words. She paced outside, ostensibly to catch her breath but really to see if he'd show up; she was soon shooed inside by overeager cab drivers who could tell she was a tourist (the fanny pack was just the beginning) and wished to take her anywhere on Earth for way too much.

On the escalator going down and in, Allie called Dan's cell and told him she was on her way, her parents shouldn't worry, let him break it to them that she'd be late. Maybe—she thought with hope that was really fear that was really disillusionment—they might not mind so very much.

Dan was still on the road, alone in his truck without even bread along for the ride, and was relieved and conciliatory. He told her what train to take, something she could have learned for herself if she hadn't again made herself helpless.

After she boarded, Allie watched out the window to see if Tony would come running in, last-minute, like someone from another movie—a romantic one this time—and maybe he'd get stuck on the train because he'd taken so long to say he loved her, and he'd have to actually go upstate with her, and that would be the end. But he didn't come, or had gone to the wrong car.

The train pulled out—it was a commuter model, with cushioned seats unlike the subway and still sort of crowded, for there'd been back-ups due to the disruptive bag. Allie stared at the receding platform and thought about the boy. She cried in great choking, child-like sobs, hoping the humiliating sound would be smothered by the train's exhaust. Then she dried her face on her bare forearms, for she had no tissue or even sleeves.

By going to her home, the train seemed to be taking her back in time. Yet—like everything else on Earth—Allie was actually going forward. Slowly, she felt even angrier now than before she'd come, more prone to punish, and this was a mere glimpse of how she'd be later in her life.

On her cell phone, she dialled 911 and spoke loudly enough to be heard by the operator but low enough not to disturb her seatmate, a man dozing fitfully. She didn't know the boy's last name or actual address, but she knew his first name and the number on his family's phone, and she thought someone could use the information.

"He was dark, probably foreign. Maybe he had something to do with planting that bag."

Even though he was innocent, he might be taught a lesson and given a good talking to. She didn't say her own name and hung up when they asked.

Then the train went into a new tunnel, one so dark she could no longer see herself. And in it, she fell asleep.

The alert, in which the boy had not believed, was about to become very real for him. For Allie, it would quickly become an edited, censored, self-aggrandizing anecdote she repeated to her family and friends back in town. And, inevitably, it would fade like a flower, until it was a memory as distant, foggy, and half-forgotten as a dream.

BOMB SHELTER

Was it the beating of his heart? Maybe it was nothing at all, this thumping he heard around him. Or maybe it was something approaching on big fat footsteps. Or something that just *announced* an approach: a drumbeat, a fanfare, a—what was the word?—a herald.

Whatever it was, he could not deny the sound in the empty apartment. There was no furniture left to absorb the sound, no lights for him to identify anything making a sound, and, since he sat on the floor of the ground floor apartment and knew it wasn't beneath him, its source remained a mystery.

Shivering, Selwyn pulled the blanket around him. Sometimes, beyond his bloody face, he could see his breath and, fascinated by it, he said a few words to watch the little cold clouds form.

"Now I know," he said, the "N" sounds particularly good at propelling the, what was it, condensed air? Steam? That didn't sound right; he was so ignorant about everything.

He didn't know why he didn't just get up and go: everything had already happened, and he had to be out by morning, six hours away. But in truth he felt as if he was awaiting something now, and the sound—which, as he'd already thought, was premonitory—seemed to bear him out.

"Now I know." He'd said it automatically, but he'd obviously meant it somehow, so he had to wait, also, in a sense, to catch up with his unconscious, to learn the origin of why he'd uttered it. Besides, there was no easy way to stand, nothing left to hold onto—another unconscious allusion to his present circumstances—no chair or anything to hoist himself up, so he stayed where he was.

Selwyn's teeth started chattering as in a cartoon. It was colder in the country: a banal observation, he knew, but one he had never stopped thinking—or saying, when he still had people to talk to—and now he thought it again. He had thought it the day he showed up from the city, fleeing after *it* happened—and here he wasn't being coy, just so hated considering the actual event by name; that's how sensitive, high-strung, thin-skinned, call it what you will, he was about it—and the country had only gotten colder, in all ways, since then.

"You want to copy the whole thing?" Ray the computer man had asked the day before he fled—"whole thing" meaning whole hard drive—and Selwyn had agreed. What was he leaving anyway, besides the possibility of imminent violent death along with everyone else in Manhattan? What had he ever accomplished there, in a place where "accomplishment" meant only one thing (making money) and "where everyone is big-time," in the words of his father, who hadn't been born there as Selwyn had, who had come there seeking this very kind of accomplishment, was challenged by it—unlike Selwyn, who had only been intimidated by it—and who had actually become a famous novelist well before Selwyn's current age of forty, and who would have surely considered leaving the city like this the worst kind of cowardice, public violent cataclysm or no, and who had only himself "left" two years ago at the late age of eighty, unwillingly and brutally escorted by the bouncer leukaemia.So why not just put his whole hard drive onto a zip, the very name connoting speed and a cocky, comical—what was the word for when you washed your hands of everything?

"Okay, here's how you do it then," Ray the computer man had said, and explained right there in the store for free. That's how nice everyone was being in the first few days after *it*.

Why not just copy his bank records, personal letters, unsuccessful attempts at every career from journalism to academia, put them in his back pants pocket and fly as far as fear would take him?

It turned out to be about ninety miles north. Even now Selwyn could see the black and hunchbacked mountains through the curtains he had kept (paid for and so not had repossessed) and only partly closed, the skiing area that gave the place its history, glamour, and cachet.

None of those fancy digs had been for him, however, no house—of course, he could only afford to rent an apartment much like the one he had just abandoned in the city, though smaller and cheaper and located not in a pre-war high-rise but in a little development of eight shabby mock-houses, "Gleeful Terrace," on the first floor of three and one of six other flats. His bomb shelter.

Most of his neighbours were elderly and seemed both glad and confused to see such a healthy (though pale) single man in early middle-age (with no car) in their midst. Had he moved up there for a job, his aged upstairs neighbour wanted to know?

"Uh, yes," Selwyn said, even though he had just up and quit his job proofreading the backs of cereal boxes, a gig that hardly paid at all, and he was living only on a small inheritance from his father.

Actually, Selwyn couldn't say why he had come—panic—because in the country no one actually understood how bad it had been in the city, and those who suspected refused to accept it. Here things seemed to have stayed the same for centuries, regardless of the trends and changes "down there": the disaster to them was like when they first installed that subway or those electric traffic lights down there, a distant, modern event, the ripples of which would eventually reach them, but not now, not yet, wait a few years, why don't you? Also, everybody there acted so laconic and countrified and self-sufficient-like that to give off even a trace of his actual trauma was to appear horribly, hopelessly weak, and what kind of a way was that to move in?

"Uh, yes, I'll be working here," he said again, to the excruciatingly cute and dangerously young college student/waitress at Hilly's, the town diner, who seemed oddly attentive to him. Since he'd never received any kind of attention from similarly cute and young acting student/waitresses in the city, he assumed it was his very newness and maybe even his age that made him exotic and of interest. Still, as he always had at home, he mumbled so quietly that he had to repeat himself several times to be heard.

"Yes, I'll be working here. I said, I'll be *working here*." And finally, lying very loudly, "WORKING HERE."

Still, it was safer not to engage her, and safety was, after all, what he had come there to find. It was safer, too, not to actually *ask* the owner of the local bookstore, Left Brain, if he had a job for him instead of just assuming, from the relative emptiness of the place in the two and a half hours he spent browsing in it, that he couldn't possibly need another hand. (It was the only local place he could even conceive of working, since his other jobs, such as they had been, revolved around correcting other people's writing—most recently "The Story of Spelt," on the back of the Succor Flakes box, which had had only one grammatical error anyway, which he considered too unimportant to even dare mentioning.)

In his new home, he was no more assertive. The heat was faulty, the toilet kept running for forty minutes after being flushed, there were nails sticking up at the entrance to one closet after a carpet had been removed and not replaced, and a paint job of the kitchen had never been completed. His super assured him that these chores would get done soon, but Selwyn didn't press, said in fact, "No rush," even though the bottom of his left foot was covered in band-aids after he had first entered the closet barefoot. And so the super, a tall, skinny, bearded man named Tim who could have been anywhere from forty to seventy years old, believed him and did nothing. Similarly, his aged upstairs neighbour, apparently still nimble enough to move his fingers up, down, and across, often practiced a mournful cello until well into the wee hours, but Selwyn let that go, too, apart from a few timid taps on the man's door that might have been answered if they'd only been heard.

Most days and nights he just spent sitting alone in the apartment, which he had begun to furnish with nice pieces bought on credit—why punish himself further by looking at unpleasantness all day? Hadn't life been unpleasant enough recently?—and marvelling at how absolutely silent it was at night outside cities. On New Year's Eve, for instance, which had been deafening until dawn in his old digs, and which he now spent in the same solitary idleness as every other night, he counted only one dim, distant, drunken cry of "Whee!" outside, which on closer consideration, could have been a coyote being hit by a car.

Now, as he sat waiting and shaking in the dark, covered in blood, there were no such sounds from outside—or upstairs, either, the cello man having died weeks before and his apartment yet to be rented. Besides, he would never have mistaken the thumping or whatever it was for the old man's music, even for the occasional merry slapping of the cello he did when his sad song would suddenly for a strange second shift into a jazzy little tune before sliding back to sadness again.

Selwyn, of course, could not forget the last time he had heard the music. It had been on the night, a few feet away from where he now sat, he had first gone into his new laptop to retrieve the copy of his hard drive that Ray the computer man had helped him create. He had intended to use funds left to him by his father to pay his first month's rent.

The file was empty.

At first he thought there was some sort of mistake. The title of the file was there, so was the little cartoon image of the file—and that's as far as he could go in describing it, "little cartoon image"—but, inside, where all the information about his finances had been, there was nothing.

For several minutes Selwyn could do no more than pace and clap his hands, impotent and infuriated. Where *was* the file? And again, his knowledge of how and where things were actually "located" on computers went no further than the word "where." Then he decided to check the copies of all the other files to make sure they at least had been made.

His personal letters, some sent in response to receiving condolences on each of his parents' deaths, others apologizing to women he'd dated who thought him too mild or too "nice," his applications for employment, unanswered or rejected, his abandoned short story, novel, play, screenplay, sitcom pilot, piece of "creative" nonfiction, and poem—all *appeared* to be present, for all retained their little cartoon images and titles ("Jennylett," "Alicelett," "Untitledshorstor"), but like a contaminated neighbourhood where the names and addresses remain outside of houses with no one left within, all were empty, too.

His face and chest became hot from disoriented fear. Selwyn made the first call he had made to the city since fleeing.

"Uh-oh," Ray the computer the man said. "Oh, no. Whoops."

"What do you mean, 'whoops'?" Selwyn asked him, feeling dizzy and sinking into a canvas chair he had just charged.

"Well, it's like this—" and Ray went on to remind Selwyn about the "shortcut" he had placed on Selwyn's desktop, because Selwyn hadn't wanted to move each and every one of his files onto the zip; it would take too much time. This had been a way—remember?—to copy only one big document onto the zip as opposed to lots of little ones. Once Selwyn had moved all the little ones into the shortcut, that is.

"You did put all your files in there, right?" he asked.

Selwyn didn't immediately answer. He had just assumed—idiotically, it turned out—that all the documents had been *in* the shortcut already, that Ray had put them there. Or something. In other words, he had done nothing of the sort and soon had to say so.

"Uh-oh," Ray said again, very quietly this time. "You just saved the shortcut then."

Tears began to come to Selwyn's frightened eyes. "Yes," he confessed, hardly knowing what the hell he was even saying. "I just saved the shortcut."

The path, the method, the way of solving something had been saved; the thing that needed solving had been lost—or, more precisely, left on and chucked out with the computer Selwyn had dumped outside in the trash with all his other stuff on the day before he fled.

"Well, look," Ray said, "that's not *my* fault."

Ray, who had been so generous just days after *it* occurred, was now, just a few weeks later, no longer so generous. Had he and everyone else in the city already returned to their old ways? Had so much bloodshed right before their eyes already been absorbed, accepted, and forgotten? Suddenly, Selwyn felt cut off, abandoned, permanently out of reach.

He could not return to where he had been before, physically or any other way—he was not as insensitive as Ray. In fact, he was the most sensitive man of all—of all who hadn't been directly or physically affected, that is—and he hung up the phone cursing Ray and all those others getting on with their lives simply because they had survived and were literally unscathed, because, by not being like them, he was officially and utterly isolated and alone.

And what could better prove his solitary exile than what he was staring at: a blank space where all his work, correspondence and—corny as it was to say—hopes and dreams had been? He was now wandering naked in the wilderness—and by his own choice, his terrified haste the reason for the action that had stripped him. No, it was worse than that—he was a shell, a husk; everything inside of him had been erased but he was still apparently to others alive.

Once he had reached this conclusion about what he was, he was exhausted. Selwyn fell asleep on the desk in front of the laptop, which, while still running, eventually and slowly closed its own eyes, went into oblivion, and fell asleep with him.

He was awakened by the cello sounds from upstairs—the perky change, to be exact, that his neighbour momentarily made before shifting back into misery. The sprightly segue seemed oddly longer than usual tonight—never-ending, actually—and Selwyn pulled a clock radio closer. It was three A.M.

Jesus, he thought, am I the only one in the building who hates hearing this? Or is this how it is up in the country, live and let live past the point of absurdity? The little jig grew more and more lively, stopped for a second, then restarted; Selwyn could have sworn that the man had slowly turned the instrument around, spanked it, then turned it back again and gone on playing, in an elderly imitation of how Jack Lemmon played in *Some Like It Hot*.

Shocking himself, Selwyn flew out of his chair, left his apartment, and in seconds was outside the old man's door. He didn't tap timorously this time; he banged with the force of a full open palm. After a second, the jaunty music guttered out in a discordant note. Then the old man was standing before Selwyn, fully dressed, in plaid shirt and pleated pants, as if it were the middle of the day.

"Yes?" he said innocently, and more than slightly startled.

"Can you stop it?" Selwyn said in a belligerent tone he barely recognized as his own.

"Can I stop what?"

"Stop what. The music. Of course."

"The music?" The man actually rubbed his chin, in an old-fashioned I'm-taking-in-new-information way. "Why? Is it bothering you?"

"Look—" Acting almost without volition, Selwyn leaned in close to him, nearly nose-to-nose. "Let's not play games."

"I'm not. It's just that no one's ever been bothered by it before."

The man, appearing "interested," was clearly really flustered, clearly really needy of keeping to his custom of playing hot and cold cello at all hours of the day and night. It was as if someone had threatened an animal he owned, Selwyn thought, with a contempt that was the opposite of the usual "compassion" he showed to anyone irritating him, and that prevented his taking any action.

"That's it," he said conclusively, and pushed past the man. The instrument itself, leaning against an elegant old wood chair, was too big to deal with. But the bow was nice and light. Selwyn snapped it up, then placed it "protectively" under his arm.

"Well, we'll see," he said. "We'll see what happens now."

And with that, followed only by a weak, mewing-like whimper from the man, Selwyn left the room and slammed the door.

The bow was placed in a corner of his apartment like a spoil, a scalp, and Selwyn stared at it with a sense of petty, gloating triumph—another new emotion for him. Each time he passed the old man after that, his neighbour was obviously always about to beseech him, and Selwyn always shot him back a look that said, don't push me, you'll be sorry, and the man backed off.

Early one afternoon, Selwyn was appealed to by proxy. Tim the super came to the door and opened it with his own key.

"Oops," he said, seeing Selwyn, who was still sitting staring at the bow. "I assumed you'd be at work."

Nice try, Selwyn thought, with a flash of hatred and then—without even intending to—shot out, "Nice try. That's a cheap trick. Next time, knock."

Tim seemed pushed off-stride by so quickly being called on the carpet. He began stammering an explanation that his tenant didn't let him finish.

"Maybe you can get by with that up here in the boonies," Selwyn said, "but I'm not from here."

"I'm well aware of that," the super said, trying to evince a sense of cynical humour but only succeeding in looking as if he had entered the far end of his forty-to-seventy age range. "Believe me, I know." He pointed a now-shaky, suddenly liver-spotted hand at the implement in the corner. "I just came to pick up a piece of Merce Caldwell's instrument."

"Oh, you have, have you?" Selwyn stood then, and though shorter than the lanky upstater he now moved with an intimidating bantam scrappiness. "Well, why haven't you come here about *anything else*?"

With that, he grabbed the super by the back of his plaid shirt and pulled him harshly towards the closet, which he opened, the man recoiling from the door coming only inches from his face.

"Look at those nails! Look *down* at them! Do you know what damage they've already done to me? Do you know how long ago you promised to fix them?"

"Yes, I'm very well aware—" Tim stuttered, trying hopelessly to retain some dignity "—that I said I would—"

From there, Selwyn hauled him to the other sites of neglect, first nearly sticking his face into the wall of the unpainted kitchen "—Look at that splotch! Do you know how long ago you promised to—" and last, jerking him into the bathroom, where the super finally fought free, obviously fearing where his face would be directed to acknowledge the faulty flushing of the toilet.

"I said that I'll do it!" he cried, cheeks aflame. "Though I seem to recall you were in no hurry before!"

"I was lying!" Selwyn yelled, elated by admitting it. "I was lying to be nice!"

"All right then! But if I were twenty years younger, you wouldn't stand a chance!"

Selwyn knew that, at whatever age, the man was fit and feisty, so he didn't argue. He just, with relish, rubbed it in. "But you're *not*, are you?"

The super looked at him with the kind of revulsion he reserved for the most pestilential vermin; to Selwyn, it felt good. The older man made a sudden feint to retrieve the bow, but—as his tenant had started bobbing in goalie-like anticipation—he reconsidered and reluctantly fled the room.

Once he was alone, Selwyn felt something that went way past an indecent sense of success. He experienced a rush of arousal unlike any he'd ever known, an acknowledgment of great power inside himself, regardless—or because—of how meanly and inappropriately he had expressed it.

Looking at the laptop still sitting before him—now sporting a screensaver of a grotesquely animated cow jumping over a madly grinning moon—he knew what had caused it. He had thrown his old self in the sewer, along with all the money his old self had owed, the people to whom it had (pathetically) appealed, the jobs to which it had (pointlessly) applied. All of his weakness had been washed down a drain, and bubbling back up, overflowing, inviting his submersion, was only one element: aggression.

Selwyn listened for the thump, but it had subsided. Or had it? He didn't know.

That night, he had been ravenously hungry. Still with no wheels, Selwyn nearly ran the ten blocks to Hilly's, the diner, where he ate like an animal: burger, bacon, and bun, topped off by a piece of chocolate cake suffering under a huge and oozing scoop of ice cream. This was a far cry from the man who had known and bought every brand of low-fat yogurt and fat-free cheese in the city.

"God, that was good!" he cried and slapped his distended gut. Then he paid for it with nearly the last of his father's cash, but he didn't care.

The student/waitress gave him his change, watching him with her usual avidity.

"What are *you* looking at?" he said, making her and himself jump.

"Nothing? What do you mean?" She had that tentative, teenage, every-one-of-my-sentences-is-unsure style of speaking.

"I was just kidding," he said, aware he'd come on strong, amazed he wasn't mumbling—*as if!* or however the hell teenagers talked today; he only knew what he saw on TV. "Sorry." He sensed he was being unbearably sleazy but just hoped she was green enough not to know.

"Forget it?" she shrugged.

Now he realized that he had underestimated her idea of her own experience. She seemed to think she had a completely clear understanding of what he was—which was wrong, but *whatever!*—and felt she was not too young to know how to handle it.

"You're a writer or something?" she said.

"Yes—how did you know?" he said, immediately.

"You've got that pale, sort of pompous look?"

She laughed, and then he did, too. How could he be offended? She wasn't teasing him; she was teasing someone else, a man she thought he was. And since it was the man he had always wanted to be, why would he mind? In fact, he could be that person now; he could be anyone at all.

"You're an English major?" he asked.

She nodded. No wonder she had been eyeing him: he fit perfectly the fantasy of a tough yet neurasthenic novelist she had been taught. Here was one right in the town where she worked to pay her way through school. He was like her homework assignment.

Selwyn, of course, had always been tormented—partly by his father, but mostly by himself—but now he had become a tormented *artist*, and that made all the difference.

"It's a hard row to hoe," he said suavely. "It's just you and that blank piece of paper, in the boxing ring, circling each other."

"You're mixing your metaphors?" she said smartly. "That's not very good writing?"

"I'm not writing *now*," he said testily, his transformation into this man complete enough to include his touchy, insecure, kneejerk reactions. "Not at these prices."

His comment quieted her; she backed off then walked away. Had he insulted and scared her? So what if he had? Stupid kid, he thought, as this new man, bitter and sage. He'd find himself a *real* woman.

Then he got his answer as to what impact he'd had. She returned to his side and, in what seemed an apology, filled his coffee cup again.

"On the house?" she said, as a secret.

When he took her back to his apartment—and who cared if there were no couch as yet, this new man could use the floor—he completed her assignment in a way she could never tell any teacher. And he warned her, too, about confiding in a counsellor or a parent or—worse yet—a reporter.

"Why would I want to do that?" she asked, still acting as if she were old enough to handle this, too prideful to admit how hurt she was by how horrendously he had treated her. Tears hid in her eyes, waiting for the chance, once she was alone, to fall. "Get, you know, real?"

Before he made her walk home, he grabbed her bag and took her tips for the night. He was, after all, almost broke. Then, by himself, he opened his window and howled like the most dangerous wild dog in the world. And no one in that dumb hick town dared answer him.

Because they never do, things did not go backwards. Selwyn soon spent the last of his money—mostly on beer, even though he'd always been a one glass of white wine man in the city, and firecrackers, buying them for the first time and setting them off in forests and on the sides of roads.

To finance himself further, he shifted his focus to the diner, for his young girlfriend was an impeccable inside source. After an evening of excruciating (for her) intimacy, he forced her to promise that she would pilfer from the register. This kind of robbery went on for weeks—with far more efficiency than he would have expected—until she entreated him tearfully to let her stop: there were suspicions, and she needed to keep her job to stay in school. He angrily agreed, but at a physical price, her vocal response to which upset his neighbours much more than an old man's music, and caused them to bang on all the walls and ceilings.

With four-legged cunning, he kicked away the artist now like a skin in spring and shifted tactics again, to take advantage of the stupid trusting nature of his community. Hardly anyone in the apartment complex (and how "complex" was it compared to where he'd come from? Not at all!) locked their door, or if a lock was turned, it was old and vulnerable. During the day, Selwyn entered the apartments of those still young enough to work, and, after the departure of ambulances, church cars, or casino buses, the homes of the elderly. When he got tired of preying on his own little house, he started stealing from those that surrounded it, eight in all.

It took a while—for the idea of a crime being committed in the country spreads slowly, because it occurs rarely and so is believed reluctantly, as opposed to the city where it is always immediately accepted, no matter what the circumstance and whether it's true or not—but people began to catch on. Fliers were posted in the laundry rooms beside and in marked contrast to the benign, hand-drawn ads for babysitters or "chest of drawers for sale."

"Has cash been stolen from your apartment?"

A complex-wide meeting was called and, so as not to attract attention, Selwyn went. He sat right amidst the others—it was a good turn out and not all old, since he'd been democratic in his thievery—and though unshaven and unable to remember the last time he'd bathed, he tried only to be obtrusive by craning his head to hear better what was said. Still, more than one neighbour moved away.

A dumb and dumpy local cop spoke: hallway "watches" were to be established, and Tim the super (whom Selwyn could have sworn stared at him suspiciously the whole time) promised to change all locks.

Selwyn realized he had been all too clever, because now not only did he have to stop stealing, for it was too big a risk, but the new security would mean higher rents, so there would be more that he couldn't afford.

Soon he maxed out all of his credit cards. His furniture, which had arrived so recently, began to get repossessed and carried out in broad daylight, before the prying eyes of other tenants, some of who spied from behind their Venetian blinds. One day, the fliers in the laundry room contained a police sketch, which while looking nothing like Selwyn did not look unlike him, either.

Selwyn started to grab milk cartons from the stoops of neighbourhood houses, where in the early mornings it was—amazingly and luckily—still delivered. He was chased by dogs when he swiped bowls of their food from backyards.

Though it was moving into mid-winter, he turned the expensive and erratic heat off in his apartment. His skin—so sensitive when he himself had been sensitive in the city—cracked and bled. But he rarely saw his skin now, so bundled up was he in unwashed coats, blankets, and sheets.

The last call he made before they disconnected his phone was to the city, to the store where Ray the computer man worked, to recommend his firing. He said that he'd sue them for how that idiot had compromised his computer! So what if he had actually enjoyed the impact of Ray's "incredible incompetence?" It felt good to give him up.

He learned the upstairs man had died of a sudden stroke, his unusable cello on the bed beside him.

Now he just sat, humming to himself, on the floor of his place. Occasionally, there would be a knock at the door and at least once, someone turned the knob. But Selwyn never saw another soul until the day he heard an indefinable sound in the hall—a rustle or a scraping or something—and his curiosity tweaked, fiddling his nearly frozen fingers before they could be used to reach and hold, opened up.

His super was there, his back to him, on his way out of the vestibule. He turned, with a look of nasty delight that removed years from his face.

"One way or another!" Tim laughed. Then he rushed away without another word.

Selwyn watched him go, perplexed—until he turned to close the door. There he saw, Scotch-taped upon it—the reason for the rustle and the scrape—an eviction notice.

Now he merely waited. He had a week or so, he couldn't remember exactly what he'd read on the door. If he didn't move much, he wouldn't even need to eat. He would simply hibernate, another way for an animal to survive in the natural world.

After a week or so, late one night, there was finally another sound at the door. It was not a knock or a turn of the knob or a cutting and a pressing of tape—it was a big-bodied push at the door's weak wood, probably from a shoulder as it always was in films. And, as in a film, the door—probably as poorly made as one in a studio, though in this case chiefly because of the landlord's cheapness—burst open, the one crummy lock breaking from its place and flying to the floor.

An ugly, muscular young man of maybe nineteen stood there. He wore jeans and an untucked shirt—plaid, of course; it was the upstater's uniform, the pinstripes of his particular prison. He was silhouetted for a second by the light from the hall—a very dramatic and again movie-like entrance. He used the light to scout the place until he saw whom he was seeking: Selwyn, curled up in his cold corner of the floor. Then he closed the door again, and all was black.

His eyes sore from the sudden flash, Selwyn shut them and only heard heavy boots approach. When they stopped, he slowly squinted up and saw the shadow of this big beast above him, one that had definitely been drinking a lot of cheap beer.

"Jesus, it's cold in here," the young man said, slurring his words so they were almost unintelligible. "And look at you, you're pathetic."

He went on to say, in stunted sentences Selwyn could barely understand, that he was either the boyfriend or the brother of Selwyn's waitress and unwilling accomplice. Though Selwyn had virtually forgotten her, apparently he had made more of an impression.

"You know what you done to her, man? She can't eat, she can't sleep—" or was it "peep"?

Either because he loved her romantically or as a relative, he was going to avenge her by "kicking the crap" out of Selwyn, no matter "how big a famous writer he was," or "how build-a-ferry-white" he was.

It certainly was colder in the country. As soon as Selwyn (sort of) heard this, he saw the hands of the man, which he acknowledged were bigger than his own, turn into fists. He was momentarily shaken. But he soon felt the courage of the small and graceful dog against the big and clumsy one.

He started with a foot kicked directly up between the man's legs, yanking him off-balance, and the merciless rout went on from there. He sprang up, jumped him, and fought with every weapon he had—from teeth to elbows to obscene insults—becoming a different monster every minute, from werewolf to vampire to snotty and superior jerk. He fought him long after the young man was defeated—and at the end, his enemy literally crawled out, leaving his blood all over Selwyn, gasping still sloppily, "This isn't the end of it," or "This *is* the end of it," Selwyn wasn't sure.

Selwyn sat back down again. He had enjoyed every minute—it was the purest, most thrilling experience of his life, the culmination of it all.

That had been two nights ago.

Now a small shock of sun began to come through the curtains, but did nothing to warm the place up.

"Now I know," he said, the clouds forming, the outside inside.

He knew that this realization was what he'd been awaiting. The outside *was* inside: all the rage and cruelty he had so recently feared in the world had been in him the whole time; it was what he had been fleeing his entire life. He had been his own bomb and his own bomb shelter.

By coming to the country, he had—well, he had just saved the shortcut, and the way wasn't enough. He had needed to embrace the scum, abuser, and thief within him—and the killer, too, for who knew what would have happened if his prey had not escaped?

He would return to the city that day, just as soon as they threw him out, and add all of himself to its otherwise blank and shapeless and formless environment. *It* did not matter, might well as not have happened. There was no outside world, had never been, not without what he imposed or withdrew from it.

He was too busy thinking this to hear the thumping again. Perhaps it had come too quickly or too close to his head to be heard, the hot water forcing its way through the old frozen pipe. He was sitting on the floor against the radiator, turned off.

For whatever reason, he couldn't move to escape the explosion that contradicted at least part of his conclusion, the spray of water one hundred and fifty degrees, as hot as the water in hell, if there was such a thing, and if hell—like this world and like the evil in this world—really existed.

OLD TRICKS

Will emptied all the ashtrays, though nobody smoked; he had stopped years ago, and there were only a few candy wrappers to shake out in the trash. Then he ran a vacuum around the place perfunctorily and briefly dusted with a new, easy—you could hardly call it an appliance, it was just a stick with a sort of cloth attached, though apparently it was a goldmine for whoever had been smart enough to invent it; he owned one, didn't he? Afterwards, he wasn't winded, his energy was high, he had done a mediocre job of cleaning because he was nervous and excited, not because he was tired—he never was, never even considered being—and his mind was racing like this because he was eager, not addled, or however someone his age was always portrayed.

He didn't feel his age, sixty-five, however that was supposed to feel, and he didn't look it—believed he looked fifty-five if that, since he was still in shape and had a full head of grey hair. The woman he was awaiting and quickly cleaning up for was twenty-eight or thirty, and that's how he felt, too: young.

Will had straightened up the bedroom last and least, merely plumping (was that the word? His mind was moving again, but out of jitteriness not because it was foggy or cobwebby or whatever word was always used in news stories about "seniors" who hit the gas when they mean to brake and sail and crash into benches full of innocent people in public parks) the pillows, because he did not want to press his luck by preparing a room into which he might not be lucky enough to persuade his guest to go. An undergraduate would have felt the same; there was no difference in attitude between them, regardless of their ages: they were both young.

Will's wife Jane was young, too—youngish, no student but forty-one, and she would be away at work all day. For years, Will had been an art teacher in the city's public schools (representational work, he could never abide abstraction) and he had met Jane—who was in the mayor's office as an educational liaison—three years ago at a function. She had thought him charming and slightly rugged, which he supposed he was in a way, an Army veteran and all, which most of the young men she knew were not and never would be; he had thought her, well, classy, to use an old-world word, and beautiful, to put it mildly, and things had progressed from there. He said theirs was a Tracy-Hepburn kind of relationship, a reference she only vaguely recognized, and so one he soon stopped making.

Some of her female friends had wondered aloud at their age difference, but Jane said she liked her work, didn't want kids—Will already had two sons from two earlier marriages, each ended by divorce—and she never liked conventions anyway, and maybe she liked older men, what do you think about that, she'd say and laugh, somewhat but not too defensively, he didn't think. They had gotten married right after his retirement, and with their combined savings, had bought a house ninety miles north of the city, which was where he was now.

Will had looked forward to staying all day in the house, free at last to paint, which his teaching schedule had never allowed, while Jane commuted with the occasional sleepover at her old digs in the village, which she had kept; he had at long last let his own apartment go.

Now Will swiftly stacked some newspapers but didn't bother to throw them away. If things hadn't turned out exactly as he had hoped, whose fault was that? How was he to know that, in a matter of months, staying home all day to paint would be unbearable, that he would get nothing done, that he would miss the contact of students and faculty—despite how often he had hated them both—and that if he had really wanted to stay home and paint he would have found a way to do it all those years ago, would have made it a priority in his life instead of a constantly deferred—intentionally, it turned out—dream?

And it wasn't Jane's fault that she was who she was—a somewhat cool woman without a great deal of interest in romance or sex or much of anything except city government, who seemed to like having him at home, safely ensconced, where she could keep an eye (or, since their main form of communication had turned out to be the telephone, an ear) on him. Her father had been largely absent and maybe this was her way to control and corral an older man, said one of those friends, an amateur shrink Will couldn't stand and whose suggestion Jane immediately and testily rejected.

It was no one's fault that, far from free, Will felt at once put out to pasture and into a cage, if such a thing was conceivable; both abandoned and imprisoned, treated as a pet and a threat—it was just the way things turned out, that's all, that was the extent of his thoughtfulness. Though he thought he'd tired of it, he missed the city, sometimes dreamed of himself as in a science-fiction film, a giant reaching from an ocean to embrace the skyline, but suddenly caught and stuck in quicksand (which was the country? He was no "brilliant" interpreter of symbols, like Jane's friend) and deterred, kept ever at a distance. He missed action; it was too early for him to be entombed; he was alive and so, to his way of thinking, he was and always would be young.

Will straightened a framed poster on the wall from a Monet show at the Met, which had been an inspiration at first and now was merely an irritant. The whole house—starkly modern in design, airy and blindingly bright, isolated off a main road and built in the middle of a sort of swamp that led to the woods—had been inspiring at first and now seemed cold and inhuman, jagged and angular. The staircases alone, you had to walk to the side like Groucho or Milton Berle or some other comic, and these were old references he had to remind himself to avoid when she showed up, and not *she*, show some respect: Angela.

It had taken him a while to meet Angela, taken him a few "sightings" as if she were a celebrity or an exotic bird—he wasn't sure he'd seen her at first. Will had been spending his days in a small truck he'd acquired, driving aimlessly around the town—which was considered one of the region's most prestigious, populous, and "busy," but to him now seemed dead, depressing, and in these weekdays during the summer, stultifyingly dry and hot. He would cruise to the few areas of interest—an art exhibit at a school, a book sale at the library, even the farmers' market on days when he could convince himself he cared about produce, which he never had. And one day right before he was ready to keep on driving, straight to the highway and back down to the city and maybe who knew where from there, he was sure that he saw her.

She had been at all these same places, a slim, appealingly plain woman with dark blonde hair and sunglasses, as if she were following or perhaps preceding him there. They had never acknowledged each other—and it had taken an effort not to, since they were usually the only ones around—they had simply silently admired (or in Will's case endured his view of) the local landscapes being displayed or browsed the old books being offered or felt and/or sniffed, in Will's case with false expertise, the fruits and vegetables. Even on this day, when it was obvious they had similar interests—or just were alone with an identical desire to find something, anything, to do—Will was too unsure of the situation to say anything and had begun to go away again. Then, in a good-humoured voice, she had stopped him by asking, "So? Where are we going to go tomorrow?"

He only smiled, didn't respond right away. If he wasn't mistaken, he thought he heard a trace of an English accent, maybe one fading but still fighting to stay alive after years in the U.S. He could have been a clever guy, good with the comebacks, but he only said, "Right, right," and made it clear that he saw what she meant, that was what mattered most. And then he was emboldened to extend his hand and say who he was, and both their skins were similarly sticky and wet and their spoken names—"Will," "Angela"—seemed to merge in the moisture that was made in their palms and forge a pact, the same way children do—did they still?—when they spit on their hands and shake. In other words, they had been linked to each other from the very start.

They had lemonades at the "quaint" local deli, which was now utterly empty. He was right, she was from overseas originally; she didn't say England, but it was implied, and she shared his boredom with the town and, while never specific about her circumstances—she didn't wear a wedding ring—said she had fled the city to change her life and had taken a job there in the Chamber of Commerce, which Will had noticed was a stand-alone storefront on the main street, not even air-conditioned, more like a shed than an office. Angela was the only employee and so spent much of the day out, driving anywhere to avoid being there.

"It's like a coffin," she said.

Will, of course, understood: he, too, had recently unearthed himself, risen from the grave, refused to go under and become a ghost. He was not explicit but mentioned being married—why not, she'd seen his ring—and Angela didn't answer, she barely blinked. The lemonade, the languid afternoon, the lack of any others in the place—it was for Will like being a teenager on a first date in the middle of July at the end of the Earth. He felt that time had been suspended, that it hung there as heavy and lifeless as the humid air.

In his life, he had never known the moment when he left the particular, protected, exclusive world of youth. Unlike other men with younger women, he never perceived the possibility—and they knew it grew greater the older they grew—that he was being played for a fool. He didn't promise young women things; he didn't intend to teach them. He approached them sentimentally or erotically, as a young man might, as himself. He was doing so now, and this was what Angela seemed to see: the eternal Him, as he'd always been.

Still, Will was discreet, patient; he didn't even touch her hand until the third time they met in the same place, still swapping stories about their loneliness—and even then he made sure that the nosy and annoying owner (always eager to engage in boring talk about rustic things like canning and riding and planting) had stepped away. He drew Angela's face on a napkin—a perfect likeness and the best and really the only work he'd completed since coming to the country—and gave it to her as a gift. Then he invited her to his house and she agreed to come, and everything was clear to them both.

He only worried about being discovered. He'd been unfaithful to both his wives and neither had known; his second ex-wife had died without knowing, so what had been the difference? None. Maybe he'd been betrayed by both of the women, as well; he'd probably never know now, either. This was bigger than guilt: it was as if he and Angela had wandered into each other in a fog, like actors in an old movie about London, or stumbled into each other's arms, like lovesick zombies or something—he was never good with similes, he only knew it felt too right to refuse and he was sure she felt the same.

Now, on the day they had decided, unbearably eager for her appearance, Will kicked a last dust ball beneath the couch. If he breathed heavily, it was from want, not from an age-related constriction of the lungs. He had done enough, the house looked lived-in but not inhabited by shut-ins or lunatics; she would not be repelled. Soon he heard tires rolling slowly on the gravel of the drive, a purely mechanical motion that irrationally he was aware promised pleasure.

From the window, he watched Angela leave her car. She was wearing her sunglasses and looked glamorous in a Jackie O sort of way—that was an old reference, too, even that—though also awkward and even nerdy, an endearing combination, tilting a little in her flat shoes on the gravel, almost falling over before righting herself. Her imperfections meant she was alive, Will thought; only the dead could not be improved. He opened the door before she even rang the bell.

"Well," she said, "here we are again, as we always are. In the middle of nowhere."

It was hard for Will to answer. He had been worried about her reaction to the new environment, but there had been such a quick connection made, the remark soldered them together so suddenly, that he was both relieved and aroused, in a state of infinite calm and impatient desire, the way adolescents are when they get a first crush, deeply sure and totally panicked, and why they call and hang up, call and hang up, just to hear the other's voice, reassuring and rattling themselves—or how they did, Will thought, before technology both increased and obliterated secrecy.

In the sterile and impressive house, which Angela scoped out politely but with thoroughness, she looked younger than ever. Will was aware that she didn't remember Watergate let alone World War II, and while it might have been unseemly to others, it didn't matter at all.

She looked out the picture window, which took up most of the wall, and saw the sort of swamp and where it led.

"You ever go walking in the woods?" she asked, her accent still staying alive on "wa" and "woo."

Will shook his head. "I'm always afraid I won't come out again."

She nodded—a way of saying me too, and it excited him to see it.

Then, without warning, she went into his arms, and since she was only slightly smaller, bowed to place her head upon his chest like a child, her open lips near the silver hair apparent above the buttons of his shirt. Will could smell her strawberry shampoo, a kind used by even younger women, and after hesitating, stunned for a second, he slipped his hands around and held her with a powerful feeling of protectiveness and need. When she pulled away, there were tears in both their eyes and he was sure for the same reason.

"Is there a bathroom?" she said. "Or when you move into a place like this, do you never have to go again?"

"No," he said and smiled. "You go more often because there's nothing else to do. It's up the stairs and to the right."

As she walked up the leaning staircase, the angle of her ascent didn't seem real to him, because he felt so dizzy anyway. He could not believe the intensity of the emotions that had grabbed hold of him. He and Jane had made a mistake getting married, that was clear (and would be to her, as well, once he explained, or maybe he wouldn't even have to), but still, without it and their ill-advised move to the country, he and Angela would never have met, so had it been essential? Or would there have been no need to meet, since their meeting had been a reaction to the torpor and malaise of the marriage? He knew it was all intertwined, but how exactly? Will knew he was not a clear thinker, he was a picture man, but he couldn't stop the boyish barrage of ideas occurring to him now. Love was like a stick that upended a rock under the ocean and flooded the area with little fish—that's what he felt. Suddenly he realized he'd never used that word—love—about this experience, but knew now the word was right.

He had experienced the feeling at some point in all of his marriages and a few of his affairs, but never so passionately. He moved to and stood at the end—the beginning?—of the stairs and waited for Angela's return like a young groom impatient for the appearance of his bride and the start of their ceremony.

Will waited for what began to seem a strangely long time. He knew that, since he was in this state, even an instant without her would seem an eternity, but still. He checked his watch: Angela had been gone for almost twenty-five minutes.

Cautiously, not wanting to seem like he was spying on her—or worse, having an older, parental, you-feel-hot-to-me-let-me-kiss-your-forehead burst of anxiety (when it was after all the opposite: a timeless I'll-break-the-door-down-and-drag-you-off type thing)—he started slowly up the stairs. When he reached the top, not liking to but having no brighter idea, he listened at the door. Hearing nothing, once, gently, and—if it was possible—with good humour, he tapped upon it. Still there was only silence. Finally, affecting an amused and affectionate tone meant to dispel any sense that he was snooping, hysterical, or simply a strange man, he said, "Angela?"

When there was no answer, he turned the knob. He knew that no door in the house had a lock, which was something he had intended to change when he thought he would be staying. Then he opened up.

Angela was curled upon the bathroom floor. She was entirely naked except for her shoes and a thin gold choker he hadn't even noticed she'd been wearing. Her clothes were piled up neatly upon the closed toilet. For a second, in his shock, Will thought he saw bright red sleeves upon her bare upper arms—a strange fashion, he thought. Then he slowly realized he was looking at lines of blood that started at her wrists and ended at her elbows before dripping down and pooling in the hollows of her knees, which they were resting upon.

The medicine chest behind the mirror was open and a small but still sharp pair of scissors sat in the sink, an implement of Jane's that Will assumed Angela had used to jab herself with until she opened her veins. There was also an empty bottle of pills beside it, the cap nowhere to be found.

Will stood gripping the sides of the threshold like an obedient man in an earthquake. He was totally immobile and for once his overactive mind was empty but for the facts of the sight before him. The one detail he made sure to retain was that Angela was still breathing.

He saw that her little handbag—which he hadn't even been aware she was carrying—had been placed upon her carefully arranged blouse and pants. Will reached into the room gingerly, as if sneaking something from the bedside of a sleeping thief, and grabbed the bag by its thin hoop handle. Then he pressed it to his chest, primly and absurdly, and turned to go. He knew that there might be information inside that he would need when he called an ambulance.

As he approached the stairs, he didn't consider the threat to him in doing so—the explanation, inevitable lying, and possible exposure—he only knew it was essential that someone save Angela's life and he didn't know how to do it himself. He had been confined to the base during his stint in the service and his only physical dealings with someone dying had been seeing his elderly mother expire in a nursing home. Also, as a child, he had—unfortunately—forced himself to watch his pet cat being put to sleep, a process which turned a sick but living creature into something as stiff as a fossil frozen for a century, haunting him for the rest of his life and inspiring a painting he had once started but never completed.

His mind was starting to fill again with thoughts like dirty, drowning water, and to avoid them, he moved ever quicker to the crooked stairs. His first step was more like a skid and his hand slid off the thin, attractive, useless railing. Will rolled idiotically down, pinballing off the sides of the walls.

When he hit the bottom, he was as curled as Angela, though fully conscious and cognizant of startling and unprecedented pain coursing through his right ankle and left knee. He glanced up and saw that the little handbag had jumped from his hand and opened, its meagre contents strewn upon the rug like breadcrumbs leading to her identity: a credit card, a driver's license, and a photo of Angela with a man and baby boy Will could only assume were her ex-husband and son.

Will's upper body so far felt only sore not broken, so, carefully, he propped himself up on his elbows then placed his hands on the floor for leverage. He felt like a character in the old movie *Freaks* who was just a head and torso and lit a match without any limbs, and he didn't care how old the reference was. He pushed himself up enough to test the weight on one leg, then the other, and found both to be equally unbearable. Still he stood, then tried to walk, hopping from left to right, holding onto the wall, knocking down Jane's framed pictures of her family, that annoying Monet poster, and a Fritz the Cat clock as he went. At last, he reached the small table where the phone was, tears dripping from his chin like raindrops. He sank slowly onto a hard wood chair, his opposite knee and elbow so savaged he was surprised they weren't sending out those shooting pain signals that were always in cartoons. He dialled 911, staring at the liver spot that now seemed so prominent on his shaking hand.

—∾—

The EMS people came quickly, their siren piercing the silent street. Three young paramedics—two men and one woman—got cursory information from Will before rushing up the stairs to the bathroom. Will had meant, of course, to cover Angela, but there was no way he could reach her again, not on the legs he had now. So he simply sat on the same chair, immobile and slumped a little forward, like an invalid in a doctor's waiting room.

In a few minutes, he watched the men bring Angela down on a stretcher, under a sheet that came to her shoulders, her wrists bandaged, an oxygen mask on her mouth. Her clothes were in a plastic bag tied loosely around the wrist of the lady medic, who followed.

"I think she'll be all right," she said kindly, and Will felt a final tear fall from his eyes, not from pain but pure relief.

"I hardly know her," he said helplessly, without her even asking. "She had just come by for—" what was the least incriminating occasion? "—tea."

Then he gestured at the documents and picture still lying on the rug which he could not even consider stooping to retrieve. The woman bent and scooped them up, plus the handbag, which Will had also helpfully pointed out. Then she took down his name and number and the men hustled Angela out the door to the ambulance. None of them had looked at him with any suspicion at all. While relieved, Will soon realized it was for the worst reason: they could not imagine that he and Angela could have been in this world in any way romantically involved.

"Can we do anything for *you*?" the woman asked in a clearly pitying tone.

"I'm *fine*," Will said, annoyed now, but the force of the statement sent a new and terrible sensation down his legs. The woman only smiled, slightly, then nodded with a wholly irksome kind of understanding, and was gone.

A few hours later, over the phone, a doctor told him that Angela was out of danger, fine, expected to make a full recovery. Will said that that was wonderful to hear. Then he offered to make himself available for any questions, even from police, if need be. But the doctor—sounding, infuriatingly, amused, Will couldn't help but think—said only that he'd be sure to pass the information along. Will left a message at Angela's hospital room, but it wasn't returned; the next morning, he was told she'd been released.

Over the next few days, no one called Will at all about the incident. If word got around the small town about it, he was not made aware. Finally, a week after his and Angela's date, he received a small letter with no return address. It was a hand-written note from Angela, which was short but still somehow rambling.

She said that her depression had led to her divorce and the loss of custody of her child, and her psychiatrist, a man of Will's age, had recently died. She had now been put on a prescription for a new pill she hoped would be effective, and she would be moving back to the city. She was sorry she had caused Will any trouble and wished him luck in the future. Will thought he could hear her slight English accent on the words "shan't" and "mustn't" which she used several times in regards to their relationship. She left him no way to get in touch with her.

As he put it down and folded it away, Will realized that the letter proved what so many might have suspected: a woman her age would have to be crazy to want him.

—~—

The reckoning shook and sobered him, but soon he had other concerns. He began to regret not responding more honestly to the female medic's question about his condition. His belief that his ankle and knee would simply improve turned out to be unfounded, and after both became purple and bulging, he was forced to seek a doctor's care. His ankle was said to be severely sprained and wrapped, and the ligaments of his knee were torn and it, too, was taped. He was given crutches and a cane to walk with for the next six weeks.

Jane had apparently not heard (or maybe just disbelieved) any word of the incident, and she readily bought Will's white lie that he had tripped down the stairs while running to get an art reference book. At first she showed sympathy, but when Will's condition not only didn't improve but seemed to worsen—leaving him ever more hobbled and dependent on pain pills which made him weary and a little groggy, in contrast to his usual robustness—she began to lose patience. Now she occasionally called him "Grandpa," which she had only ever done once and with affection after love-making, and his slightly slurred speech brought the polite requests, "Speak clearly, for goodness' sake," and "Please don't sound like you're in an old age home." When his memory, also weakened by the pills, faltered, she snapped a correction at him, tightly smiling, and in front of company.

Now trapped all day at home, not able to drive, his paints and easel lying beneath a layer of dust and his mind dulled by hours of daytime television, Will began to feel desperate about what seemed Jane's growing disdain for him. Far from negative or even mixed about their marriage, as he had so recently felt, he started to fear her rejection, for in this state, at his age, who else would have him? He would be lonely for the rest of his life, and so he became clingy in ways that clearly annoyed her.

Soon Jane began to stay overnight more often in the city, citing work obligations. There were frequent calls to the house with no one on the other end, or quickly hanging up when Will answered. If he checked the Caller ID machine, which could catch the name and number, it always said "Unavailable" or "Anonymous."

—~—

One dusk, Jane had stayed away in town again. Not having turned on any lights, his cane at his side, unshaven for the entire day, his face full of grey stubble like the old men he used to see in bus stations reading paperback westerns, Will felt disgusted with himself. Defiantly, he stuffed the cane into a closet. Then, holding onto pieces of furniture as he proceeded, he managed to move to open the back door and walk outside, unassisted.

It was a horribly humid day near the end of August. He had neglected to use bug spray, and mosquitoes and gnats swarmed his face; it was more of a swamp than he'd even suspected. His feet squished in the mud as he pried apart tall grass. But he didn't stop. Soon Will was pleased by his progress and laughed at himself for taking so long to try this and test his mettle.

But eventually the sweltering heat made him feel a little swoony. His shirt became soaked with sweat and his skin began to itch and sting. After a few more minutes, he panted more than breathed. His legs ached so much they shook. The sun had almost set, but if possible it seemed even more stifling. Will felt that if he kept on standing, in one minute more he would fall down.

He stopped. He had gone far enough, as far as he could go. Slowly, Will turned back. The house was at too great a distance to reach, and when he turned the other way again, to his horror, all he could see were the woods.

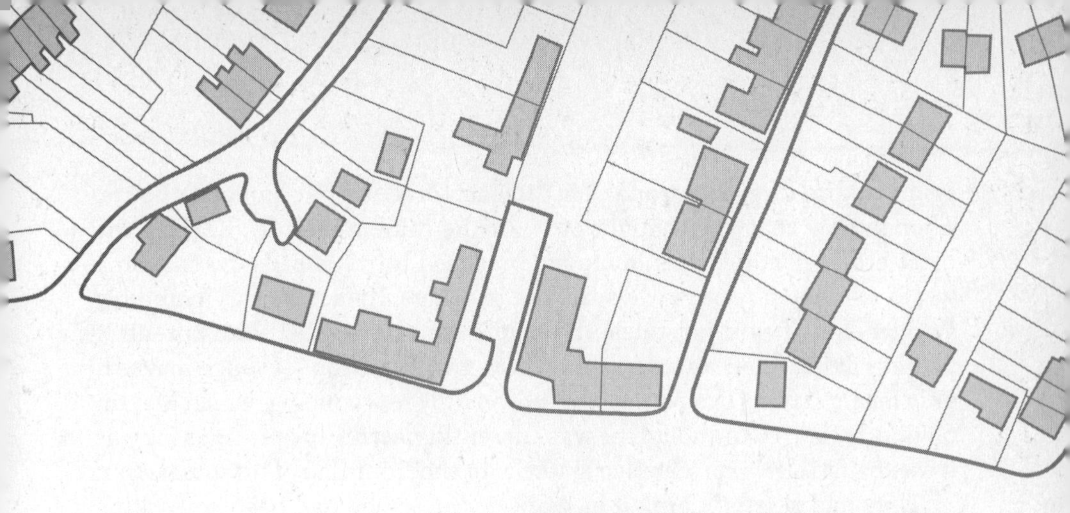

THE DEAD END JOB

They were supposed to be doing something at work, and they were. *She* was doing something anyway, talking to him while sitting beside him on super-structured swivel chairs imported at great expense from Finland (or some foreign place) in her office, which had been presented to Isabel as an incentive to take the job—she wouldn't be working in a cubicle, in other words—and which had actually become a boon for them, since it was small enough for them to be close together—"conferring on data"—without arousing suspicions when she did this, when she told him stories about herself to excite him and he touched himself through his jeans or—if he was feeling bold enough—unbuckled and unzipped his pants and touched himself directly.

They had started doing it a few weeks ago, during lunch hour when the rest of the office emptied out. She had learned that Martin didn't eat lunch, hardly ate at all, unlike herself who felt even at twenty-three that she ate too much, even though others thought she was being silly, others found her attractive—Martin did, at any rate, though it took him forever to say so and, come to think of it, maybe he never actually had. He had just moved toward Isabel like an object on a ship's table sliding amidst a storm at sea. Maybe his not eating enough explained more than his—not entirely unappealing—ultra-slimness, it had caused his—how should she say it?—lack of strength in a certain area, something she had discovered during their first date, if you could even call it a date; it had been more, again, a kind of gravitational drift in each other's direction after hours. Though now that she thought of it—as he came forcefully, hearing the most erotic part of her monologue breathed into his ear—he was only weak sexually in certain ways and not in others. In fact, he was incredibly avid when he heard her tales; she might even have called him potent, if potency didn't imply an interaction with another person—though maybe it only meant having the potential of powerfully reproducing, which Martin obviously had, even though he was currently wasting his precious (or was it inexhaustible?) reproductive material in the front flap of his underwear.

They had started doing it at work because they had been so fucking bored. Not that Isabel had expected to be thrilled exactly, collecting data in a company that made security systems—let her get this straight—so that "passive requestors" could strengthen the "trust realms" between "insecure" computers, so that web browsers could better "make requests" of—oh, the whole thing had been so lame to begin with, and so was anybody working in it. But, well, she had needed a job and the industrial park was within driving distance from her apartment (the first she'd ever had, gotten right after graduating college where she had studied art history—as useless a major as she had been warned it would be). This was sold to her, too, as another incentive, the short commute, though now in fact she would have preferred a longer ride in the morning, since pressing her foot to the pedal and turning the radio knob were more actions than she performed at work, more of a physical and mental workout, and she was only half-kidding.

Martin had not been her first office mate: Rita had been there to begin with, a nondescript woman of fifty who, to Isabel's amazement, had already worked there for ten years, and who had a heart attack and took early retirement two days after Isabel arrived (Isabel was not the reason, as she had been solemnly reassured by her boss, Owen, as if she ever would have imagined that she was; though, in fact, the reassurance actually made her consider it for a second). Martin arrived soon after, at about half Rita's salary, Isabel assumed.

He was, she immediately noticed, her own age, dark-haired and not unhandsome, though so slight as to seem positively fragile. Isabel had never fantasized sexually about being physically bigger than a man, but in truth she wasn't the most experienced in this area, having gone through college just racking up short relationships with an aspiring and seemingly pot-addicted musician—mostly because they lived on the same hall—and an acting student who had said he was bi-sexual, but whom she soon learned was homosexual, or at least would be—he confessed while leaving her for a male stage manager—after his experience with her. *Their* affair, too, had come about through inertia—they had been at the same cast party and left at the same time, and this, it turned out, was the most they would ever have in common.

Martin and she had quickly formed a tighter bond, one based on incredulity at the fact of their daily tasks—disbelief that they were meant to merely man computers, waiting for data, feeling as suffocated as those at battle stations in wartime submarines but nowhere near as necessary (Martin had said this; he'd been a history major). The two were nearly stunned by the idea of doing this all day, unnerved enough that they couldn't even laugh about it, until, one night on the way home, after they'd each had two beers apiece at a nearby bar, they couldn't *stop* laughing.

Even here, the torpor of the job had taken its toll, sapped their spirits; they hadn't actively chosen the bar, Martin had just caravanned behind her car until Isabel shrugged, put on her turn signal, and he had followed. In the same sleepwalking way, they had gone to her place afterwards, since he still lived with roommates, one of whom slept out in the open, on the living room couch.

They had watched an animated movie for a while, one that both had seen several times without even liking. Then, neither being the aggressor, they simply moved closer on the couch like commuters making room for others on a crowded subway car, freeze-framed the film, and got close enough to touch.

Martin's hands had skittered over her like bats, and she had darted her tongue into his mouth as if trying to reach something under a couch where it had not been vacuumed for years. While each had made the least amount of effort possible, both became aroused—it had been ages for Isabel, after all, and she heard Martin moan in what sounded like agreement when she rubbed his half-erection, her wrist pressed somewhat painfully against the clump of keys in the right front pocket beside it.

Yet by the time she'd returned hopefully from the bathroom—carrying a condom, which she'd taken discreetly from a bowl of free ones in a progressive bookstore downtown—wearing only her panties but still holding against her the T-shirt she'd taken off, self-conscious as ever about her size, she found that Martin was already pulling back on the pants he'd partially yanked down and was reaching again for the remote.

He gave no explanation (later, she understood he'd been too embarrassed, or at least too unhappy with himself to speak), and at the moment she blamed herself, and then him, and then herself again, and sat there feeling strange, still gripping the unwrapped condom with her right hand and the T-shirt with her left as he began the movie again from the place where they'd stopped it.

While they watched—or while he did, and she stared into a middle distance, wondering if she was blushing (it seemed like it) and, if so, whether if it was from anger or embarrassment or both—without a word or muting the movie, Martin turned and began touching her again, fingering her through the side of her underwear and occasionally moving her T-shirt away to inexpertly but intently suck her nipple. He did it, she thought later, out of guilt and obligation, or as a kind of good form and fair play (he was a WASP after all; he had said so over drinks, though he had gone to school on a scholarship), or from an excitement that (and here she began to feel compassion for him and not contempt) he was unable to fully feel but only witness and acknowledge, the way one smells food that one doesn't actually crave but understands others eating. Why ever he was doing it, he made Isabel come, a bit more intensely than she usually made herself in the evenings, her experience diminished somewhat by the accompanying sound of a song sung by cartoon flounders in the movie, along with which she suspected Martin was quietly humming, though it might have been more of the agreeing-with moaning he had done before.

Afterward, he pulled away, leaving her to readjust her underwear and fully pull on her shirt. The fact that he had even done it after appearing impotent (because he lacked strong enough blood circulation or didn't desire her in that way or didn't eat enough—he had only nibbled at the nachos in the bar, while she ate almost all of them—or was, well, ill) somewhat endeared him to her, and she placed an elbow upon his shoulder, as if they were players on a high school soccer team or something, as they watched to the end the movie they still thought mediocre.

As the credits rolled—and Martin finally pressed mute—Isabel thought she should say something to comfort him, in case he felt at fault.

"I bet you've had more exciting evenings," she said to take the rap, though she knew—or at least suspected—she was unworthy of such punishment, a tiny residual doubt notwithstanding.

"Oh, hey," Martin said, after a long and tortured pause, direct expression clearly—along with other kinds of human interactions—an ongoing and excruciating trial for him. "It's you who had to . . . I mean, I hadn't been . . ." and that was the best he could do to grab back the ball of blame.

Then there was an even longer pause before, not able to look at her, he asked, "When was the first time you—you did it?"

Isabel was surprised, even taken aback, by his inquiry. For a second, she didn't answer. He took her silence as a rebuke and said, "Sorry, maybe I shouldn't have . . ."

But that he had had the energy to ask her *anything*, had taken an initiative that wasn't to make up for a failing (as when he'd touched her) or express a negative emotion (as, at work, when he had once "mistakenly" deleted incoming data), so impressed her that she felt obligated to reply, if only to encourage him to continue.

"It was, well, in high school," she said, "at a boy I knew's house."

Slowly, he asked her another question about the encounter (which had been with Bailey Glynn, arts editor of the high school lit mag, *The Long Island Epiphany*), and then another, and each time she answered, because as she did so, she sensed a commitment from and curiosity in him that she had never seen and did not want to quash, uncomfortable as she was revealing details which up till now had been known only to Bailey and herself.

"He undid my bra, and then we thought we heard his parents pull into the driveway, but it wasn't the case; strangely, that seemed to make him harder, and—"

"What did you do then?"

She told him about her first fumbling yet erotic experience with fellatio, distancing herself from the event by pretending to describe a movie she had seen and, accordingly, embellishing it here and there, which both allowed her less unease and increased his avidity. The almost entranced quality of his arousal (his eyes closed, his mouth slightly open) grew more and more marked as she kept talking.

"And were you excited?"

"So excited."

As she reached the peak of her story, Martin began to undo his pants with great haste, as if he simply could not wait a moment longer. She was surprised by the strength and size of his erection now, as if he were another person, had a whole other body, when she talked to him like this. Before he could touch his penis she did, and before she could touch it more than once he came, so loudly and powerfully that he sounded as if he was in pain and had to place a hand on her arm to steady himself, as if he was afraid of what was happening, though this only made her excited and not concerned for him.

Afterward, Martin looked down and saw that his semen had shot the entire length of his bare leg and onto her couch, some of it even hitting the TV remote inches away. He said nothing, just rose to pull one, two, then three tissues from a nearby box and start to fastidiously clean up. Before he had finished, Isabel had tugged his hand toward her, pried the tissues loose from it, and placed it between her legs: he pushed three fingers inside her, and she held his hand there and came again, this time much more deeply and electrically than she had before—than she ever had, she later admitted only to herself.

Each briefly looked in the other's eyes, aware that both were alive in ways that were unknown to other people in the office, and that neither would have known if neither had exposed—sacrificed—something (he pride, she privacy); that both had *done* things that night and been rewarded, in other words, the opposite of how they spent their time at work. Then they looked away, each secretly knowing what would happen next.

Isabel and Martin didn't discuss or arrange it: speaking to each other was not their strong suit (especially not his). Yet the next day, after staring immobile at information on a screen before pressing a button to distribute it, when no one was passing their door, she quietly asked him what else he wanted to know about her, and he answered her question with another question—"What was the next time you, etc."—and she answered his question with an actual answer, and that made him ask another question with an urgency he showed about nothing else (had maybe never shown about anything else), and she answered again, his excitement exciting her (her power to excite him exciting her), until he nonchalantly placed the base of his palm quickly against the large lump that had grown below his belt, and she naughtily brushed it once or twice with her elbow and ended the exchange, Martin gasping and seeming almost lifted up in the air by the wild rush it afforded him. Then Isabel excused herself and went into the ladies' room where she locked herself in a stall and made herself come, too, which happened almost instantly and left her so sweaty and aromatic that she realized her "natural" deodorant didn't work and probably never had, she just never had known for she had never tested it with enough effort.

As weeks went on, they got the routine down to a science, knew when to stop if they heard sounds in the hall, when to swivel away from each other, when to start up again. One day, Martin stayed out sick with a cold and called her from home. This was physically easier for her—Isabel only had to eyeball the hall and not physically disengage from him if the coast wasn't clear—yet it took some getting used to, it being more impersonal.

"What did he say about your tits?" he asked after she had quietly described an event.

"That he liked them."

"That's all?"

"That they were big. That I had nice ones."

"Then what did he do?"

"He kissed around, then licked around and bit around my nipples. He wouldn't suck them. He was tormenting me."

"Did your nipples get hard?"

"So hard."

"What did you do?"

"I begged him to suck them. And he said I'd have to wait."

"Were you wet?"

"So wet."

"What happened then?"

"He made me promise that I would swallow his come if he sucked my nipples."

"And what did you do?"

"I promised that I would."

"And did you?"

"Yes. Later."

"I really want to hear about that."

There was a brief pause on the other end of the line as she heard only Martin's slow, slightly cold-congested breathing. Then, "I'll call you back," he said and hung up.

She made up the stories, of course, having long since exhausted her actual experiences, which she had fictionalized in the first place as to make them virtually unrecognizable. She saw herself as a kind of Scheherazade, though only vaguely aware of whom that was. When Isabel looked up the name online, she saw that the analogy wasn't perfect but close enough to make her feel connected to an oral tradition, in a line of great raconteurs.

Yet after more weeks, this remained the only connection she could feel. Martin never stopped wanting to hear her "memories" (which she assumed he knew were padded with details picked up from porn films she saw online, actually had researched at home in her idle hours, the sites not being "safe for work," and then made less mechanical and cold when she offered them up as her own), but this remained the extent of their physical relationship. Soon he was not requesting to do it after work anymore but only in the office, and didn't reciprocate by touching her (for she, being shyer, refused to have that done in public and still insisted on going to the ladies' room by herself, and then even stopped doing that). Isabel began to feel their actions were fading into another form of passivity—more work, in other words, a new and modern job, the pressing of a penis the same as that of a "send" button, etc.

It was around this time that their boss, Owen, requested her appearance in his office after five.

Isabel had spoken to Owen just two or three times—once when he assured her she hadn't caused Rita's heart attack; once when she rode the elevator with him after only he and not she had carried an umbrella in that morning's thunderstorm, and she had tried to laugh off the water literally dripping from her hair and clothes and pooling on the marble floor of the car, and he had smiled, politely, seeming she thought repelled, and another time she couldn't remember. He hadn't even hired her; it had been an obese woman named Cybil in Human Resources.

So she had been startled when Owen poked his head in her and Martin's office only a few minutes after Martin had excused himself to clean up in the men's room. Owen had an open and expectant look, as if about to ask if she wanted anything at the store, he was making a run ("I'll fly if you buy," they used to say in college), but that couldn't be it, of course.

When she walked to his office later, it was with trepidation—an instinctive reaction to being summoned by someone in authority, she thought—but she also had a flickering hope that she was about to be fired, though if the cause was her office adventures with Martin, that might turn out to be embarrassing, maybe even featured on the evening news, then splashed all over the Internet where her parents could see it.

When she sat opposite him, though, Owen didn't mention Martin and only wanted her to do some special project on a freelance basis; he would understand if she were too busy.

"Busy?" She was unable to keep a tone of comic disbelief from her voice and was immediately sorry about it. "I mean, no, I don't think so. All right. Thank you."

Isabel needed the money, after all—and she tuned out when Owen explained about the mild tax complications that "freelance" would mean, "estimated" or whatever. She concentrated instead on looking at Owen, who was forty-two but whom she thought was either thirty-five or fifty. He had a boyish, snub-nosed face surrounded by greying hair, reminding her of a modern painting in a gilded frame from another century. He didn't meet her eyes as he spoke, yet what he said couldn't have been more simple, innocent, and non-incriminating. Was he avoiding something else of which he *was* ashamed? She didn't know. She had walked in wondering why he'd chosen her and left convinced it could have been her or someone else; maybe he'd just stopped by her office after counting to ten.

When Isabel got home, there was a message on her machine from Martin. In it, he implied an interest in hearing her talk over the phone that night, having apparently enjoyed it when he'd been ill, unlike Isabel who'd had mixed feelings. Isabel meant to call him back, yet by the time she'd finished the assignment for Owen, it was midnight and too late. She'd completed the task in just one night, despite the several Owen had assumed it would take. Since it had been no more interesting than what she did at work—seemed more boring, actually, like spending a vacation in her home—Isabel was surprised by her diligence and went to sleep without comprehending it.

The next day, she politely demurred when Martin nodded suggestively at the empty hall during lunch hour. They had sometimes missed other opportunities—for instance, when they had had to attend day-long, company-wide meetings after which both confessed they had fantasized about doing it in front of the entire workforce, which had fuelled and made more exciting their next encounter. This was the first time Isabel had actually said or at least shaken her head no, and she could see the disappointment—which was deep—on Martin's face. At day's end, he waited for her to accompany him out, but Isabel simply said she would see him tomorrow.

"I'll call you?" he said, or asked, as if unsure whether he would, or would be allowed to by her, it wasn't clear which.

As soon as he was gone, Isabel walked quickly to Owen's office, hoping he hadn't left for the night. She carried the work she had done, which she had printed out and placed neatly in a folder. She could have emailed it to him but wanted to deliver it in person, she didn't know why.

"Well, well," Owen said, impressed, using a way of talking that was older than his youngish face, as if his greying hair were talking or something—Isabel couldn't express it coherently to herself. "Thank you. I had no idea you'd do it so . . ."

Suddenly Owen couldn't finish the sentence—and the final word was almost certainly "fast" or "quickly;" he appeared too appreciative and that made him too emotional. Or was it something else? For whatever reason, his eyes filled with tears.

Standing before his desk, Isabel didn't know what to do. Had she somehow sensed this aspect of Owen—an instability—and complied with the job so quickly out of compassion? She was suddenly unaware of so much, though many things were presenting themselves. She only knew that something had been building in her, begun by her losing interest in—growing to resent really—Martin. Unintentionally, the older man had stepped into the spill of a searchlight Isabel had been shining around, and now she had stopped it; he had her full attention.

"May I close the door?" he asked, still choking up, and Isabel nodded, as if to say please do.

When he retook his seat, Owen again spoke without looking at her, but occasionally met her eyes and glanced away, testing new waters of trust.

"My wife," he said, "I don't—I don't mean to put her down. She can't help it. I know depression is a disease, that's what the doctors say. I understand that. But she sleeps hours and hours a day—sometimes all day. I bring her books and newspapers—I brought her an easel with an expensive palette, for she used to paint. They all go unused. She's taken every pill invented and none has worked for more than a week. What am I supposed to do? Nothing? That's what it feels like she wants for me to do, not to leave her but to leave her be. How can I? She stays behind a closed door that seems as big as that space monolith in that movie where—oh, of course, you wouldn't know it, you're too young."

The idea of Isabel's age had stopped his confession, returned him to reality; Owen swivelled to the side, seeming grateful that *something* had.

Isabel felt a bit offended. She *had* seen that movie, or at least part of it once—had heard of it anyway—and besides, he was too young to have seen it originally, either; he wasn't *that* much older. In any case, she knew that in the only way that mattered, they were the same: Owen was a person going to waste, as she was.

"I *do* know," she blurted out, and thought she sounded even younger, a child asserting sophistication. It made him smile—mostly with his eyes, if that were possible, as he barely moved his mouth—and that hurt her even more.

Still, her youth meant something to her: Isabel waited for him to speak before continuing the conversation—not because he was her boss, exactly, but because what he was going through was something she hadn't experienced, the depth of his despair was something she had never known. Wasn't that worthy of respect or at least silence? This wasn't about her impressing *him*, after all, though she wanted to, had to force herself not to keep trying, to make him know that she understood him, understood everything, even though she sensed she didn't.

But Owen wouldn't respond, so Isabel had no better idea than to leave. When he saw her start to go, he rose at the same time, actually making a decision, moving toward her as she moved to the door. He was faster than she, because he wanted to get where he was going more.

Owen stood before her, no longer on the verge of tears, as if feeling beyond what tears could tell her. He offered himself as a desperate supplicant, without any other options, beyond all embarrassment.

"Please," he said. "Please. Use me."

At first Isabel didn't know what he meant. Then she realized that she was fighting knowing and did not resist as he came closer, in fact she placed her hands at his hips to help. Soon he was near enough to whisper, "Anything you want. All for you. Use me."

As he undressed her, he discouraged her doing anything in return, shaking his head or murmuring "No" when she as much as raised a hand to touch him. She felt she was being prepared—anointed, that was the word—for some ceremony, saw herself in a Roman movie scene, a princess stripped, bathed, and placed naked under robes by female slaves. In that case, though, they would have been careful how they handled her, not wishing to offend—and, moaning, Owen was stroking and kissing every inch of her he could after he removed her one good white (un-ironed) shirt, then her bra, her skirt, and, as he placed her with her help upon his—slightly cold—leather couch, her underwear (it had been too warm that morning to wear tights).

Still fully dressed, he moved down her, and she spread her legs, not sure but daring to assume that's what he wanted. Then he said softly but she was almost sure, "I want to lick the alphabet on your clit," and that's what he did, speaking each letter before he formed it (with surprising efficiency) upon and across her, something she suspected *he* had seen in a porn film, but a good and imaginative one that she had missed. By the time he licked the three lines for the stems or the arms or whatever they were called of the "E," she came, feeling more naked even than she was, though this was how he'd wanted her; she was only obeying him by allowing him to submit, or something.

Then he laid his head against her thigh, breathing with what seemed like relief that he had actually had an effect on anyone, made an impact—that he might be remembered by someone for doing something. She didn't dare to reach down and touch his head (the grey hair of which she now decided she liked, without knowing why), though it was her impulse to at least acknowledge how good he'd made her feel. Soon he had recovered and was undressing himself, moving her gently (again with her subtle assistance) so that she lay beneath him. "So big and beautiful," she thought he whispered, though she wasn't positive and couldn't say "What?" because that would be weird, given what was going on—though she was curious, wanted to hear the compliment. She realized he already had a condom, was taking care of everything, was supremely adept at assisting—her sexual valet in a sense, her "man" as they called it in old comedies about butlers, and the word had so many meanings now, she thought, as he entered her, and she realized she was sort of babbling to herself, because she was so nervous and so aroused. As he pushed into her, he knew what she wanted though he hardly knew *her*; he was catering to her, customizing her account, as it were, her AOL or whatever, in bed. Soon she stopped feeling guilty about giving nothing and decided to go along, for that's what he wanted, to enjoy being on the receiving end, *accepting* now an action in a way it had never been before.

That he was acting for himself *and* for her—that he was aware of what effect each push was having, that *her* pleasure caused *his*—was something new. She thought of someone rowing and how the digging of his oar into the ocean moved his boat, rippled the water, and built the muscle in the rower's arm, a seamless situation. Now *she* was the water, or merely made of water, and when he pushed into her, he was, well, not like the oar exactly, but like an entire man disappearing into a wave, which was her. She now knew what "so excited" meant, and it was different from what she had pretended it meant with Martin, when it had meant nothing, when it had been something from a porn film and bullshit.

"Oh, my God," she said helplessly as he pushed particularly hard and pressed the front of his abdomen (which she noticed was flatter than Martin's, despite his being so much older—fifteen or forty-five years—though she had only briefly glimpsed Martin's soft stomach through his unzipped and partly pulled down pants) against her clitoris. She thought of a dolphin, as if she was still in an ocean, and how it butted against you or something when it liked you and you swam with it. He (or maybe just his erection) was like a strong and slippery dolphin, rock hard but really responsive, and making that little chirping radar sound, which she now realized was coming from her own open mouth.

"It's good, it's good," she said, and again she hadn't meant to say anything at all.

Then, suddenly, he stopped moving, obviously could move no more without ending everything, which meant that she was on, it was up to her. Instinctively she wrapped around him, inside and outside: outside with her arms—and inside she had never known she had such flexibility, like when you realize you can bend a finger back all the way without breaking it, only this was better. She had never known that she could be tender with a grown man, not just her baby sister or her old kitty cat Monkey, kissing and kissing them—she was *passionate*, that's what she was, and why had it been embarrassing to say before now?

Coming with him felt like (she could not stop comparing things; it made her feel safer to do it, put things in perspective so she wouldn't feel she had entered an environment alien and disorienting—it was still her own life, she had not gone insane, you know?) that trick where the magician pulls out a tablecloth and all the plates stay put: she was the tablecloth, the table, *and* the plates. And he came, too, immediately after, or actually during, though she suspected he'd started a little ahead of her, could feel him doing that pulsing that of course came from his heart and had been weaker in her hand when it came from Martin. And Owen's sound was bigger: Martin's was like air going out of a balloon and Owen's was like one bursting, like a whole float in, say, the Puerto Rican Day Parade, or he was a terrorist exploding himself along with everything else, and she had made him into one. That was so exciting that it made her come again, or maybe it was just the end of her first orgasm, an aftershock, like they say there are in earthquakes.

"I can't stop," she said, and perhaps that was another trick, because she wanted it to continue and thought saying that might be the spell to make it so.

Then he placed his lips against her temple, where her hair was wet and slightly stuck to the area above her ear. Would he say he loved her? She didn't think he did; she didn't love *him*—she didn't fool herself, she wasn't a baby. Maybe she wanted him to say it so she could feel superior, could feel less than he and so more in control. (She had read once that the young are more powerful in young-old affairs, because, well, they live longer. But what about her uncle's second wife who was twenty years younger and who died first? Who was more powerful then? Her uncle, obviously, who was still alive.) Soon she didn't care about creating distance. She found herself kissing him, too, his cheek, which was not unshaven but getting there with the night coming on; things were changing, growing all the time, and now she knew it, this was proof.

Her boss had wanted to work for *her*, and that was what he had done; he had not been lying, been, what was the word, rhetorical, and that made her want to serve him—not serve, that was subordinate and not what she meant—to give to him, to know what he knew, to get pleasure by giving pleasure, to feel the connection or current, the wet finger in the spilled liquid that was then stuck into a socket, only good and shocking, not bad.

She took him into her mouth even though he protested, weakly, that this was not for him but only for her, tried to insist and sincerely, not coyly, not to get what he pretended not to want. But she wouldn't listen and soon, her breasts intentionally squashed against his leg, she kissed at the grey pubic hairs she had not noticed on him before (and which, for reasons she could not articulate, excited her in a new and discombobulating way). It was only seconds after she started, sort of forced him to experience it, had hardly moved her mouth on him, was just getting ready to do her stuff, or figure out what stuff would do the trick for him, that he came. More than melting in her mouth (as crass girls in college called it), he seemed to completely disappear, his head tilting back, his eyes closing, his arms laid flat, his hands opening as if going under in that ocean again—or better, being pushed off a cliff by coming. It almost scared her. She suddenly knew how lonely he had been and yet he hadn't used it against her but *for* her, had wanted to deny himself until she wouldn't let him anymore (or was the denial his way of getting over the guilt of sleeping with a young girl who was his employee? If he got nothing, in other words, what had he done wrong? He would be a kind of sex saint).

But then she didn't care what was his way to explain it to himself, was just glad that she had given him this, given him *something*—God knows she gave him nothing at the job—and soon he seemed to reappear, to float up to the surface again and exist, and she moved to lie against him. He buried his face in her sweaty neck, maybe ashamed of how much he had shown of himself, uneasy about how much she knew him now, though she liked knowing him—he knew *her*, so why not?—secretly wanted to know him more, to know everything, even though she suspected that it would be impossible, would probably never happen, that this was as close as they would ever get, this instant, this afternoon.

—~—

Isabel didn't see Owen often after this. Only once did they meet in his house, when his wife was away. While Isabel was there, the door to the bedroom stayed closed, and she could imagine how its dark (was it oak?) wood might have to him a vexing and mysterious power—intergalactic or timeless or whatever it had been in the film—if always in that position. They used a den but mostly stayed in the bathroom, where he washed her slowly in the shower, aroused as he always was by fulfilling a function, being employed, even if the need was one he had created in her. She did *need* him now, just wanted him, had had trouble waiting for him from the time they entered his home. Otherwise, they met in his office whenever they could, for he had obligations, and—without saying so, without saying much of anything—they both regarded their time together as a gift, could not be greedy for more, just had to be grateful.

Isabel barely spoke to Martin now. Her duties seemed less stultifying, filled as they were with subtext, the numbers on her screen changed into symbols of longing found on another planet or formed in the future. But Martin seemed even more frustrated. Isabel could hear him sighing from where he sat, and she believed it was both for her benefit and a genuine expression of dismay. She was sorry for him but not guilty, no matter how much she thought she ought to be.

One dusk, both were alone in the elevator going down, though she usually avoided exiting the building with him. They rode in silence until, a few floors from the lobby, Martin spoke a rare, completed sentence.

"I know that you go with him," he said.

Isabel started, and the little bell rang as they hit the ground floor, seeming to underline his remark. She didn't respond, only walked quickly ahead and away from him, but she knew that things were different, had entered a new phase; she could feel it, and he had made it happen.

The next day in the office, Martin kept on talking to her in the same clear voice he had either always had or acquired for the occasion, feeling he had no alternative.

"Why don't you tell me about doing it with him?" he said.

Isabel didn't answer, just kept looking as if interested at her screen, though she knew it was absurd to try and fool him in this way.

"I want to hear about you and him," he said, and his voice conveyed at once the sincere need to please himself and punish her, which was new; before he may have been selfish but not unkind.

Isabel turned to see him and he didn't avoid her, kept staring at her as he had been the whole time. Her response was reflexive, though this reflex was also new.

"I won't," she said, and saw him appear shocked, not because she had officially ended something between them, she didn't think, but because he was being denied something obviously available: brand-new information that would no doubt be exciting and could have been given to him easily, as if newspapers were being thrown from a boy's bike onto everybody's lawn but his.

As Isabel pushed by him to leave early (being privileged by her association with Owen, she did not need to explain herself), she realized that Martin had always thought her stories were true, and this made her feel differently about him, though in what way she wasn't sure.

—∞—

For a few days, to Isabel's relief, they sat in virtual silence. Finally, Martin addressed her on their way into a meeting, among a crowd in which it would be hard for her to reply.

"I told her," he said.

"What do you mean?" she whispered back. "Who?"

"His wife. About you and him. I left a message on their machine."

Isabel stopped, bumped by another employee trying to get past. Waiting to be alone with him in the hall, she reached out and grabbed Martin, got hold of his shirt, which she nearly ripped and which he yanked back, annoyed, so she wouldn't. They stood there staring at each other, Isabel nearly shaking with rage both at him and her own inarticulateness; it was as if, with a few words, he had taken *everything* away.

Martin didn't look triumphant; he seemed shaken, even shocked by her reaction. He then grew apologetic and stammered, reverting to his old, un-socialized self.

"I-I-I had to do something," he said at last.

—∞—

This was right before the weekend. On Monday, Isabel arrived late and Martin was already there. He sat faced away, his complexion pale, his chin in his palm, the computer screen before him blank. Was he sick again, she wondered? Or just afraid to acknowledge her?

Soon she noticed a general absence of people around. When she looked out in the hall, many doors were shut, others open to reveal no one but a briefcase or bag hastily, even indifferently tossed in a corner or on a chair. It was like a science fiction film in which a plague breaks out—or a bomb drops—that kills people but not things. She wondered if a meeting had been called without her knowing, but now that she knew Owen, she was always in the loop.

Isabel walked out and after a few steps began passing others. All were either heading toward Owen's office or returning from having been there. There was a feeling of people drifting to and from a crime scene or a free outdoor concert at which some were turned away. Isabel could not remember there ever being this kind of purposeful movement in the office, such urgency, concern, and curiosity. Had the company been sold? Owen been fired? One woman was in tears. Isabel heard someone say, "I can't believe it," and another, "They found him in his house," and a third, somewhat snottily, "I would have thought it would have been his wife."

Isabel began running through the hall, her feeling of fear in action, and soon was nearly flying. She knew that if Owen's door was closed, it would be bad news—or would it be if his door was open and people were in his office crying the way she was not yet allowing herself to cry?

Now she was running faster than anyone ever should inside, with too much speed to be contained in the office, as if she were about to burst out of it at any instant. And it was true: she would be, in a way, exploded into life by death as soon as she rounded the corner at the end of the hall.

THE SON HE NEVER HAD

Weeks after he came home from Florida, Ben looked at a picture of his son. He had never thought he would approve of someone being punished, especially in such an extreme way. He had never approved of any kind of punishment, not the corporeal kind certainly, not even spanking, when he had been a young enough parent for it to matter.

Ben's son Alan, though, *had* seen him as punitive, not physically but emotionally, when he had been young, young*er*, a college student, at the age to be cruel and accusing in order to separate himself from his parents—or so Ben had read in a self-help book, in order to soothe his rattled nerves after twenty-year-old Alan had lashed out at him ("Don't you see what you're doing to me?" In public, no less, in a restaurant. "Don't you see how it fucking makes me feel?"). Ben had driven home, shaken, after the whole horrible evening—driven only with his wife, Miriam, for Alan had escaped into the night on foot, worrying his mother, who was also worried about Ben's driving. "Alan's at that age, he doesn't know what he's saying," she said, though she was clearly upset herself. "Watch where you're going, you won't solve anything by getting us killed."

It was all painfully ironic now, of course—the car, the reference to death—because of what had happened: Alan at thirty getting killed in an accident, his car crashed into by a driver making an illegal left turn. Ben had flown to Florida to collect the body, Miriam being unable to accept the event enough to accompany him. The two were old enough now that their emotional characters had coalesced, both totally disoriented by what had occurred.

In truth, while time had shaved away some of Ben's horror about Alan's old outburst (he believed he had always loved and encouraged the boy), he was no more knowledgeable about it now, just old enough to close himself off to upsetting events as a way of not confronting them. It was an energy thing, an adjustment to the depletion of his energy with age. He had no more wisdom about it in the airplane flying over Florida, staring out at clouds as if they were his life experiences: amorphous, passing quickly, and helplessly navigated through.

Ben refused to consider how he would respond to seeing the body, as others might have done, and so he wasn't afraid. The plane even had a rough landing—he heard a few people cry and at least one pray—but he never doubted that he would get there alive, fell asleep in fact as they descended, and was only awakened by the bump as the wheels hit the tarmac. Everything was all right as he had assumed—not even imagined—it would be.

Then there was the cab ride, the air from the open window feeling so pure and warm (so unlike New York) that he found himself smiling as it brushed his face, like his mother's fingers when he was small. He had even asked the cabbie to please turn off the air conditioning—something he never liked, not even at home in hot weather, it was bad for the environment, which left Miriam miserable in the summer and having to take an Ambien at night; he had never taken a pill to sleep in his life. He was sorry to see the trip end, because the air felt suddenly hot and unhealthy when they stopped at the hospital. The cabbie's fingers were wet when he handed Ben his change; it had been stifling the whole time, apparently, and Ben had not noticed.

When Ben looked up at the hospital, he thought that his son might still be inside and alive: it was a place for those sick but surviving. Then he remembered he was meant to go to the morgue, which was in the basement, and he tried without success to shake off the last speck of hope inside him, the way people brush leaves from their clothes after sitting on the ground and one little stem or stalk still sticks to them.

Then there was the walk down the basement hall to the morgue, during which Ben diverted himself by remembering the last time he had been to Florida, twenty years earlier with his family. He was able to see in his head the hotel marquee advertising the comic playing there—now world-famous, but then just starting out. The image also included a painful slice of his young son off to the side, dressed as a space robot, a costume he endearingly wore almost everywhere back then (when he and his son were such pals, before Alan had inexplicably screamed at him), and so he stopped thinking of that and concentrated instead on counting the clicks that his and the attendant's shoes made on the waxed floor before they reached the morgue door.

When the drawer was pulled out and the blue sheet pulled down, Ben closed his eyes—discreetly, so the attendant wouldn't notice. He told himself it was unnecessary, the ritual was archaic (why make it "official"? Who needed to know?), and said, "Yes, that's him," quickly, though not so quickly that it would seem perfunctory. Then he heard the sheet being replaced and the drawer closed, squeaking, he noticed—it needed oiling, the hospital should look into that—and opened his eyes again.

Suddenly panicked, he realized it could have been *anyone* he had identified as Alan. For a second, Ben thought that it might have all been a mistake—it wasn't Alan, Alan was still alive. (And so wasn't it irresponsible to misidentify the young man really there? He probably had parents, too.) Then he stopped thinking that, for it was part of the hope still stuck to him that he had wished to forget.

And it didn't matter anyway, for soon he was handed a plastic bag of his son's belongings—wallet, keys, and cell phone—with a label containing Alan's name visible on it. Unless this was another mistake—if the hospital couldn't oil its own drawers, maybe it could mislabel its—then he stopped thinking that, too. (These ideas seemed to have come from someone else's voice in his head—Miriam's voice, for she was the one always saying foolishly hopeful things, and now that she wasn't there he was creating her comments himself, having grown used to them and needing them now. So he turned down the other voice but didn't silence it, the way he merely lowered the volume but didn't mute the television when Miriam kept talking during baseball games.)

When Ben looked down at the plastic bag, he was surprised by the quality of Alan's possessions—the actual leather of his wallet, the best and most up-to-date phone. He wondered: had the cops been tempted to steal what they found on him, the way cops sometimes screwed hookers when they arrested them? As a kid, Ben remembered having little respect for cops, secretly felt *less* safe when he saw them on the bad-part-of Brooklyn streets—thought they *caused* trouble by their presence, that their swaggering power was a provocation. But maybe he was only remembering this now because he was being transported to the police station in the back of a squad car, and so suddenly he was thinking like a criminal or a "perp."

He was surprised by how hostile he felt about the tree stump-like head of the cop in the front seat. When he found himself using the words "fuck you" in his fantasy, he stopped, deciding he'd had enough—"fun" wasn't the right word—whatever it was, for the day.

"Air conditioning okay?" the cop asked, after he turned it on.

"Sure," Ben lied, feeling a little self-conscious about his secret, aggressive emotions.

He looked out the window, at nondescript malls and patches of scrubby, unsold lots of land—and at gated communities, too, at developments where you had to have money to move in—and he thought of his son, who could apparently afford to use this state as a hideaway or weekend getaway from New York or whatever he had considered it, who had done better than his old man. But wasn't that the way it was supposed to go? Ben had only heard inklings of this through other family members, because Alan had never shared any of it with him—not money, of course, which Ben wouldn't have accepted even if he'd needed it, but his pleasure at *making* money, at accomplishing anything. Alan acted as if his achieving whatever he had and keeping his distance had been a way of avenging himself on Ben—but for what? For whatever Alan had yelled at him about in that restaurant so long ago, that's what. Alan had never *stopped* yelling, in a sense, by never coming around (only keeping up with Miriam, occasionally), not even to flaunt himself, to say, I can afford to go to Florida every weekend now, what do you think about *that*?

Suddenly the air conditioning reminded Ben of the morgue, of being trapped in a box, still conscious, alone with thoughts he didn't want to have, and he found himself pushing desperately at the button on the car door to lower the window. Warm air rushed in like water that didn't drown but allowed you to escape. It was as if he were trapped in the car underwater with the windows closed (something he feared so much that he always read articles about it when it happened to someone, learning you were supposed to open the windows as your car flew off a bridge into a river *before* you landed and went under, so you could swim out and survive. But who would ever have the wherewithal to do that, he wondered. Would *he*?), fat tears upon his face as if that water were splashed all over him.

"Okay, here we are," the cop said, glancing in his rear view at Ben.

He was taken into the station and sat before a second cop, one with a crew cut who spoke in a funny, somewhat southern accent (Ben hadn't been aware there was such a thing in Florida). He privately translated the odd pronunciations ("Flahida" for "Florida," "fand" for "find," and "tahmes" for "times") so he would not feel hostile toward him, still feeling weird about pretending to buck the first cop in his mind and eager for this one's help. So he could say that Alan was still alive? Would showing him respect cause that to happen? There were fewer gaps now between the arrival of troubling thoughts, like stacked-up planes or birds—no, bugs, he had to bat more of them away like it was an infestation—and it made Ben feel small and helpless, which he hated more than anything else.

"First of all, my condolences," said the cop ("Braun" was the name on his, well, brawny chest). Ben was appreciative of that, because the cop seemed discreet about expressing emotion, as opposed to being gushy. He told Ben about the accident tactfully, but not sparing him any details: how the other driver had hit Alan's car probably while he was texting, something which Ben didn't do and didn't understand why anyone would do—especially while driving. It was an assessment Braun seemed to share, or so the disapproving tone he used on the word "texting" implied, which drew the men closer; Braun even leaned in, conspiratorially.

"He was driving a Toyota," the cop said, offering information but also passing judgment: he knew the kind of car that Alan was driving (a Lexus) and thought it was "Ironic that his car was hit by the other car, because they hardly belonged on the same road—one car cost so much more and handled so much better than the other it was like a bum accidentally knocked a tycoon off a curb into a street and he—the tycoon—was then run over by a bus. Why were they even walking on the same block, you know?"

It was a rhetorical question. Then Braun pulled out a page that contained two digital mug shots. Seeing the other driver's face confirmed the unfairness of it all to the cop, confirmed that the two men had had no business being together on the same stretch of street. No wonder it had ended in disaster.

"This is the guy," the cop said with disbelief. "Mel Tremaine."

It was true: Mel Tremaine was, well, there were no other words for what he was but white trash: a pony-tailed, pock-marked, sad-eyed example of lower-class, biker-style American man, with one of those patches of blond hair pocketed beneath his lip, in a place that seemed vaguely pubic and—threatening, Ben thought. It was a little way to say, "I'm the underside of the world, but you don't have to turn something over to see me—I'm looking right at you." This kind of person had killed his son? Negligently, while texting—who? His girlfriend who was also his "baby mama"? (Ben sometimes couldn't help seeing the awful reality shows that Miriam inexplicably liked, and like it or not, this was one of the insensitive expressions they had introduced him to.) This realization was so disorienting that Ben felt literally unsteady in his seat. The cop reached out to keep him from falling, but at the same time handed him the printout of the pictures as a keepsake—and why would any parent want them, for God's sake? Wasn't he being clueless and inconsiderate?

"I'm okay," Ben said, grasping to keep a page falling from his fingers onto the floor.

The cop appeared shaken after seeing Ben go pale. He aggressively assured the older man that "The book will be thrown at this guy," with charges ranging from texting while operating a motor vehicle to misdemeanour death by motor vehicle, and maybe even involuntary manslaughter.

"Because your son," Braun said with what he meant to be solicitousness, "was a very successful man. He contributed. He wasn't like this—character that killed him. He still had many things to achieve. He was far from finished. If only it had been the other way around, there would have been a lot less . . . loss."

Ben was trying to listen over the new voice that he was hearing now, which was Alan's in that restaurant so long ago (his head felt like a North Korean home where propaganda was on the radio twenty-four hours a day and couldn't be turned off). He remembered now that Alan had accused Ben that night of hiding behind "judgmental decency" and "self-righteous sanctimonious liberalism" in order to discourage his son's ambitions; he'd acted as if Alan wanting to achieve so much was immoral, might hurt others, was a question of fairness, when it was really only him—Ben—being competitive, not wanting to be out-shone by his son, wanting to keep Alan at his—Ben's—own second-rate and mediocre level of life (which was a middle-class Long Island existence as opposed to being *really* rich). Braun's voice grew louder as Alan's grew just as loud inside Ben's head: "Your son was who the country was made for, not this—freeloader. How'd this guy even afford the phone he was texting on? There should be a higher penalty for killing someone better than you, for taking a person of great accomplishment out of the world and leaving yourself in his place with absolutely nothing to offer." Ben realized that, years before, he might have *defended* such a person as Tremaine to Alan, seen him as worthy not just of sympathy but help, *his* help, just the kind of "liberal" judgment that had infuriated Alan, that he had equated with Ben's discouragement of him—and being discouraged by his father, Alan had said that night and Ben now remembered, felt like he was eliminating him, killing him, his own son! "*His* father should be ashamed. But *you*, my friend, have got a lot to be proud of." Alan's voice and the cop's were merging now, saying the same things, the things that Alan had said in the restaurant, and now there was only one voice: Braun's had become Alan's, though the cop didn't seem to know it, was starting to tidy up as if making to move on. Had he been mortified by what he had been saying, even screaming? Now that he had had finished and fallen silent, Ben wasn't sure if Braun had said anything at all: maybe it had been Alan's voice in his head the whole time.

—∾—

The first cop drove Ben to the hotel where Alan had been staying, where he always stayed on these weekends away. With a slight Spanish accent he said a swift goodbye, wearing a sympathetic expression (or was Ben imagining that, too, and the cop just couldn't wait to be gone?).

Ben looked up at the hotel, a huge corporate monstrosity as metallic as a giant robot or a great big tank set up on its side, that's what it looked like to him. (He preferred cozy, modest bed and breakfasts, the communal dining rooms full of small talk, which Miriam couldn't abide but which he enjoyed; he found it calming, a way to connect to others by—call them clichés if you like—shared simplicity and a lack of pretension.)

He identified himself and asked the pretty but plastic girl at the desk for Alan's room key. She gave it to him without question, clearly knowing what had happened, looking at him, he was sure this time, with—it went past sympathy—pity, which he didn't like, which made him feel diminished.

"The room's already paid for, as usual—the whole weekend," she said, throwing him a bone, offering him a perk (what would it make up to him?). He only winced a thank you. (See, this was why he favoured smaller hotels; no one would have said such a thing.)

Alan's room had a "Do Not Disturb" sign on the doorknob. It was a lavish suite, all marble, steel, and leather on a top floor with a wraparound view of the beach—a secret and superior view, a surveillance of it from a safe height, Ben thought. When he walked into the bedroom, he saw that Alan's clothes were still strewn everywhere. They were good clothes, too, even Ben knew and he knew nothing about clothes: a cashmere sweater chucked onto the rug, a pair of khaki slacks bunched at the foot of the bed as if just kicked off. Black socks and a pair of blue underwear had been stepped out of and dumped on the threshold of the bathroom, the light of which had been left on, as if Alan had been getting every ounce, inch—cent!—from the huge room that he could, milking it while he might. Ben turned off the light, saving someone money—if not Alan anymore, who?

He sat on the edge of a reclining chair, not comfortable with easing into it, feeling unwelcome, to be honest. The whole size and feel of the place reminded him of Alan's outburst in the restaurant, the room more of Alan's revenge on him, a thing he now horribly understood. Ben tried but couldn't literally blink the thought away.

He hadn't reserved another room for himself anywhere, or a car—the cops had been kind enough to chauffeur him, for a while, anyway—and that was unusual, because he always had while travelling (if he and Miriam went from one town to another on a vacation, he even booked from the first place to the second; he never arrived anywhere unannounced—that was acting entitled). He hadn't been thinking, had barely made his flight on time and hadn't taken advantage of the reduced "compassion fare" available. Could he do it retroactively now and get the price lowered? Why would he even think of such a thing now, of saving money? Well, the room had *made* him think of it, because money was what the room was all about, what Alan had been—he didn't complete the thought, yet he couldn't stop. The room didn't remind Ben of shelter or comfort but just of money, bills flung from the window onto the beach, money landing on spit-white water and drifting into the distance, away from land and human hands, eaten by birds and fish, nourishing no one, wasted.

Then, in the carpet as if he had conjured it, he saw actual cash: dollars casually dropped there like Alan's drawers but looking more like—what, poisonous weeds that were flourishing in its fringe? He heard a faint, monotonous voice and realized the radio had been left on, tuned to a twenty-four-hour financial network giving international stock updates, constantly, indifferently, as if someone insane were talking behind you at the movies and wouldn't stop.

The bed was unmade, rumpled—do not disturb. Feeling a sudden crushing weariness, Ben was tempted to fall onto it. It seemed so soft—was it silk? Something expensive, he didn't know. He noticed a squeezed-out tube curled in its covers like an infant or a pin-up in a men's magazine. When he squinted, he realized it was one of those lotions, jellies or creams for easier—fucking. He remembered opening Alan's door without knocking when he was a teenager and finding him with a girl on the bed—she was wearing only a bra and blue jeans, big breasts—and while Alan yelled Ben had closed the door, and neither mentioned it ever again; he hadn't remembered it until now, looking at the lotion (she was one of so many girls Alan had—used, use the word—a way of behaviour which hadn't been fair to them; Ben had never been with anyone but Miriam). Then, tipped forward in the chair as he had been in the police station (the cop hadn't been compassionate, just fawning and overbearing—an asshole, like most cops, admit it), still not wishing to sit back into the overpriced cushion, Ben fell asleep. His head bowed as if praying or paying his respects, though he was doing neither, the word "escape" the last thing he thought before falling as unconscious as his son, though for him it was only temporary.

—~—

Ben was awakened by a heartbeat loud enough that it filled the entire room, as if his son's stopped heart had restarted and grown big enough to be everywhere around him. Then he realized it was music—loud music, even though muffled by the ceiling and the carpet in the room above him. Ben could mostly hear—feel—the bass, which thumped constantly and pitilessly, as if an incantation meant to drive away demons (or just other hotel guests—less wealthy ones, like Ben).

Ben groggily considered phoning the front desk and threatening to call the cops, something which he'd heard big hotel people hated, for it was bad for business (they'd actually put an end to a party in another room to avoid it). Then he asked himself: what did *he* care? It wasn't *his* room. Alan would probably have enjoyed the horrible music, would have been inspired to use more of his—jelly—with the bass in the background, egging him on to—use it on himself? Or on who? Some victimized woman he paid for, probably. Ben hated thinking about it; it sickened him for so many reasons. He rose and picked up the phone, not to call the desk but to get local information; then he hung up before anybody answered, remembering that you were practically charged for *looking* at a phone in such a place, and who would pay? (What did it even mean, "the weekend was paid for," when the renter was dead?) He used his own cell phone, feeling independent, free of corporate fees, and dialled "Free 411," then had to listen to ads, found it wasn't free after all—nothing and no one ever was in this goddamn country—before he was told by the recorded operator Mel Tremaine's address.

Ben asked the new person at the desk (a buff corporate type, squeezed into a suit so tight it looked like a big, blue, body-sized tattoo) to call him a cab, a weird request for so late at night, he knew (it was about three A.M.), but hotel people were used to it, or paid to be discreet, right? This "dude" stared at him with openly amused curiosity, either because he was too smug just to do his (potentially useful) job or because Ben was too old to be behaving so oddly (sweating like a drug addict and speaking at an unnatural speed, because he hadn't eaten all day, not even the nuts on the plane).

"There you go," the young man said, barely able to keep from laughing (or was Ben imagining all *this*, also?) when the cab arrived.

Ben had no plan for what he would do when he arrived at Tremaine's place. It was, he noticed without surprise, in a tacky part of town full of condemned tract houses, the worst kinds of fast food chains (what was "Mojo's"?), which were still open, and more stray animals than humans at this hour. When the driver stopped at the house, Ben saw it was no better and even marginally worse than the ones beside it, dumps protected by barred windows the way they were in movies about tragic and gang-infested ghettos Ben had seen on HBO.

"I'll be back," he said. "There'll be a few more bucks in it for you."

The driver agreed to wait, probably wanting to see what Ben would actually do. (Get out? Here? This guy?) Ben left the car and approached the path, at first refusing to even glance around for fear of seeing who was there, yet unable to keep from advancing. With every step, he grew less uneasy, until he felt calm, safe, and among his own kind.

When he reached the door, he froze, not from fear but fascination. The cab's front bulbs had caught and pinned him like a prison spotlight. They had also exposed the sign on the door's gated grill. It was a foreclosure notice issued by the company that Alan had worked for.

—∾—

Ben flew back to New York with the mug shots the cop had given him folded neatly in a side pocket of his suitcase. When he got home, he called the Florida police department, learned when Mel Tremaine's first court appearance would be, then wired money for his bail. Ben fully expected the accused would not be allowed to leave the state, and he questioned whether he had the stomach to return, or felt he could or should leave Miriam alone, for there was no way she would come.

In the weeks ahead, he kept the newspapers from Miriam, though he needn't have bothered: she was still interested in virtually nothing and slept most of her days away. (Ben wondered why they hadn't made a greater effort to have a second child after Miriam's miscarriage; he tried to stop and to forget he'd even wondered, but he could not.)

Sometimes, if Public Radio was on, the name of Alan's company would come up; it could not be avoided as its selling of so many faulty mortgages, and the resulting foreclosures, was often the lead story. But Miriam never seemed to register it, or at least made no comment and gave not even a glance at Ben.

So it was up to Ben alone to keep watch. He rarely turned off cable news, checked online as often as someone decades younger. He was relieved to see no mention of the car accident and no description of it being not *accidental* at all but intentional, a punishment, the stalking and assassination of someone wealthy and predatory—though didn't "assassination" apply just to world leaders? No, he remembered, they had said it about John Lennon years ago. And anyway, there was no evidence anyone had been meant to be *killed* by the car, just banged up, warned, and scared a little.

After it seemed no more news would be reported on a given day, Ben would go to bed, relieved that at least for now there wouldn't be worse charges for Tremaine than the ones the cop, Braun, had predicted.

As time went on and still nothing else came out in the media, Ben allowed himself to breathe easier, to actually expect nothing worse would happen—that no other shoe, as the expression went, would drop.

—∾—

One afternoon, his wife still asleep, Ben wandered into the living room. He stopped and looked at the family pictures on the piano (an instrument

Miriam used to play beautifully but which she had been abandoning in stages even before the accident). Feeling a little lighter, with something from him lifted, he picked up a snapshot taken on a bridge above the Thames on their first family trip to Europe.

His son was then about twelve, already starting to leave childhood but still waiting to enter adolescence, where temptation and rebellion awaited. He certainly was a long way from where he was today, living uneasily as an adult, restless and with a self-destructive anger, as well as a ponytail, a "soul patch," and—though Ben wasn't sure, could only imagine—tattoos. The sense that he had failed as a parent overwhelmed Ben now, but before he could bury the feeling—for otherwise it would bury *him*—he experienced a rush of self-justification. How much more could he have done? He had not beaten, molested, or otherwise harmed the boy. Were we not responsible for ourselves, all alone in the world? And what did we really know about what anyone did and why?

Then—this idea not keeping the other upsetting one at bay—Ben felt something new, his fingers pressing tighter and tenderly around the frame of the photo. He secretly felt (and don't tell Miriam, though she never listened to him about anything now) proud of Mel, for even if the boy had taken a violent turn—turned the wheel for the wrong reason, not to get somewhere but to get *back* at someone—at least he had done it in a righteous cause, to defend those who went without and to punish those who took from them, like the rich young man killed in the other car. This idea, misguided as it was, had been good and was, Ben knew as he pressed his lips to the boy's face behind the glass, one that he had instilled in him. He had not failed, it turned out, as Mel's father.

Ben would take the car to do some shopping—Miriam had done nothing for days; there wasn't even coffee in the house. As he left the house, he saw a sign upon the door he hadn't noticed, even that morning when picking up the paper. The notice might have upset others, but it made him smile. It said: "Foreclosed." It was the truest sign of solidarity with his son, gave him a total sense of identification with him, with someone else in the world. He left the door ajar.

Then Ben drove, forgetting where he was headed, wondering: whom might he hit? Who might hit him? Who would be guilty or had been all along? He would never know the answers, and neither, he thought, would anyone else on the Earth.

HOME INVASION

He didn't know that someone was inside his home; he sensed it, the way you sense when you're coming down with a cold, a subtle shift in how you feel, like fatigue or a stuffed nose (his usually started with a pain in his left ear).

When he stopped being utterly disoriented by the idea, he found that he was afraid in a way he had never been before. (And wasn't being disoriented a way not to feel afraid, to replace it with a more acceptable emotion? He thought he'd seen a report about that once.) Living isolated for so long had sharpened his perception of any alteration in his routine, even in the routine "aura" of his apartment, yet it had also given him no way to adjust to change, and certainly no way to accept it: there was no explanation that wouldn't be awful; no one would have broken in with *good news*, would they?

Quickly, surprising himself, he segued to a preservational instinct, a desire to beat back any threat—not to himself but to his "roommate," a word he had never thought to use even ironically, but one which he now employed to give himself a perceivable "companion" to protect, a conventional sense of someone he could save. The image was invigorating or at least less paralysing than fear. He found it even enlivened him physically, made him swell his chest as if in anticipation of a fight, the way he'd seen athletes in stories "suck it up." Whoever was hiding—lurking, that was the word—in his apartment (and now he swore he not just sensed but actually saw the shadow of someone scramble across the floor) would have *him* to contend with!

Daring to move, he made his way to where the potential target of the intruder was. He stood sentry-like before the object he suspected was about to be damaged or destroyed by his uninvited guest.

But why would he, she, they want to do anything to the Centre? (Centrepiece was, of course, its full name, "Centre" being one of the many nicknames others had invented for it, not out of affection necessarily, but simply from restlessness that resulted from always having to use one name for something so ubiquitous in human life, the nicknames ranging from "Centre" to "CP" to "Ciece" to the "Erp" or the "Earpiece," depending on the mood and maybe the age of the speaker. He was middle-aged, typical, and somewhat timid, so he always used the most common and least comic "Centre.") He had long since forgotten the meaning of the name, how it described the *central* place it took in people's lives, yet as he considered whether to use the thing to call for help, he was reminded of the totality of the Centre's functions and this made him reconsider the intruder's designs. She—and it was a she, he was suddenly sure; there had been something about the small shape of the darting figure—wanted to *steal* his Centre, not disable it. And realizing this gave him a new clue to her identity, or at least the kind of person she was.

Who else would want to swipe it but someone who didn't have one, who lived outside, underprivileged, "at risk," or whatever they called it, deprived of all that the Centre could provide? On Centre talk shows, he had often heard of break-ins committed by these types—urban legends abounded about them, some describing committed atrocities so awful they could only be apocryphal (or were they?)—and now it had actually happened to *him*. It was hard to believe—yet now he heard the sound of steps in the near distance, barely audible as if taken by bare feet (which would make sense, for these "outsiders" had no money—or shoes—dispensed by a Centre), dragging toxins or whatever all over his polished floor. This made him even more afraid—no, angry, and that gave him more energy.

Now he channelled (which was an unconscious pun, given the dialled adjustments on the Centre) his anger into indignation, for the break-in was making him late to work, even though, of course, he made his own hours working for the Centre and filed his own time card at the end of the pay period to get his groceries, medicines, etc., from it. This gave him a new thing to feel—high dudgeon—instead of fear.

"Okay!" he yelled, blocking the Centre's screen just in case she suddenly jumped out. "Let's do this! You and me!"

There was no response. He began to feel foolish, as if he'd imagined the whole thing. Then, slowly and it seemed timidly, a young woman peeked out from behind the packing crate for the new exercise bike he'd ordered from the Centre and hadn't yet thrown away. Her features were as small and delicate as a kitten's, her short hair crudely cut as if by her own hand with a rusty knife. She spoke a word he of course couldn't understand for she had not learned her language from a Centre. Yet the intensity of her tone and the tears she shed afterward made him perceive it to mean, "Help!"

That was the last he saw of her for a while. He didn't fool himself into thinking that she'd left: he heard her breathing heavily from her crate-hiding place whenever there was no other noise. In fact, that night, he kept all noises off—music or stories from the Centre—out of a perverse desire to be sure that she was still there. He didn't shift the crate and reveal her, in the way you kept a cereal box or a spoon in place to hide a cockroach you knew to be there, in order to timidly maintain the status quo—not to have to kill it, in other words. Was it this kind of compassion (or cowardice) that made him refrain from even reporting her now? Or had the sight of her and the sound of her frightened voice made her seem less intimidating? She wasn't there to rob him. Despite what he'd heard, there were apparently people from the outside who just got lost and stumbled their way inside, like that fly the other year, banging against a window it didn't know couldn't be open and which he had to kill with a rolled-up tax form sent by the Centre that he hadn't filled out.

It was more than that, of course: the woman's breathing was the first real sound of another human being that had ever been inside his home. So he listened to it rapt, as he might a professional singer on the Centre performing a hit that he himself had hummed. The sounds were sort of the same but completely different. And that's why he sat up, suddenly, in his chair, when her breathing stopped.

He realized that he had fallen asleep, lulled by her inhaling and exhaling. The silence awakened him like a warning.

He walked cautiously to the crate, but even after reaching it still heard nothing. With a foot, he knocked it to the side and saw, to his surprise—and he had to admit, relief—she was there. She was curled in a ball, her chest barely rising. He realized that she was wearing rags. While he'd been unconscious, she had not risen to secretly get food or even water from the Centre; a thin crust encircled her white lips.

With the first feeling of panic he'd had since she arrived—panic was different from fear—he ran back, hands shaking, and dialled the Centre's adjustment for dinner. Then he brought back his own favourite: fried chicken, peas, and a Diet Fresca. He left the steaming food near her nose, unwilling to so much as tap a part of her bony frame. As he pulled away, he was stopped—stunned—by a gesture of her own.

Her eyes still closed, the woman slowly reached out and took his hand in thanks. The second she glanced his palm, he felt a heat so savage that he began to scream, and black smoke wiggled from the circle of skin she had immediately burned away.

~

In the days ahead, he didn't pay much attention to his job or the countless distractions the Centre provided. He was more engrossed by the spectacle of the woman's reawakening, her growing less scrawny and stronger—her face, even her hair, filling out—as he tended to her. He even experimented with the kinds of meals he served, something he had never done by himself (the Salisbury steak with cooked carrots and Strawberry Yoo-hoo was one he'd have to remember).

Of course, he kept a distance from her, putting the plates down as if for a dog ever since their terrible encounter. She felt guilt she couldn't disguise (especially since she had remained unharmed) and smiled with obvious relief the day he put on a smaller Centre-dispensed bandage, forcing herself to stare as if as penance at the sphere of red wet welt that had replaced his palm and was only now starting to scab.

He thought she was being hard on herself. He didn't blame her. She didn't know—as neither could he—what effect the outside would have on those shut-in. Was it the air or whatever environment was out there? Or merely the contact itself for which he hadn't been prepared, against which he had never, like an infant, developed an immunity? He didn't know.

They couldn't discuss this, of course, having no common language. But that didn't stop her from talking anyway, once she started to recover, charmingly indifferent to his understanding, chattering away as if fully comprehended. He began to get an idea of what she was expressing—and she eventually added physical gestures, standing to mime swimming or fighting or struggling to do *something*. It was her own recent life story she was telling, he realized—how she had arrived by accident, fallen in and entered through some section of pipe that led to an air duct, maybe. It was a gripping tale, far better than anything that might have been on the Centre at the same time.

Also entertaining—and even moving—were the little tunes she softly hummed as both were starting to sleep, she still behind the box where she insisted on staying as if not deserving better accommodations. The music was not exactly what he was used to hearing on the Centre, but still interesting once you got used to it.

One day, he verbally admired the strange little bracelets (made of, what, shells? Stones?) strung around her wrists and ankles. She explained with a few words and concise movements that she'd made them herself—she sold them to others on the outside; it was her job. She was industrious—you could be out there. It was fascinating to him.

That night, he stayed awake as she slept. He watched her from his chair, a slice of her back visible from neck to knees behind the box. Her shirt—one of his own, actually; her ragged T-shirt now sat in a pile of his laundry waiting to be washed in the Centre—had ridden up, exposing the side of her bare waist, which was pale, freckled, and slightly fleshy now that she had begun and not ceased to eat. Fidgeting in his seat, he could not stop staring at it. The wound beneath his bandage began to itch, as if to warn him. He averted his eyes from her. Then he could not help it—he sprang up.

He approached the Centre. He set the adjustment and, three different times, made love to it—two times more than was his usual nightly practice. At the end of the last event, he lingered with his arm around it, thinking of it now as "Ciece," the friendliest and fondest of the nicknames, before going to sleep. He realized it was the first time, except to eat, he had used the Centre in days.

"Help?"

He spoke easily to her in his own language now, having realized that his tone of voice, facial expressions, and hand gestures would get his meaning across. He was holding up the crude bracelet he himself had made, responding to her—sometimes impatient—prompts on how to do it and using coins, buttons, paper clips, and parts of food containers for this purpose. After his request for aid, she was politely encouraging, but then opened her hand and wiggled her fingers to indicate that he should hand it over. Given that he hadn't had any of her materials—unknown to him and from the outside—he thought he'd done pretty well; however, after she in a few seconds rearranged and improved the sway of the objects on their string (a rubber band from a bag of Centre s'mores), he realized how much he had to learn.

When he had passed the jewellery to her, she had conscientiously as ever avoided touching him, which given their close proximity sitting on the floor had required almost balletic skill that she was willing to employ if it meant not burning him. His appreciation of this was unspoken, yet he secretly inhaled her natural perfume, equal parts skin, sweat and—was it smoke? He felt like the blindfolded chef on that Centre cooking show.

Other things remained unsaid as well. Both knew, for instance, that this "braceleting" art or craft, call it what you want, had long since superseded his doing his actual job (which involved receiving, processing, and then resending facts and figures, things which now seemed so boring he couldn't begin to figure out the words and gestures to explain it). A red square blinked on the Centre's adjustment for his job, signalling a next to final notice of his absences, something which had only happened once before when he came down with a flu he had gotten from a tiny hole in one window he later plugged with an epoxy. The eventual consequences: docked pay then withheld groceries, and then—well, either he would return to work or he was dead, and in that case, there would be a slow and complete shut-down of the Centre. Unspoken, too: there would not be food enough for two forever and she was strong enough to go now, whenever she wished.

That night, as she slept, he sat awake in his chair, the work warning the only light in the apartment. When his eyes adjusted, he could see again her torso, revealed by the box, her shirt hiked even higher than usual. The signal spotlighted her elegant spine—the bones that led to her brain, *her* Centre—as if it was a path on the floor of a darkened room in a museum, a way to get out. He swivelled and stared at the triple-thick window, at the slightly shaky, shimmering grey sky that was all he'd ever seen of the atmosphere outside. He knew the glass could only be broken open, unless there was some other odd other way to escape—the air duct or whatever—that he had never learned.

He was willing to make the leap, and leap was what it might be: she would know he didn't know a thing. If he survived, his life outside would be a reversal of fortune, a shift in his status, a come-down; while that scared him, it intrigued him, too, or so he thought.

He rose. For a second, instinctively, he steered toward her then he took a turn. He stood before the Centre, frozen in its light, then shifting uneasily as if it could see him and judge him (like someone he saw in a story on the Centre who thought a painted portrait on a wall had accusing eyes), though he knew that it did not.

He did not know how to shut it down, for he had never wanted to. The front was smooth. He came close and strained to see a few knobs at the back, the whole area dusty from lack of use. He reached his good hand, could only get it in a little before his forearm, crushed against the wall by the Centre, forbade him going farther. His fingertips managed to turn the first knob, but that did nothing. He touched the second—he'd never get as far as the third—and with an effort spun it twice. To his surprise, this dimmed the light of the Centre's screen. With a grunt, he plunged in again and twisted it a final time. The light went off entirely, but the Centre's familiar hum was audible: no matter what he did, it was and always would be on.

He snapped on an overhead light, which startled her. She sat up, blinking, her young face looked weirdly wrinkled by her being so rudely awakened. She appeared beyond beautiful to him: a faun, a newborn, or an angel, whatever image there was for the most hopeful and least cloying creature, he did not care. In a second, he was beside her and beginning to explain.

He flicked one of his best made bracelets, which she had endearingly attached to her wrist. He indicated the idea of them working together. He pointed at the window, at her, at him, and said "We," a word he knew now would make sense. Before he could finish his final and most foolish gesture—to cross his heart—before he could say the word that was so basic and yet so hard to express and understand, she was way ahead of him and had agreed—her shrug said so—to anything he wanted.

Her smell was more powerful now: impossible to describe, except that it was hers alone and could only ever from now on be imitated by others. Her lips parted—not in a smile; he had seen many of those—a way to say something new, to convey a want that was at once welcome and treacherous. He saw the fast rise and fall of her small breasts beneath his own washed shirt, the beauty, even the existence of which he had tried to avoid acknowledging.

And suddenly he had placed his hands under the shirt and onto her sides, her waist, the area he had seen so often at night. He didn't stop; she could not, either, even though the fire burned him, even though he shrieked so loudly it startled neighbours in the building he didn't know he had. Dusky smoke filled the place like fire on a grill from which the grease was never cleaned.

—ɷ—

In the morning, he sensed something different in his home, the opposite of the first inkling he had had it seemed so long ago. He had an acute perception of solitude, different from the one he'd always known—worse, for absence had been added to it, and loss. Was it more awful than the physical pain he was in now? He didn't know: as someone wise once said on a Centre talk show, when you've got abysmal alternatives, why choose?

To be honest, he couldn't see whether she had gone or not. He could hardly turn in his chair, and his eyes were nearly covered by bandages (which the night before, diligently, weeping, she had followed directions dispensed by the Centre and helped him to put on). He had to depend upon a feeling for the once again altered "aura" of the place—and of his knowledge of her, of her sense of right and wrong, of how and how much she loved. And, sure enough, the sun eventually set without a sound or sight of her.

He was startled to think of never seeing her again. The idea of mourning was a mystery to him—everything on the Centre had always stayed the same, or only ever been added to (more meat for meals, new shoes, even another job if he wanted one, though he had always stayed with what he had). He didn't cry, though he wanted to, fearing initiation into a kind of grief from which he would not return the same.

He turned his attention to the Centre, the warning work light of which had reached the final level: orange. To his surprise, just as he'd been acknowledging the thing's consistency, he saw that a new adjustment had been added. Maybe it had been there the whole time; he'd been paying it so little mind. He didn't rise to reach it, though his feet were his only parts that were unscathed. Out of curiosity, he simply switched to it with the clicker.

And there on the screen he saw her. She looked at him with an excited expression, as if she'd been waiting for him to turn to her. Was it his imagination? He didn't think so. He believed that she had found her way inside it as she had his home, gone through whatever were the Centre's equivalents of pipes and air ducts, a process he could not begin to imagine. It was her way to love him without risk, to protect him from herself, to never leave.

He smiled back. Then he couldn't help himself, he cried—not just because he was so relieved to see her, or so moved by the enormity of her gesture. He cried because he had already begun to—and knew he would forever—miss the irresistible agony of a human touch.

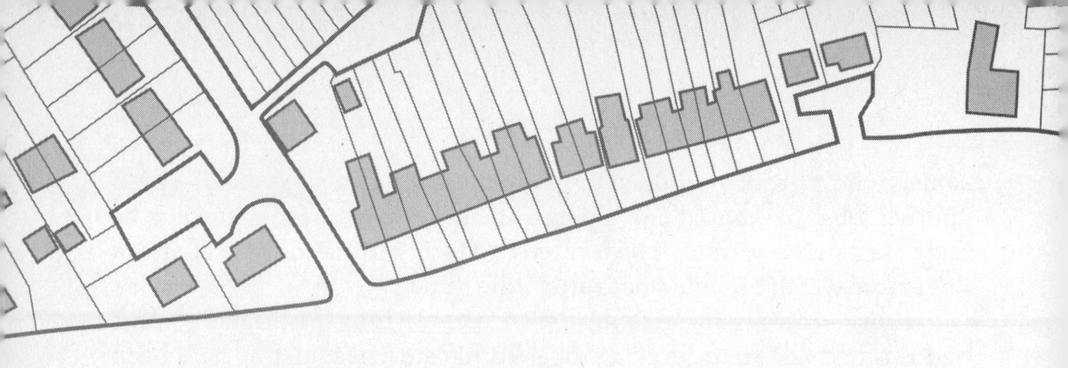

ACKNOWLEDGEMENTS

Not long after 9/11, my beloved wife Susan Kim and I rented an apartment north of New York City as a kind of bomb shelter. Soon I was sitting around there, totally and loudly bored out of my skull. Sick of my complaining, Susan said, "Why don't you just . . . I don't know . . . write a *story* or something?" So I'd like to acknowledge her exasperation and impatience as the reasons this book exists. Plus her love, support, and notes.

I'd also like to thank Brett Savory and Sandra Kasturi of ChiZine for their innovative sensibilities and excellent taste, Andrew Wilmot for his immensely helpful edits, Erik Mohr for his superb cover, and Andrea Somberg of the Harvey Klinger Agency for her dogged efforts on my behalf. Finally, I'd like to thank my therapist, Catherine Silver. It's great to get this book published, but I'll be keeping my appointment next week, as usual.

PUBLICATION HISTORY

"The Family Unit" was originally published in *Natural Bridge*, No. 22, Fall 2009
"Hole in the Ground" was originally published in *Café Irreal*, Issue 22, May 2007
"What the Wind Blew In" was originally published in *SNReview*, Summer 2007
"Stray" was originally published in *The Literary Review*, August 2008
"The Unexpected Guest" was originally published in *Gargoyle*, No. 53, 2008
"Long Story Short" was originally published in *Foliate Oak*, Volume 4, March 2008
"Versatility" was originally published in *Hamilton Stone Review*, Issue 19, Fall 2009
"Modern Sign" was originally published in *The Literateur*, Oct 29, 2009
"The Happy Hour" was originally published in *Skive Magazine*, Issue 13, December 2009
"Alert" was originally published in *Sliptongue*, March 2008
"Bomb Shelter" was originally published in *Brink*, May 2008
"Old Tricks" was originally published in *Straylight*, Volume 2.2, Fall 2008
"The Dead End Job" was originally published in *Sliptongue*, March 2010
"The Son He Never Had" is original to this collection.
"Home Invasion" was originally published in *[Pank]*, No. 4, September 2009

ABOUT THE AUTHOR

Laurence Klavan wrote the novels *The Cutting Room* and *The Shooting Script*, which were published by Ballantine Books. He won the Edgar Award from the Mystery Writers of America for the novel *Mrs. White*, co-written under a pseudonym. It was made into the movie *White of the Eye*. He and Susan Kim wrote the Young Adult novel *Wasteland*, and its sequel, *Wanderers*, which were published by Harper Collins. The third installment in the series, *Guardians*, will be published next year. Their graphic novels, *City of Spies* and *Brain Camp*, were published by First Second Books at Macmillan. *Brain Camp* was a Junior Literary Guild Selection and a Scholastic Book Fair Selection. His short work has been published in such print and online journals as *The Alaska Quarterly*, *Conjunctions*, *The Literary Review*, *Gargoyle*, *Louisville Review*, *Natural Bridge*, *Failbetter*, *Pank*, *Stickman Review*, *Ellery Queen's Mystery Magazine*, *Albedo One*, and *Morpheus Tales*, among many others. He received two Drama Desk nominations for the book and lyrics of *Bed and Sofa*, the musical produced by the Vineyard Theater in New York. It also received two Obie Awards, five other Drama Desk nominations, including Best Musical, and an Outer Critics Circle nomination for Best Musical. It made its London debut at the Finborough Theatre and was nominated for five Offie (Off West End) Awards, including Best Production. His one-act, *The Summer Sublet*, is included in Best American Short Plays 2000–2001. His theatre work is published by Dramatists Play Service. He lives in New York City.

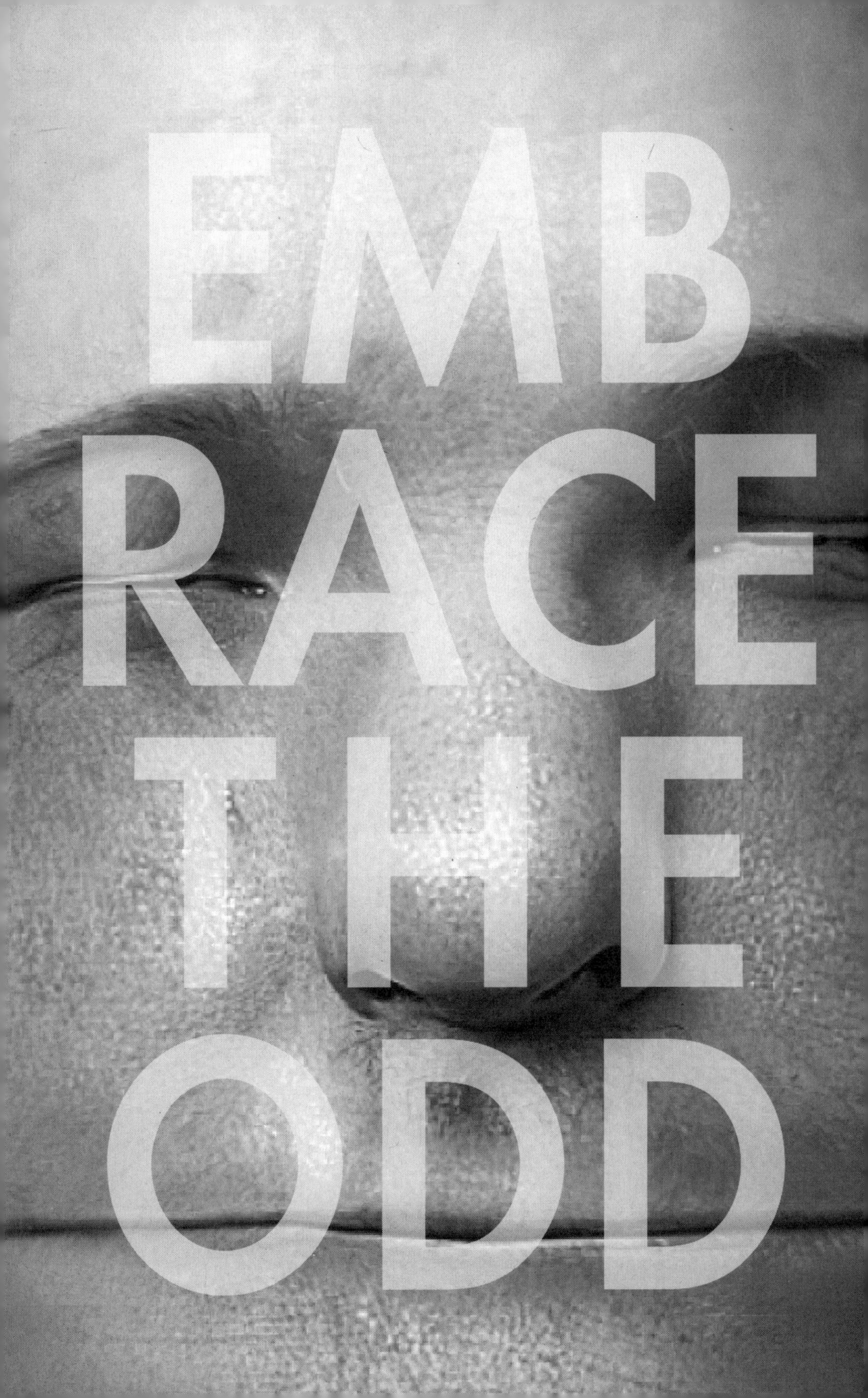

EMB
RACE
THE
ODD

WE WILL ALL GO DOWN TOGETHER

GEMMA FILES

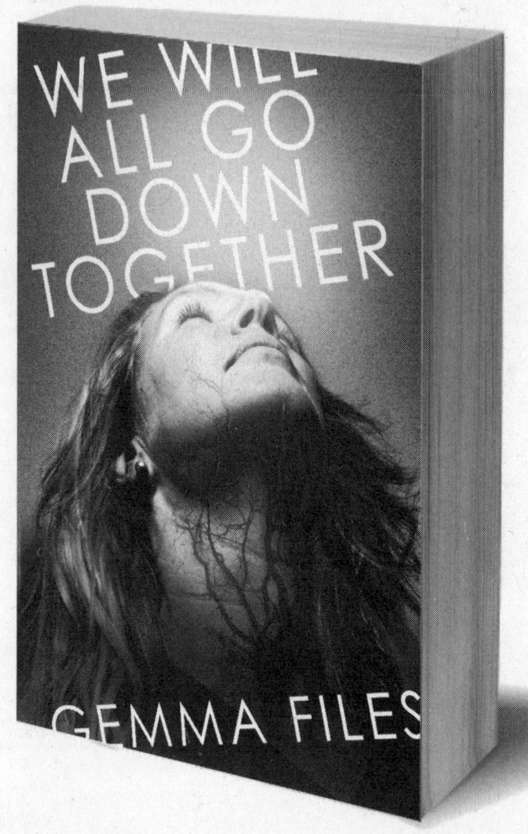

In the woods outside Overdeere, Ontario, there are trees that speak, a village that doesn't appear on any map and a hill that opens wide, entrapping unwary travellers. Music drifts up from deep underground, while dreams—and nightmares—take on solid shape, flitting through the darkness. It's a place most people usually know better than to go, at least locally—until tonight, at least, when five bloodlines mired in ancient strife will finally converge once more.

AVAILABLE AUGUST 2014

978-1-77148-201-1

GIFTS FOR THE ONE WHO COMES AFTER

HELEN MARSHALL

Ghost thumbs. Miniature dogs. One very sad can of tomato soup . . . British Fantasy Award-winner Helen Marshall's second collection offers a series of twisted surrealities that explore the legacies we pass on to our children. A son seeks to reconnect with his father through a telescope that sees into the past. A young girl discovers what lies on the other side of her mother's bellybutton. Death's wife prepares for a very special funeral. In *Gifts for the One Who Comes After*, Marshall delivers eighteen tales of love and loss that cement her as a powerful voice in dark fantasy and the New Weird. Dazzling, disturbing, and deeply moving.

AVAILABLE SEPTEMBER 2014

978-1-77148-303-2

CHIZINEPUB.COM CZP

FLOATING BOY AND THE GIRL WHO COULDN'T FLY

P.T. JONES

Things Mary doesn't want to fall into: the river, high school, her mother's life.

Things Mary does kind of want to fall into: love, the sky.

This is the story of a girl who sees a boy float away one fine day. This is the story of the girl who reaches up for that boy with her hand and with her heart. This is the story of a girl who takes on the army to save a town, who goes toe-to-toe with a mad scientist, who has to fight a plague to save her family. This is the story of a girl who would give anything to get to babysit her baby brother one more time. If she could just find him.

It's all up in the air for now, though, and falling fast. . . .

AVAILABLE OCTOBER 2014

978-1-77148-174-8

ALSO AVAILABLE FROM CHITEEN